Beautiful Stranger

A-List novels by Zoey Dean:

THE A-LIST

GIRLS ON FILM

BLONDE AMBITION

TALL COOL ONE

BACK IN BLACK

SOME LIKE IT HOT

AMERICAN BEAUTY

HEART OF GLASS

BEAUTIFUL STRANGER

If you like THE A-LIST, you may also enjoy:

Bass Ackwards and Belly Up by Elizabeth Craft and Sarah Fain
Secrets of My Hollywood Life by Jen Calonita
Haters by Alisa Valdes-Rodriguez

and keep your eye out for
Betwixt by Tara Bray Smith, coming October 2007

Beautiful Stranger

An A-List Novel

by
Zoey Dean

 LITTLE, BROWN AND COMPANY
New York ᴠ Boston

Little, Brown and Company

Hachette Book Group USA
237 Park Avenue, New York, NY 10017
Visit our Web site at www.lb-teens.com

First Edition: September 2007

The characters and events in this book are fictitious. Any similarity to real
persons, living or dead, is coincidental and not intended by the author.

Produced by Alloy Entertainment
151 West 26th Street, New York, NY 10001

ISBN-10: 0-316-11352-2
ISBN-13: 978-0-316-11352-6

10 9 8 7 6 5 4 3 2 1
CWO
Printed in the United States of America

To Dianne.
Loyalty is everything.

New York was real and California was not.
T'was ever thus.

—Lauren Bacall

Black Silk Christian Dior Gown

There were many things that Anna Percy loved: classic novels written in the nineteenth century, the antique diamond stud earrings handed down from her grandmother, the idea that a person could, if she really wanted to, reinvent herself. But at this moment, she wondered if the thing she loved most of all might not be slow dancing with Ben Birnbaum.

The orchestra was on a raised platform draped in white and gold, built for this very occasion. The music was smoky and jazzy—very retro. Anna had never heard the song before, but she didn't care. It was the first slow number since she and Ben had arrived at the lavish wrap party for *Ben-Hur*, and the first time she'd been in his arms all night. Transnational Pictures—the studio behind the *Ben-Hur* remake—was hosting the affair at one of its soundstages in its studio complex in Culver City.

"Maybe we should blow this off and go somewhere else," Ben murmured in her ear. His breath sent shivers up and down Anna's spine. Said spine was quite visible, in a black silk Christian Dior gown that appeared modest in front but slid below the waist in back. If Anna had been the type of girl to give much thought to what clothes said about the girl underneath them, she would have mused that the dress was much like her on this particular August evening: modest on the surface, offering only a glimpse of the heat beneath. The reason she knew about that heat had everything to do with the boy with whom she was dancing.

"I can't do that to Sam," she whispered back, which was true. The star and director of *Ben-Hur* was Jackson Sharpe, America's best-loved action hero, and his daughter, Samantha, was the closest friend Anna had made since she'd come to Los Angeles seven months before. Anna couldn't very well duck out on her.

Besides, going somewhere more private with Ben was not in her game plan for the evening. She intended to take things slow. They had fallen for each other too hard and too fast, right after Anna arrived in Los Angeles from New York. In fact, it had happened on the plane from LaGuardia to LAX. She'd come to California to spend the second half of senior year of high school, to live with the father she'd barely seen since her parents' divorce in middle school. She'd come here to try something new, to—here was that word again—*reinvent* herself.

Anna Percy, of the old-money, Upper East Side Manhattan intelligentsia, had wanted something more.

She'd gotten something more. She'd gotten Ben Birnbaum. Ben was the first and only guy with whom she'd ever made love. From the very beginning, the experience had been whatever was two steps higher than fantastic on the Bliss-o-Meter. In fact, it defied every scale of measurement Anna had ever known or even imagined.

For one, Ben was knockdown, drag-out, take-your-breath-away handsome. Every feature seemed at once chiseled and effortlessly boyish, adding up to nothing short of a six-foot, blue-eyed, tousle-haired Adonis. She still remembered how her stomach had flip-flopped the first time she saw him, in the first-class cabin of that same NYC-L.A. flight, when he'd stood to take off his Princeton sweatshirt. For another, he radiated confidence unlike any other guy Anna had met: he was comfortable in his own skin—or whatever his skin was in. Tonight, that was a vintage Armani tuxedo with purple-tinted cummerbund and breast handkerchief. Anna found his looks, and pretty much everything about him, devastating.

Yet their relationship had been plagued by secrets, and at the end of July, Anna had made a momentous decision. She'd taken a step—five steps—backward, and told Ben she wanted to roll back to "dating." She wanted them to really get to know each other, without sex getting in the way. Ben had been her first, and being with him was so good she feared the constant flood of endorphins in her cardiovascular system was clouding her judgment.

To be honest, there was another guy involved too. During the latest off-again patch of the on-again/off-again cycle of Anna-and-Ben, she had met Caine Manning, who worked at her father's international investment firm. Anna had boldly told Ben and Caine that she wanted to date both of them at the same time. Somewhat to her shock, they'd agreed to her plan. She was proud of her decision—it wasn't the kind of decision she would have made back in New York. It made her feel much more in control of her love life than she had in a long time. In theory, at least. When she was within a few feet of Ben, the idea of being in control was just that: an idea.

Anna tore her eyes away from Ben's perfectly chiseled jawline and looked around her. Transnational had transformed the soundstage, a cavernous building only slightly smaller than an aircraft hangar, into a huge, 1940s-era speakeasy. This had nothing to do with *Ben-Hur* and everything to do with what the studio hoped would be Jackson Sharpe's next project for them, a remake of the 1940s Humphrey Bogart classic *Casablanca,* about an expatriate speakeasy owner in Nazi-occupied Morocco, considered by many to be the best motion picture of all time.

Only a movie star with the clout and box-office appeal of Jackson Sharpe would consider remaking *Casablanca* and taking the starring role.

In keeping with the speakeasy theme, there were small tabletops, banquettes lining the walls, and cigar and cigarette girls circulating. The orchestra played Gershwin on its risers, and most everyone was dressed formally. A number of people had affected 1940s couture in honor of Jackson's next project. It was supposed to be "top secret," as was breathlessly noted on every entertainment TV talk show and industry rag and mag. In Hollywood, Anna had learned, there were no secrets.

Sam was dancing nearby with her handsome Peruvian boyfriend, Eduardo Munoz. He wore a black Ralph Lauren three-button tuxedo; she'd chosen Chloé black chiffon and lace trousers with a fitted white silk Dolce & Gabbana plumed jacket that flattered her pear-shaped figure. Anna knew how Sam worried constantly about her size ten or twelve (depending on the day, and often depending on the hour) figure, which by Beverly Hills standards was considered massive. Anna found this ridiculous, and she'd told her friend so. Sam's smiling response was that since Anna was naturally lithe and slender, with more than a passing resemblance to a younger Gwyneth Paltrow or a taller Sienna Miller, she needed to shut the fuck up.

Sam caught Anna's eye and waved one arm as she and Eduardo danced. Anna waved back, thinking she'd never seen her friend look so radiant. Eduardo was good for her—and for her self-confidence.

The song ended and some people applauded. Marty Martinsen, the head of Transnational Pictures, stepped to the tall, forties-style microphone in front of the orchestra. Martinsen was a barrel-chested bear of a man, with bushy eyebrows and a trim goatee. He wore a standard Hollywood I'm-sorta-dressing-up uniform of black jeans, black T-shirt, and well-tailored black jacket. He didn't bother to introduce himself, seemingly announcing that if you didn't know who he was, you didn't belong on this party's guest list of the thousand or more people who had something to do with *Ben-Hur*.

"Thank you all for joining us tonight. And now, ladies and gentlemen, it's a pleasure to introduce to you the star and director of *Ben-Hur*—which we believe will be the most important movie of the decade—Mr. Jackson Sharpe!"

The enormous crowd applauded and cheered wildly.

"Make way, make way, make way!"

Anna heard deep male voices calling above the applause and watched as the crowd parted. Two by two, a dozen blond, silicone-enhanced young women in mini-togas strew rose petals as they walked toward the stage. Behind them, another dozen buff young men dressed as gladiators carried a gold-leaf-covered platform, upon which Jackson Sharpe lolled and waved laconically to the onlookers. Jackson himself wore jeans and a gray T-shirt. He seemed taller than his six feet, and was in rock-hard shape. His jawline was as sharp as a straight-edge razor, and sandy hair fell over one of his blue eyes. When you were America's best-known action star, and the camera loved you as much as it loved Jackson, you dressed to please yourself and no one else.

Sam sidled up next to Anna as the throng cheered her father, who was now clasping his hands overhead like a victorious heavyweight champion after a knockout.

"I have to hand it to dear old dad," she told Anna over the noise. "He knows how to make an entrance." Sam stood on her tiptoes and tried to gaze over the heads of the crowd. "Have you seen Cammie?"

Anna shook her head. Not only had she not seen Cammie Sheppard, she didn't *want* to see her. Just because Sam and Cammie were best friends since forever didn't mean that Anna had to like Cammie, too—especially since Cammie had taken an instant dislike to her from the moment they met. Anna suspected it was mostly because Ben was Cammie's ex, and if Cammie couldn't have something she wanted, she didn't want anyone else to have it either. Recently Anna and Cammie had been

sentenced to do community service together over a trivial trespassing-on-a-private-beach regulation. Anna had
almost kind of started to appreciate Cammie's moxie and
charm.

But then Cammie had made it quite clear that if she
broke up with her current boyfriend, Adam Flood, she
was going after Ben. And in general, what Cammie Sheppard wanted, Cammie Sheppard got. She would have no
qualms about jumping into bed—table, locked bathroom
stall at a trendy club, whatever—with Ben. Every time
Anna thought about it she felt as if she couldn't breathe.

"There she is!" Sam suddenly exclaimed.

Anna looked over to see Cammie sashay over to Ben,
wrap her arms around his neck, and give him the softest,
tiniest of kisses on each cheek. Ben looked amused. Anna
forced a tense smile, though she wished a movie extra in a
gorilla suit would come in with a coconut cream pie and
apply said pie directly to Cammie's freshly powdered and
lipsticked face. But in the world to which Anna had been
born and bred—the gracious world of the *This Is How
We Do Things* Big Book (East Coast WASP edition), dis-
playing any kind of negative emotion publicly was simply
Not Done, even with the help of a costumed extra. See
Chapter Eleven: "The Art of Ignoring."

The whole thing would have been easier to shrug off if
Cammie didn't look like . . . well, like Cammie. Crown-
ing her tanned, toned, curves-in-all-the-right-places five-
foot-eight body, Cammie's strawberry blond locks shone
with the same luster as her yellow satin Maison Martin
Margiela sleeveless gown. Its loosely plunging V neck-
line left just enough to the imagination, which is to say it

boldly featured the best breasts available on today's market. Anna thought the whole Camilla Sheppard package should come with a warning label: BEWARE: HIGHLY FLAMMABLE. She took a step back to make room as Cammie edged toward her and Sam.

"Wake me when that's over," Cammie said without preliminaries, tossing her curls off her face as she nudged her chin toward the stage. Having hugged Marty Martinsen, Jackson was now going through an off-the-cuff but seemingly endless list of thank-yous to various people who had worked on the two-hundred-million-dollar epic that was his *Ben-Hur*. Anna thought it would be impossible to remember the names of every key grip, best boy, gaffer, wardrobe assistant, dolly operator, assistant director, assistant to the assistant director, and truck driver associated with his movie, but Jackson seemed to tick the names off effortlessly. It was a remarkable, if verbose, performance.

"Where's Adam?" Sam asked. Eduardo slid his arms around her waist from behind, and Sam beamed.

"He'll be here," Cammie replied confidently. Anna knew that Cammie had given Adam, who was in Michigan on vacation with his parents, an ultimatum: He needed to be back in Los Angeles in time for the wrap party or their relationship would be toast. However bitchy this sounded, Anna recalled that it was an extension of an earlier dictum that Adam "get his ass back" to her two weeks ago. Anna couldn't imagine forcing someone she loved to make that kind of decision. But then again, she couldn't imagine being Cammie Sheppard at all. Only Cammie would look at an ultimatum extension as generous. And only she would decide ahead of time that if things didn't work out with Adam, she was going after Ben.

"There's Dee." Cammie waggled her fingers in the direction of Dee Young, who was just arriving with her boyfriend, Jack Walker. Jack and Ben had both just finished their freshman years at Princeton, where they'd quickly become friends. Jack was in Los Angeles for a summer internship in the Fox reality TV department. Anna recalled how they'd met. Dee had just been released from an upscale psychiatric institution and needed a date for senior prom. Cammie had promised that she'd find Dee a date. The date turned out to be Jack. The rest was history.

Diminutive Dee wore a petal pink dress so short that Anna hoped she had on more underwear than Britney or Lindsay—even Anna, no fan or follower of pop culture, knew about their ventures into no-panties land. Instead of a tux like Ben or Eduardo, Jack—who bore a passing resemblance to music icon Beck—sported a retro pink-and-black sports shirt from the forties and black peg-legged pants. He'd recently grown a small soul patch like so many of the young guys who worked in the world of TV.

"You guys, hi!" Dee cried in her breathy voice.

She was tiny and adorable, with shaggy blond bangs that covered her eyebrows. After spending time at the Ojai Psychiatric Institute near Santa Barbara, she seemed like an entirely different person. While Anna had found the old Dee just a bit too cosmic for her tastes, it couldn't be easy to go through what she'd gone through, and Anna really liked the new and improved Dee. "Hey, guess what? Jack got time off from Fox and we're going to Hawaii. Evolution is working on their new album at my dad's studio in Maui."

Anna was surprised. Last she'd heard, Dee was feeling crowded by Jack's talk about marriage and their future together in New Jersey. Apparently, Jack had been getting dangerously close to the *M* word with her: Marriage. And now they were going to Hawaii together?

"When are you leaving?" Anna asked politely.

"Tomorrow," Dee answered with a grin that didn't mar her pink lip gloss. "Hey, I've got a great idea. Why don't you and Sam and Cammie come visit me?"

While the idea was tempting, Anna knew she only had a few more weeks here in Los Angeles before going back east to start college at Yale. She was about to make the most polite demurral in history when Ben came to her rescue.

"Want to get some air?" he asked, gently touching her elbow. "There's a buffet outside."

"Go ahead, you guys." Sam nodded. "My dad's still just getting started with his thank-yous. Check it out. There goes Parker."

Sam pointed to the stage, where her father had moved on to introducing his cast, and inviting them up to the stage. One of those actors was their friend Parker Pinelli, who looked like a cross between James Dean circa *Rebel Without a Cause* and a young Brad Pitt in his *Thelma & Louise* period. Tonight he was wearing jeans and a red Windbreaker to heighten the hey-he-looks-like-James-

Dean comparison. Anna had to smile at that. Parker was the only guy there besides America's Most Beloved Action Hero who was casually dressed, and it made him stand out—in a good way. Up onstage, Parker shook Jackson's hand warmly.

"He should be shaking *my* hand," Sam joked. "He got that part because of me."

Anna grinned as Parker edged in next to Jackson. Parker had played the part of a stable boy who helped prepare Jackson for the big chariot race, and Sam had reported that Parker's scenes were excellent.

"How 'bout we take a break?" Ben repeated. He moved his feet restlessly. "We can come back when the speeches are over."

A break seemed like an excellent idea now that Anna had paid her requisite respects to Sam. Anna told her friend she'd see her in a little bit, and then she and Ben snaked through the crowd to the rear exit of the sound-stage. From there they walked across the Transnational lot—a collection of low-slung buildings, streets with false storefronts used for filming, warehouses, and one ultramodern structure that was the company's corporate headquarters—and then out the main gate and onto the scruffy streets of Culver City.

Los Angeles was full of *über*-hip neighborhoods. Culver City wasn't one of them. It was better known for auto-body repair shops and used furniture outlets than Porsche dealerships or designer storefronts.

"Sorry to drag you away back there," Ben commented as they walked arm in arm. "A little dose of Jackson Sharpe being charming to his cast and crew goes a really long way. Same thing for industry parties. You know those girls who were throwing the rose petals? I think my father did them all."

Anna laughed. Ben wasn't talking about sex. He was talking about plastic surgery. Ben's father was plastic surgeon to the stars, responsible for the good looks of most of Hollywood's talent over the age of thirty—both male and female—and quite a few under that age who probably didn't need any work to begin with.

Ben had grown up around show business, and had told Anna many times how unreal that world was to him. When people wanted something from his father, they were his dad's best friends. After they got what they wanted, they were gone. That was one of the many reasons he'd decided to attend Princeton rather than a school in Southern California. Anna, who'd been accepted early decision to Yale, had thought quite a bit about how much fun it would be to meet him in Manhattan when they were both at school in just a few weeks, as it was about the same distance from New Haven as it was from Princeton. On weekends, she'd hop on the train and be there in an hour and a half. Ben would be waiting for her at Grand Central, where he'd whisk her into a taxi, and they'd fly uptown to her empty Upper East Side town house, where they'd—

"I'm thinking about not going back to school."

Anna stopped walking and gazed up at him. "*What?* Why?"

"Well . . ." he began. His voice seemed strangely loud, until Anna realized it was because there was so little traffic in this neighborhood. An orange-blossom-scented breeze ruffled his thick, dark hair. "You know how I started the Monday night thing at Trieste?"

Anna nodded slowly. Trieste was the club of the moment. Located on Hollywood Boulevard not far from the corner of Vine, a line of hopeful partygoers snaked down the block on a nightly basis, eager to be admitted. Ben had a summer job there and recently he'd started a Monday night event where the pounding sound system was turned off, drinks cost half their usual price, there was no dancing, and poets, playwrights, and various other artists could perform in a decidedly nonclub atmosphere. Trieste Mondays, as he called them, had already become quite successful.

He took her hands in his. "Don't laugh at what I'm about to say."

"Never."

"I've been thinking that I'd like to open my own club."

Anna looked at him wordlessly. A club? He wanted to drop out of college and open his own *nightclub*? But Ben was so smart. And he hated Hollywood. He'd just said he was sick of industry parties. Running a Hollywood club would be like doing industry parties seven nights a week.

"So . . . when did you get this idea?" she asked cautiously.

"I've had it for a while." He let go of one hand and tucked his own into the pocket of his tux pants. "I get really excited about it, you know? Not another beautiful-people, let's-keep-out-everyone-from-the-Valley bullshit kind of club. Something entirely different. One that's accessible and just . . . cool."

Anna couldn't help but notice the enthusiasm in his voice—he was livelier than he'd been all night. Still, you didn't just throw away an Ivy League education. She waited to see what else he would say.

He ran a nervous hand through his hair. "I sit in class at Princeton and my mind is a million miles away. I study, take exams, write papers, and I just don't even know why I'm doing it. Being there doesn't make any sense."

"But maybe it doesn't need to make sense right *now*," Anna put in. "Maybe becoming an educated person is a goal. In and of itself, I mean."

"But I just don't *feel* it, Anna," he insisted, his bright blue eyes shining in the dark night. "The best thing I've done in . . . well, in forever is to start the Monday night series at Trieste. *That* I care about. And when's the last time you saw me excited over something that isn't you?"

Anna nodded. She knew how hard he'd worked to do something different at the hip club du jour. And he'd succeeded. But still, how could opening a nightclub compare to going to one of the best universities in the world?

"Ever since my dad started Gamblers Anonymous he's been an entirely different person," Ben continued. "He took me out to dinner last week and told me he wanted us to make up for lost time. He said that whatever my dreams were, he was going to back them one hundred percent. That came after a twenty-minute monologue about how my grandfather made a lot of money in the rag and junk business back in Syracuse, New York, but never backed him in anything, of course. How everything he'd achieved he'd achieved on his own. He even paid for med school on his own."

Anna nodded. She was happy to hear about Dr. Birnbaum wanting to reconnect with his son. But what did that have to do with Ben leaving Princeton?

He stopped and turned to her, running his hands under her wispy blond hair at the nape of her neck. "College will always be there. I can go later. But right now . . . I really want to do this. And with my father's backing, I can. I know he'll support me—he'd never want to repeat what his dad did to him." His eyes bore into hers. "So what do you think?"

What did she think? She thought he should probably go back to school, but could she possibly be the one to dim the light she saw in his eyes? Besides, this was probably just one of his idle fantasies, like the plans she'd made in her imagination for weekends in Manhattan with him. She knew that if anything, Ben probably just needed to talk it through. Eventually he'd realize that dropping out of school wasn't a realistic plan.

"I think it's fantastic," she finally pronounced, and was rewarded with Ben's wide, dimpled smile. "Maybe you could do it someplace no one else would think of. Not Hollywood Boulevard, or Los Feliz. Someplace different. To show that the club would be different."

"Right, because you're such a club kid," he teased, kissing her neck softly. They were standing in the driveway of a small frame house, on a street with a dozen other small frame houses. It was a world away from the estates and mansions of Beverly Hills and Bel Air, but the location didn't matter. When she was close to him like this, she tried to remember exactly why it was she'd decided they should rewind their relationship to "dating," because all she could think about was his body and her body and—

No. That was not a productive train of thought.

The lights in the house flicked on, and Ben suggested that they turn left onto Venice Boulevard and loop back to the Transnational lot. As they strolled, they joked about club locations and names. "How about . . . an old hospital?" he asked. "We could call the club Lovesick."

She laughed, happy that Ben hadn't yet brought up the fact that if this club idea actually came to fruition, he'd be here in California and she'd be three thousand miles away at Yale. If he hadn't come to that realization yet, he couldn't really be serious, which made it easier to play along. "Gee, I don't know of any old hospitals that are for rent. How about . . ." She closed her Chanel-mascara'd eyes as she tried to think of the wildest place for a new nightclub. But as she opened them again, she spotted an abandoned auto repair shop, its wall covered in faded murals of ancient taxicabs. There were two gas pumps in front so old that they listed the price of a gallon in cents, not dollars. Through the broken windows, she could see hydraulic lifts, long neglected.

"How about . . . the Body Shop?" Anna joked, pointing a slender finger at the weedy, garbage-strewn property.

Ben rubbed the stubble on his chin. "How about it?"

She'd seen that look on his face before. "You're not serious."

"Why not? It would certainly be unique. Of course, the name sounds like a strip joint. But maybe that could work in our favor."

"You *are* serious."

"Maybe I am. It would take a ton of work but . . ." He looked at her earnestly. "But I'd be willing to do it. I really want this, Anna. Maybe it's crazy, but . . . all I can say is, I never feel this rush when I'm at school. And don't say it's because I'm only going to be a sophomore."

Anna looked at Ben's pleading eyes and realized this wasn't idle fantasy. He was dead serious, and he'd thought it through. She managed a weak smile. She was not about to be the one to say no to his dream, even if she hadn't ever realized that that dream would be opening a club. Hadn't she come to Los Angeles to reinvent herself? Well, maybe that's what Ben wanted to do, too. Who was she to judge what he wanted to reinvent himself into? Besides, just because an Ivy League education was right for her didn't mean it was right for him.

She leaned close to his ear and whispered, "Like I said, I think it's fantastic."

His lips met hers in the softest of kisses. Then he kissed her again, harder, drawing her in close and holding her tight.

But as their lips met, the small part of her brain that was still functioning couldn't get beyond the fact that if Ben did stay here to open a club, in just three weeks she'd be starting college three thousand miles away. From Yale to Princeton might have been doable, especially for a couple that was just "dating."

But from Los Angeles to New Haven? Many a relationship had died over less. The thought made her feel truly lovesick.

Thanks to Good Genes and Just the Right Amount of Silicone

"Never ask me about a guy when I'm doing downward facing dog," Cammie quipped, arching her slender back as her knees dug into her purple Styrofoam mat. She and Sam were in the last few minutes of an extreme yoga class at Yoga Booty on La Cienega Boulevard. The class had been Cammie's idea, but she didn't want to go alone. Getting Sam to agree had involved nothing more than a pointed look at her best friend's thighs, an arched brow, and five little words: "Are you putting on weight?"

Actually, Sam was looking really good these days. Not that she'd dropped a pound, because she hadn't. But there was a sparkle in her eyes and a confidence in her step that Cammie had only ever seen in Sam post-Eduardo. That was what love did to a girl.

Not that Cammie would know about love. Sure, she'd *thought* she loved Adam Flood. She'd thought he brought out a side of her that no one else ever had.

But look what that had gotten her. Stood up. Fucked over. Alone.

Damn him.

18

He hadn't shown up at the *Ben-Hur* wrap party last night. That he would choose to extend a camping trip with his parents up in Michigan, where there were more mosquitoes than mojitos, rather than be with the hottest girl ever to graduate from Beverly Hills High—namely, her—was unfathomable.

Not only had he not shown up, he hadn't even called. Hadn't texted. Hadn't anything. It was mortifying. When the night had come to an end and Adam was a no-show, even Parker had looked at her with something resembling pity. Dee had given her a tight hug and said that if Cammie wanted to talk before she left on her vacation with Jack, she'd be there. Sam had suggested a triple Flirtini.

The nerve. Cammie was a girl who pitied other girls. They *never* pitied her.

She'd thought she'd feel better if she sweated out her anger. Yes, she was quite sweaty in a hundred-and-ten-degree yoga studio. But the class was ending, and even though she was probably five pounds thinner she didn't feel better at all.

"Exzellent work!" Zazu, their instructor, called. She was a coltish eighteen-year-old brunette model wannabe, a recent arrival from Marseilles with an almost indecipherable accent and an astonishingly lithe body under tan muslin yoga pants and a white cotton top. "Breez deeply and let all ze tension leeve ze body."

"We're outta here." Cammie scrambled to her feet and beckoned Sam to follow her. She was in no mood to "breez" deeply with Zazu, thank you very much. In moments, she and Sam were stripping down to shower in the locker room.

"I can't imagine Adam not even calling you," Sam commiserated. Yoga Booty had custom terry cloth towels for their clientele, and Sam wrapped herself in one. "I mean, maybe something is really wrong."

"It doesn't matter." Cammie threw her sweaty clothes into her pink and green floral Kate Spade gym bag and caught a glimpse of herself naked in the full-length mirror. Her body was ideal, thanks to good genes and just the right amount of silicone. A recent Brazilian wax at Pink Cheeks in Sherman Oaks had left her smooth and hair-free where she wanted to be smooth and hair-free. Her high-cheekboned face and pouty red lips were set off by a halo of sexy strawberry blond curls.

Even sweaty, she was fucking luscious. How *dare* Adam blow her off! And what the hell was he doing that could be better than being with her? Fishing for walleye? Chopping wood? Mixing up a batch of delicious Tang?

Minutes later, Cammie let her anger simmer as the steamy water beat down upon her from twin showerheads. When she stepped out, she found Sam already dressed in new high-waisted Chloé jeans and a red sleeveless cashmere tank, blow-drying her shoulder-length straight brown hair at the large mirror that ran the length of the dressing room as she hummed to herself. Sam Sharpe. Humming? Looking into a mirror and evidently feeling okay with what she saw there? While Cammie was on a slow burn? That *never* happened. It was always the other way around. And she liked it that way.

Cammie quickly dressed in CK white linen shorts and a T-Bags silk-screened white T-shirt of Marilyn Monroe holding hands with Marilyn Manson. Instead of drying her hair, she twisted it into a makeshift bun and secured it with a silver Cross pen. Nor did she bother with makeup. Cammie *always* bothered with makeup, so of course Sam noticed. Looking perfect was at the top of Cammie's to-do list every single day.

"Why don't you just call him?" Sam asked, as she finished her hair and opened her H. Couture Beauty cosmetics case.

"That reeks of desperate. I'm never desperate." As if to illustrate that fact, Cammie whipped out her limited-edition Razr and turned it off.

Fifteen minutes later, they made a pit stop at the first-floor juice bar for the fresh-squeezed ten-fruit concoction of the day with a double shot of vitamin B for energy. Cammie considered taking a vegan walnut brownie, but she was sure it tasted like ass, like all the other healthy baked goods. Why waste the calories? As for Sam, Cammie was shocked to see her ordering a slice of baklava that oozed honey and nuts. It had to be a sign of the apocalypse.

"Eduardo doesn't care about whether he can serve tea on your ass?" Cammie asked. She knew it was a low blow, but she was feeling too terrible about herself to be nice to anyone else right now.

"Actually, he loves my ass," Sam replied, seemingly unfazed. She was actually chewing her baklava with gusto.

"He's an exceptional guy," Cammie muttered.

"I still think you should—" Sam was interrupted by the chime of her new Motorola Razr V3. She pulled it out of her oversized, studded white leather Zac Posen bag, checked caller ID, and then winked at Cammie.

"Hey, handsome," she purred into the platinum phone.

Cammie gritted her teeth so hard that her jaw hurt. Eduardo, obviously. Meanwhile, her own phone was so not ringing—it wouldn't have made a difference if she had left it on. She had had more boyfriends and flirtations than she could possibly count. Guys lusted after her all the time—all types, all ages. They called and e-mailed and texted. They sent her cards and flowers and gifts and she didn't give a flying fuck. Only twice in her eighteen years on the planet had she really, truly cared about a guy.

And it now appeared that in each of those two instances, the guy had dumped her.

First had been Ben at the end of junior year. Oh, she had never let on that she really cared when they were together, lest he think he had any kind of power over her. But when he'd come to Jackson Sharpe's wedding on New Year's Eve with an unknown blonde on his arm, Cammie had wanted to shave Anna Percy's naturally blond, perfectly shaped head. How could he possibly prefer that snotty, skinny, boring, over-intellectual ice princess to *her*?

Now there was Adam. They were the most unlikely couple in the world. He was nice, sweet, smart, caring, a genuinely good guy. No one would use any of those adjectives to describe her. That much Cammie knew. He'd brought out vulnerability in her that she hadn't even allowed herself to feel since before her mother died years and years ago.

And this was what she got for it.

"Yeah, tomorrow is good," she heard Sam tell Eduardo.

Hmmm. She wasn't looking as radiantly love-struck as she had been a few minutes earlier. What was that about? Then she hung up with barely a goodbye.

"Everything okay?" Cammie asked, hoping against hope for the worst.

Sam's face was white, her eyes huge. "He said we need to 'talk.'"

"Oh, shit," Cammie breathed. Everyone knew "we need to talk" was code for "I'm breaking up with you but I'm too evolved to do it by text."

"I thought everything was fine!" Sam picked up what remained of the slice of baklava and hurled it into the nearby trash bin. "I bet he's seeing that bitch Gisella, remember her? The fashion designer friend of his from Peru? The one he got involved in your fashion show? I saw how she looked at him. She wanted him. Correction. Wants him. Correction. Has probably got him. Let's get out of here."

They gathered up their stuff and headed for the door.

"No need to jump to conclusions," Cammie counseled, although it made her feel a hell of a lot better to have Sam join her in romance misery.

"God. What am I going to do?"

Sam fished her oversized white Chanel sunglasses out of her bag and popped them on her face.

Cammie would have answered, but she was struck numb when she saw who was leaning against the white concrete building, sipping from a Starbucks cup in his right hand.

"Umm . . ." For once, even Cammie Sheppard was at a loss for words.

"I'll go take a sauna and call one of our drivers," Sam

told her. At least she knew how to handle the moment. Without another word, Sam headed back into the Yoga Booty building.

Her words barely registered with Cammie. All she could think was, if Adam was going to just show up, why did it have to be the one time she didn't look her best?

He stood tall and lanky with his short-cropped, spiky brown hair. As he turned his face away from the sun, Cammie could see just a hint of the star tattoo behind his left ear. He wore baggy jeans and an old Ramones T-shirt, and he was much tanner than the last time she'd seen him. There couldn't be a whole lot of shade out on a lake in the wilderness of the upper peninsula of Michigan.

"One of your housekeepers told me you were here," he explained. Still leaning against the building, he put down the Starbucks cup and extended his arms in an unspoken invitation. *Come and hug me,* they were saying. Her first instinct was to accept the invite. The thing about Adam was, he always managed to melt her tough exterior, to somehow get to her softer core. With him, she was actually *nice.* She couldn't decide if that was a good thing or a fatal flaw, but, in all honesty, she *liked* the girl she was with him. But Cammie stayed where she was, balling her hands into fists at her sides. She was not about to throw herself at a boy who professed his love and then stood her up.

"When did you get home?" she asked stiffly, carefully keeping her distance from him on the sidewalk. His arms dropped to his sides, but his palms faced her. That was almost worse than the offered hug.

"Late last night."

Suddenly, a wave of fury swept over her. He was trying to play her. No one played her. She narrowed her eyes angrily. "I told you to be back for the party."

He scratched the tattoo behind his ear, something he habitually did when he was nervous.

"Yeah, well, here's the thing about that. I don't respond well to ultimatums." He shoved his hands into the pockets of his jeans. "You want to go somewhere and talk?"

Cammie took the pen out of her hair so that the curls fell around her face. Even though they were still wet, she knew she looked better that way. She ignored his question about going somewhere. Whatever needed to be said could be said here. "You think it's fine to just waltz in here the next day without even a phone call? You expect me to say that's *okay*?"

He shrugged. "I guess I'm tired of you thinking you can lead me around like I'm your pet pooch, deciding where I have to be and when." He reached out and touched her arm gently, oblivious to the traffic passing by on La Cienega. "I don't even think it's what you really want."

She shook him off. "I told you to come back days ago. *Weeks* ago. So actually, *you're* the one who's leading *me* around like a dog. Taking a week of vacation a month before you start college is fine. Two weeks, even. But three? Come on."

"You seem to be missing the point, Cam. Jeez, I mean, you sound like your father lecturing some sycophantic underling. I don't want to be that guy." He took two steps across the sidewalk toward her, slid his arms around her waist, and gently pulled her to him. She didn't resist.

"C'mon, let's not do this. I missed you," he murmured. "So much."

His words, though, belied his arms. He hadn't shown up in time for the party, and hadn't called either, as some kind of power play. How *dare* he? She wasn't the daughter of the most powerful talent agent in Hollywood for nothing. If anyone was ever going to make a power play and get away with it, it was sure as hell *not* going to be Adam.

Last night at the wrap party, she'd been humiliated in front of her friends because Adam wanted to make some kind of point. Now he thought she was just going to put up with it? That she'd just fall back into his arms?

That's what her head told her. But then there was this little problem with her heart. Why, why, why had she allowed herself to fall for him? Loving someone gave them power over you. And the problem with that was . . . they could use it against you. She really couldn't stand the feelings welling up inside of her, the anxiety and the neediness. She was sure some Dr. Fred–type shrink would say she had abandonment issues because of her mother dying when she was so young. But Cammie didn't care. She hated, hated, *hated* the way she was feeling at that very moment. And Adam was the one who was making her feel that way.

"Know what, Adam? Tell it to someone who cares." She flipped her hair off her face with a practiced gesture.

"You don't mean that," he insisted.

"I never say anything I don't mean."

"Cammie." Adam cupped her cheek with his large hand. Cammie knew that hand so well that she felt new calluses. Probably from a canoe paddle or a fishing rod.

It was everything she could do not to nestle into his arms, to give in to all the feelings she still had for him. But where would *that* lead? More moments of uncertainty, of her feeling vulnerable to what he might say or do. Just look at Sam, for God's sake. She had finally found someone to feel that with, Eduardo, and now he was going to *dump* her.

She ran her hands through her own hair, and was pleased when two buff guys stepping out of Yoga Booty at just that instant tarried to check her out. Adam noticed them too, she was sure. The combination strengthened her resolve.

"I meant what I said, Adam. It's over."

His jaw fell open. "Come on. You're not thinking this through."

"And one last thing," she added, keeping her voice cool and free from emotion. "You just blew the best thing you'll ever have."

Then she turned. Doing her best model walk to show off her pert and perky ass, Cammie Sheppard slung her black Kate Spade bag over her shoulder and walked away.

Whiskey Blues

"**A**nna. It's really good to see you."

Caine stood and kissed her lightly on the lips, then sat again, motioning for her to join him on the low-slung maroon divan. They were in the Whiskey Blue bar at the W Hotel on Hilgard Avene in Westwood, just steps away from the campus of UCLA. Sam had recently told Anna that the W had become her favorite hangout—displacing even the Beverly Hills Hotel—so when Caine had called earlier in the day and suggested that they meet for a drink that night, Anna had suggested the W.

Caine had laughed and accused her of becoming a bona fide Los Angeleno. Anna hadn't denied the charge, though she knew in her heart that she was a New Yorker. Mostly.

She'd dressed simply for the occasion in a taupe silk-lined skirt and a cap-sleeve empire top she'd recently picked up at the Daryl K boutique on Melrose Avenue, a pair of Christian Dior sunglasses for the drive over—coming from Beverly Hills to UCLA meant she had to go west on Sunset Boulevard, directly into the setting sun—and just a spritz of Chanel. She'd known Caine would be coming from work, and had expected to see him in one of his immaculately tailored business suits, the better to keep his many tattoos under wraps. But evidently he'd stopped home, because he wore jeans, a tight navy T-shirt, and the distressed brown leather bomber jacket he'd told Anna he'd had since he was a freshman up at Stanford. He often talked about how he had to don "protective coloration" to work as an investment advisor with Anna's father. If anyone found out that his second car was a Ford F-150 pickup truck instead of a Beemer, he joked that he'd probably be deported back to Oregon.

At the moment, though, his true colors—as well as his tattoos—were showing. His longish straight brown hair was greased up into a pleasantly stylized mess, framing a small stud earring in one ear. As for the tattoos, each decorative arm clearly displayed intricate designs below the rips in his leather jacket. There was one at his right bicep, another on the opposite forearm.

"I ordered a cosmopolitan for you." He lifted the frosted glass next to his own mug of beer-on-tap and handed it to her. She wasn't really in the mood for alcohol but didn't want to be rude, so she just smiled, thanked him, and glanced around at the wall-to-wall people. Though it was only seven-thirty, the fashionable Whiskey Blue was already crowded with an eclectic mix of studio executives, in-the-know business travelers, and the usual smattering of drop-dead-gorgeous actors, actresses, and wannabes. The bar was as big an attraction as the clientele. Clean white geometric lines, custommade orange bar stools, and a music mix that ran from alt to techno and back again brought in the people. There was also a black baby grand piano at one end. A big knot of people was gathered around Paul McCartney, who was in Los Angeles for a concert the next day at the Hollywood Bowl. He was playing a few familiar tunes for the thrilled onlookers.

"So, how are you?" Anna asked with a smile. In the two weeks since she'd set out the I'm-dating-you-both ground rules to him and Ben, she and Caine had seen each other four times—dinner, the movies, a speedboat ride on a friend's cigarette boat that was kept docked at Redondo Beach, and a ride up into the Angeles National Forest in Caine's blue truck. Each time had been just what Anna wanted. Fun and nothing more. She and Caine weren't close yet, or at least not the way she was with Ben. But that, she told herself, was the point of dating Caine. To get to that stage with him, to keep her options—and her heart—open, to be totally sure before she made any big commitments.

"I'm good. Your dad put me on a cool new deal today. Some clients want to take over another hotel in Mexico. In Cancún, this time. Your father said you helped check out the one in Las Casitas for them."

That was true. It had been back in February, and it had been one of the more interesting trips of her life. Sam had been with her, and in fact, it was where Sam had met Eduardo.

"Who owns the one in Cancún now?" Anna asked, taking the smallest sip of her cocktail. It was fruity, and the bartender hadn't skimped on the alcohol. *No more than one,* she told herself.

"Trump. A whole lot of zeros involved in the deal."

Caine took a pull on his beer. He flashed his disarming smile, then pushed the low-slung black table in front of them away a bit with his legs. "There. Much better. You look pretty."

"Thanks." Anna liked compliments as much as the next girl, but this one felt oddly removed, as if he were commenting on the Whiskey Bar's décor. Strange. But all thoughts were set aside as she felt her stomach grumble. "Where do you want to go for dinner? I don't think cocktails cover the main food groups. And I don't care what you say about the power of olives," she added with a grin.

Caine rubbed his chin. It was a strange gesture that Anna hadn't seen before. "We need to talk."

"We *are* talking."

"About something more personal," he corrected, reaching for her hand.

Oh, *now* she understood. He didn't want to discuss dinner. He wanted to discuss what would happen *after* dinner. As in, *Why don't we get horizontal so we can get to know each other better?*

"I'm not really ready for something more . . . personal," Anna replied smoothly.

He looked puzzled for a moment. "Wait, you think I'm trying to get in your pants?"

She raised an eyebrow. "Aren't you?"

He shook his head. "Although I'm sure it would be a lovely experience," he added wryly. "But what I wanted to talk you about was . . ." He looked down at their entwined hands and then back up into her eyes. "Anna, this has to be our last date."

Now that *really* made no sense. "But—but why?"

"I really was okay with the dating thing," Caine began. "You wanted to pull back and give yourself some room to breathe, figure things out—that was fine by me. But . . . you remember I told you about a girl I dated at Stanford? Bernadette?"

"The snowboarder," Anna recalled. Caine had told her about a girl who had been with him at Stanford. Hadn't she gone to Switzerland or someplace like that?

"Amazing girl." Caine got a faraway look in his eyes as he spoke of her. Anna felt herself bristling. Did he have to talk about his ex and her fabulousness while he was sitting with her, holding her hand?

She knew it wasn't fair of her at all. It had been her idea to date both Caine and Ben, so surely they both had the right to do the same. And when she'd been with Ben last, at the wrap party, the feelings she'd been having for him weren't exactly middling. If she were honest with herself, if those feelings continued, she might have had to initiate this conversation with Caine herself.

"You heard from Bernadette?" Anna ventured.

"She's leaving Switzerland and coming back to the States. She got a job with the athletics department at UCLA."

"And she wondered whether you might want to try again," Anna guessed.

"Something like that." He regarded her thoughtfully. "But she wants it to be exclusive."

Oh. So *that* was why he couldn't date her anymore. Well, he certainly had gone back to Bernadette pretty easily. Which meant he couldn't be all that into her. Which kind of hurt, she had to admit. But a bruised ego was hardly fatal—and nowhere near as bad as a broken heart.

Caine wasn't her boyfriend, and had never been her boyfriend. Not the way Ben had. She'd thought he might become that someday, when they got to know each other better, but what right did she have to expect him to hang around for a "maybe"?

"I've had a great time with you, Anna," Caine continued. Finally, he let go of her hand. "You're fantastic. I hope you realize that."

"Oh, daily," Anna joked. She was already mentally picking herself up and dusting herself off. That she would no longer be seeing Caine began to sink in, and the bad feelings of a moment ago were gone, replaced by a newfound clarity. The competition in her mind was over. The challenger—Caine—had withdrawn. Only Ben remained. It made things easier. So much easier. Because, really, hadn't it always been about Ben, all along?

Anna simply smiled at him. She and Caine had had a lot of fun. But he moonlighted at a bar where he wore jeans, fireman's suspenders, and precious little else. Could a guy like that actually be her boyfriend? It was a better concept in theory than in practice.

"So I take it you're okay with this," he surmised.

"I am. Any words of wisdom before your brokenhearted former not-quite-girlfriend heads back into the cold, cruel world?"

He took another long pull on his beer. "First of all, you're not brokenhearted. I can see that in your eyes. Second of all, Ben is going to be happiest dude in California when you tell him. Which brings me to third of all. I think he's wrong for you. So don't take this as a sign that you should jump into his arms."

"Wait, you're breaking up with me *and* telling me the other guy is wrong for me? Wow."

Across the room, Paul McCartney rose from the piano and embraced a gamine-faced blond woman half his age. Anna thought it might be his daughter, who was a fashion designer. This she only knew because Sam had insisted that Anna buy a pale pink Stella McCartney sheath dress the last time they'd been at the Beverly Center.

"What do you and Ben have in common?" Caine suddenly asked. "Consider that rhetorical. Bernadette and me? We both love an adrenaline rush. We're both rebels who know how to fit in when we have to, to get ahead. You and Ben? What's the real common ground?"

"Great sex?" Anna asked.

Whoa. It had slipped out of her mouth before she could edit herself. She could feel her cheeks redden. Maybe she was becoming more L.A. than she had realized. Even so, she backpedaled furiously.

"I'm absolutely just kidding."

Caine threw his head back and laughed, then grinned wickedly. "That's a good one. But really, it just clouds your judgment. Take it from someone who knows."

"Ben goes to Princeton, and I'm going to Yale," Anna pointed out. Her face still burned from her last ill-advised comment.

"So that means you have what in common exactly? The ability to get into an Ivy League school?" Caine took another long swallow of beer, then looked around for the waitress to order another one. "You're an intellectual, Anna. Literature, history, great thoughts, all that. Ben? He's a Beverly Hills kid. And that's just not you."

"You don't really know me," Anna pointed out coolly, thinking even as she said it that Caine knew her very well, indeed.

"Yeah, okay, point taken." He smiled, raising his hands as if to pronounce that he was backing off. "So listen, how are we going to do this? Will it be the let's-stay-friends thing, or the when we see each other in the movie line we ignore each other?" Caine spotted the waitress—a tall, thin redhead, and motioned toward his beer. She smiled to show that she understood he wanted another one.

"'Let's stay friends' never works. But let's try it anyway," Anna suggested. "You can even buy me a friendly dinner, on one condition."

Caine raised his dark eyebrows. "What's that?"

"We don't talk about Bernadette. Or Ben."

"Deal." He pulled her to him in a bear hug. It was friendly and it felt nice.

Down at the other end of the bar, Paul McCartney was seated at the piano again, but now his daughter was sitting next to him. He started a slow song that drew a round of applause from the bystanders. Then the bar hushed as the musician started to sing one of the great songs about the pain of love lost.

Wordlessly, Anna stood and offered Caine her hand. He took it and they went to the piano to listen. By the end of the song, they were singing softly along about yesterday, when all their troubles seemed far away. Just like friends would.

And she was fine with it, she really was. But his words about Ben were still ringing in her ears. *He's a Beverly Hills kid. And that's just not you.*

Destiny of Dumpdom

What does a girl wear to get dumped?
That had been the question that dogged Sam from the moment she awoke in her room—if you could call all fifteen-hundred square feet of her palaceworthy bedroom suite a "room"—on D-Day. Also known as Dump Day. Eduardo had asked—practically demanded—to meet her at noon for a walk on the Santa Monica Promenade. Sam was absolutely sure that he had chosen the promenade because it would be full of people, its usual eclectic mix of locals, tourists, and well-tolerated street people who called the outdoor mall home.

Yes, Eduardo was going to dump her in public, Sam figured, so that she couldn't—or at least *wouldn't*—make a scene. If she cried, she'd want to keep it under control, because you could bet on your Tiffany diamonds that at that exact moment a photographer from the *Galaxy* or some equally loathsome supermarket tabloid would be right there to snap her photo as she looked teary-eyed and bloated. They always picked the absolute worst angle so that the little people could gloat: *See? She might be rich and famous, but her ass is the size of a relief map of Texas!*

And then there would be the headline:

DOUBLE DUMP!! JACKSON SHARPE DUMPED BY WIFE!
DUMPY DAUGHTER DUMPED BY BOYFRIEND!

So. The all-important getting-dumped-in-public outfit. Sam spent fifteen minutes in her walk-in closet and settled on the understated look: a black-and-white polka-dot Beauty blouse, Chip & Pepper skinny jeans, and a dark Joluka denim jacket, all upgraded by the stunning white leather Jimmy Choo mules on her feet. In her Coach limited-edition gold-flecked oversize bag she stashed exactly three pink Puffs tissues. If there were to be tears—and she couldn't guarantee that there wouldn't be tears—she vowed to herself that there would be only three Puffs' worth. Her recently redone eyelash extensions would be unaffected by tears, as long as she remembered not to actually wipe them with the tissue, but rather to blot carefully. And she didn't have to wear mascara when she was wearing the extensions, hence no mascara could track down her tear-streaked face. That was even better.

At least it was a beautiful day to be dumped: impossibly blue skies, temperatures in the high seventies, and a steady west onshore breeze that made Santa Monica as smog-free as rural Montana. Even the traffic was cooperating—miraculously, there was none. It was almost as if the universe were egging her on, steering her to her destiny of Dumpdom. Sam made the twenty-five-minute drive from Bel Air to Santa Monica in less than nineteen minutes and didn't even get caught by the

lights at Sunset Boulevard and Bundy. Pulling up in front
of the Monsoon Cafe, a restaurant that her father had
once owned, back in the days when actors believed that
restaurants were worth the aggravation, she handed the
Hummer keys over to the black-jacketed valet along with
a twenty and instructions to park it someplace where he
could get to it quickly. When she was ready to leave, she
wanted to be out of there.

Eduardo had suggested they meet at the promenade's
central fountain, about a ten-minute walk north from
where she parked. In the movie version of her life, Sam
realized that she would film this walk in slow motion.
With each step she took, there'd be a flashback to some
memorable moment in her time with Eduardo, complete
with a soaring musical score guaranteed to evoke tears.
One step: their first meeting at Las Casitas in Mexico,
when he'd come across her skinny-dipping in the moon-
light. Another step: their first real date, at the same
resort, when they rode on horseback through the water
to a small, deserted island a quarter mile off the coastline,
where Eduardo had arranged for a romantic meal. Then
the time when he'd acted so selflessly, so sweetly gone
out of his way, agreeing to accompany Sam to her senior
prom.

Quite honestly, her relationship with Eduardo had
changed her. Sam knew she owed all of her fortunate
L.A. status to her pedigree and her brains, because in
the looks department, she simply could not compete.
Oh sure, she would have been in the top third in say,
Peoria—wherever the hell *that* was—but in Beverly
Hills? Money could buy almost anything in the way

of physical promotion, and girls in Beverly Hills had money to spare. Even with her sucked-in this and her altered that and blah, blah, blah, her ankles remained thick, her body pear-shaped. She did not turn heads on Rodeo Drive like Cammie did. Even petite Dee did. And Anna definitely did. But not Sam.

Eduardo—objectively gorgeous by anyone's standards—saw her differently. He thought she was beautiful. It was as if he saw her through a different lens than the rest of the world. It had taken Sam a long time to believe him, but she finally did. Talk about winning a girl over. And now he was going to pull the metaphorical rug out from under her! Buh-bye. The end. It's been fun. Let's do lunch sometime. She even knew why he was breaking up with her—her name was Gisella, and she was an up-and-coming young fashion designer. Peruvian like Eduardo, and—again by objective standards—much better looking than Sam. She had the ability and the skills to design a dress that would make her own ass a Degas in comparison to J.Lo's velvet painting. She spoke the same language. She knew the slang. They knew the same people back home in Lima. Though Eduardo tried to reassure her that he wanted her and not Gisella, Sam knew better.

How would he pull it off? Sam wondered as she made her way past a mime performing for a small crowd of tourists on her way to the fountain. He'd say they ought to make a clean break because he was going to go back to the Sorbonne in Paris in a few weeks, and she'd be starting film school at USC. It was the right thing to do.

The promenade was absolutely jammed. Street musicians weren't just allowed, but encouraged, and she

found herself going the long way around big circles of
people watching a scruffily dressed blues guitarist who
sounded very much like Robert Cray, a hip-hop dance
trio from South Central who spun on a flattened card-
board box placed on the concrete, and then—irony of
ironies—a quintet of South American musicians playing
native songs on the same locally made instruments that
Sam had seen on her visit to Peru with Eduardo right
after graduation.

It gave her a lump in her throat as she stopped to listen. Why had she come, anyway? Just to torture herself?

Because you plan to grovel and beg him not to dump
you and—

No. She might *want* to beg, but she wouldn't.

She reached the fountain and glanced at her gold
Hermès tank watch. Eduardo, who was always on time,
was ten minutes late. Oh God. What if he was the one
who didn't show up? Maybe he'd hired one of those
musicians to sing her a breakup song. Or maybe he'd
sent her a text message but her Razr was off. She pulled
it out of her bag. It was on. No text.

"Hi."

There he was. He looked serious. More serious than
she could recall. This was going to be so humiliating.
She finished the thought this time. Then she echoed his
greeting as the musicians started another song. This one
was slow and mournful. Fuck. It was almost like he'd
planned it.

"Been waiting long?"

"Not really."

"It's a nice day to be out."

"Yeah," she agreed, then swallowed hard. What the hell was going on? What were they, fucking strangers who'd just met at an industry cocktail party? Next he'd be asking her if he could give her a script to slip to her father.

Eduardo was, Sam noted, dressed for business, in a black custom-made Savile Row suit, crisp white shirt, and red tie, which meant he'd just come from his summer job at the Peruvian consulate. He hadn't even kissed her hello. One quick humpty-dump and he'd be back at the office. He probably already had Gisella on speed dial.

To hell with this. She wasn't about to wait around for the axe to fall.

"Eduardo?"

"Yes?"

"Whatever you want to say, can you please just get it over with? So then I can say whatever I'm going to say, and then the two of us can get on with our respective afternoons? I'm supposed to meet Cammie at the Ole Henriksen spa for hot stone massages. I'm hoping for a good story to tell while Olga buffs me into submission."

"You know, I think you're right," Eduardo agreed, in a voice so low that Sam could barely hear it. The fact that the crowd was applauding the band's last song didn't make it any easier to hear. "I'll be right back."

What? She watched in astonishment as he pushed through the crowd and made his way over to the lead musician, a portly, mustachioed man in a magnificent Peruvian poncho who held a lute-like *charango* in his hands. The guy smiled as Eduardo approached, and the two of them engaged in a rapid-fire Spanish conversation. Then the bandleader turned to his group and gave them some quick instructions, and they started to play.

The tune was low and melodic, almost hypnotic. As Sam watched, Eduardo listened for a few moments, then nodded his head in approval.

What the hell was he doing?

"Ladies and gentlemen!" His voice boomed out louder than the pentatonic folk melody. *"Mujeres y caballeros!* In some villages in my country, in Peru, when a man has a special thing to tell a young woman, everyone assembles on the town square. Then the man takes the woman to a quiet place and says what needs to be said. Finally they return, either to the cheers or the consolation of the people of the village."

Okay. This was how guys dumped girls in Peru? This was twisted. This was sick. Sam was not going to be a part of some ridiculous tribal ritual brought to life on the Third Street Promenade in front of an audience of strangers.

"I'm out of here, Eduardo!" She turned on the heels of her Jimmy Choos and started back down the promenade toward her Hummer. At least the valet would be able to get it quickly.

"Stop! *Por favor!"*

Eduardo's voice was so plaintive that she did stop. A moment later, he was by her side, leading her to a side doorway of the Barnes & Noble superstore, which was shielded from the crowd. "I'm sorry," he murmured. "I thought this would be fun."

"My ass it's fun," she hissed. "This is humiliating, that's what it is."

"Be patient. It will be memorable, I believe."

"I'll need a hypnotist to erase it from my memory!" Sam was getting pissed, as much at herself as at Eduardo. Why was she just sticking around and letting this whole disaster unfold on his terms? Why wasn't she being what she'd told Anna to be so many times: an active heroine, taking control of her life?

"I hope you won't have to." Eduardo lifted his right hand and held it with his fist balled, palm up. Then he opened his fist. In it was a small navy blue jewelry box. "For you."

A kiss-off gift. This was the lowest of the low. Her father, back when he'd been known for hitting on the hottest starlets of all his movies—back before he'd married Poppy (and long before he'd wisely kicked her out of the house for cheating on him)—had been famous for kiss-off gifts. There was a jewelry store in the Beverly Center that specialized in them. They were expensive baubles so that the dumper could feel better about punting the dumpee. It was actually something of a Hollywood tradition.

Eduardo had just dropped another notch in her estimation. At least she wasn't crying. She was too pissed for tears.

"Keep it," she shot back. Up went one of her hands, in case he wanted to press the box on her.

"Goddammit, Sam. Why do you have to be so obstinate? No. Don't answer that question. Just open it."

For the first time all afternoon, Eduardo grinned. For the first time since the wrap party for her father's movie, Sam felt the tiniest bit of hope for the future. Then, before she could open the box, Eduardo went down on one knee.

One knee. Hmmm. While it certainly was possible that Peruvian dump-your-girlfriend rituals differed from American dump-your-girlfriend rituals, Sam kind of doubted it involved the one-knee thing. The one-knee-thing meant . . .

But no. It couldn't possibly mean that. Unless . . .

Hesitantly, she took the velvet box with two shaking hands and opened it. Inside was a ring with a single immaculately cut diamond. It wasn't the largest Sam had ever seen. Her father had given Poppy a stone the size of Rhode Island. But this stone was startling in its whiteness. *Startling* was the right word for it. It looked like a miniature gleaming evening star.

"My beautiful Samantha. There is no graceful way to ask this question. My fear that you will reject me knows no bounds. It took all my courage to find the nerve to ask, and now I fear I cannot. Yet I shall ask anyway, because of how much I love you. Will you be my beautiful Samantha forever?"

"Umm, Eduardo?"

"Yes?"

"Can you boil that down to one simple sentence?"

Eduardo smiled and took Sam's hand in both of his. She realized that her hands were still trembling. "Will you marry me?"

Suddenly people all around them, some of the same people who'd been listening to the musicians, were applauding and cheering. Sam looked around and realized they'd drawn a crowd. An elderly Asian couple was snapping photos. A bald girl on Rollerblades was taking video.

Without waiting for her answer, Eduardo leaped out of the doorway back to where the band and the crowd could see him. "I asked!" he shouted. "Now help her answer. *Sí, sí, sí, sí! Sí, sí, sí, sí!*"

The band struck up a new song, and the crowd took up the chant. Six, a dozen, fifty, a hundred people, all shouting, "*Sí!*"

"So what do you say?" Sam felt Eduardo's arms wrap around her. "*Sí?*"

In a town where storytelling turned on reversals—where the expectations of the viewer were flipped by the screenwriter and the director—this particular reversal was too much. The dissonance between he's-going-to-dump-me and he-asked-me-to-marry-him was just too great. Sam felt dizzy and kind of nauseated. Her mouth was dry. She thought it was a miracle that she could even form the words. Fortunately, she could form one.

Samantha Sharpe, who had recently turned eighteen, who never, ever, *ever* thought she'd get married young—if at all—found herself saying, "*Sí.*"

"Eduardo, I'm only eighteen."

"Tell me something I don't already know."

It was thirty minutes later, the diamond was still in its box—though on the table between them—and they were sitting outside at a café called Pauletta's by the Sea, right there on the promenade. Eduardo had ordered a Dos Equis, Sam a lemonade. She wanted to have this particular discussion fully sober. It was one thing to say *sí* in front of a crowd just begging for a happy end to the movie moment they'd just witnessed, and quite another to move on to the actual holy-fuck-I-just-said-I'd-marry-him moment. That's why the diamond wasn't on her hand. A movie moment was one thing. Reality was quite another.

Fuck that. The voice inside her was insistent. *You said yes. You mean yes. Just put on the ring.*

"Eighteen is too young to get married," Sam pointed out. "Hell, look at my father. Forty-five is too young to be married. *No one* stays married."

He reached across the table to caress her hand. "You think this because you are swimming in the tiny fishbowl of American movie stars. My parents have been married to each other for thirty years, and they adore each other."

Sam had to admit, when she'd met his parents, they had seemed to adore each other. But they had to be what was known in Hollywood as a nonrecurring phenomenon. Also known as: a freak of nature. She did not hesitate to share this point of view with her sort-of fiancé.

He was unfazed by her hesitation. "I'm not surprised that you would say this. And please understand: I am not proposing that we start a family for a long time. But when I look at you, and I look at the last months since I've met you, this has been the most wonderful time of my life. When you find true love, you do not throw it away because of age, or distance, or a fishbowl."

"And what are we supposed to do now?" Sam remonstrated. She knew she was looking for every possible reason not to do what her heart was screaming for her to do.

"You're going back to Paris. I'm going to USC. That's not a marriage. That's a separation."

He smiled tenderly. "We can work all of that out. I'm sure we can."

"Such as?"

"There are always options. I can transfer. You can transfer. Maybe I'll defer a year and stay at the consulate here." He reached across the table. She thought he was going to take her hands again, but instead he opened the box. The diamond ring gleamed. "Look at it. It is beautiful, but not so beautiful as you, Samantha. If we want to make it happen, we will make it happen."

Well la-di-da, didn't he make it sound simple. She squinted, doing everything in her power not to look at the ring. If she looked at it, she would put it on. If she put it on, she would never take it off.

"Can I ask you something?"

"Of course."

She cocked her chin back toward the Peruvian musicians, who were still holding forth up the promenade, their music still spirited but much fainter now that she and Eduardo were sitting on the patio. "All that stuff you said, about it being traditional in the village for a man to ask a woman an important question. When your father asked your mother to marry him, did he do that?"

Eduardo threw his head back and laughed.

"I'm serious!" Sam told him.

"To tell you the truth, I wanted it to be memorable. So I had to—how do they say it?—punk you."

Damn. Well, he sure as hell had done that.

She looked at the ring. He saw where her gaze was focused.

"Don't put it on until you are sure. We will talk and talk and talk. There is no hurry."

And they talked for hours, until day turned into evening. She raised every logical argument about why they shouldn't get married. He knocked them all down like bowling pins with a bazooka and painted a portrait of a future worthy of Monet. They would travel the world. He would be a diplomat, she would be a filmmaker. They would speak two languages at home as easily as others spoke one. They would make love every day and twice on Saturdays. They'd have wrinkled sex when they got old and die in each other's arms when they were both a hundred, because they'd love each other too much to keep on living.

Finally, they were the only customers left. Their original waitress stood by, clearing her throat discreetly.

"We'd better give her a hell of a tip," Sam decided. She couldn't believe how long they'd been out there. Or what had brought them there, to see day turn into evening into night. He'd asked her to marry him. That was a ring on the table. That ring was for her.

Charlie Kaufman couldn't write anything this weird.

"I agree." But he made no move to do it.

"I have cash."

Sam went to open her Coach hobo bag, but Eduardo caught her hand. "Do you know what's in your heart?"

"Yes. A little voice telling me that you're insane."

"Thank you. Thank you very much. Look what you have to look forward to. A lifetime of insanity."

"It sounds . . ."

How did it sound? It sounded absolutely insane. Absolutely and completely insane. Which is why, finally, Sam took out the ring. Eduardo took the gleaming diamond and slipped it delicately on the ring finger of her left hand.

She adored it. She adored *him*. The ring sparkled on her tanned finger. She loved it and it made her nervous, both at the same time. She wondered if this was how every bride-to-be felt at the moment when the dream of her childhood turned into the reality of her life.

Who was she going to tell first? Her father? Cammie? Or Anna?

This was Hollywood. There was only one answer: conference call.

The Bank of Birnbaum

"If you hadn't spotted this place, there's no way we'd be here," Ben exulted as he looked around the dilapidated, neglected interior of Superior Body and Repair. "How incredible would this place be for a nightclub?"

"The question is, how did you arrange for us to get inside?" Anna asked. She peered around the place as well. It had clearly seen better days.

He shrugged. "Money talks, bullshit walks. In my case, I expressed keen interest in the property to the owner and even hinted that I'd fork over the back taxes. It's amazing how fast they got a set of keys in my hands. It's been a long time since this place was open. Half the keys were bent." He grinned as he ran a finger through the thick dust on a dented beige filing cabinet. "Not that there's anything to steal in here, anyway."

It was late in the afternoon, two days after they had walked past this abandoned building the night of the *Ben-Hur* party. Now they were inside. Ben had advised that she wear her most beat-up and expendable clothing, because the place was bound to be dusty. He was right—

the interior was so sullied with a mixture of dust, filth, and accumulated mouse and pigeon droppings that Anna had immediately donned the mouth-and-nose guard that Ben proffered. She wore an old pair of faded Earl jeans and a black Hanes T-shirt she'd swiped from her father's drawer.

Ben was similarly attired, but it was hard to tell, because the exterior windows were so caked over with grime that little natural light came through. Yet Anna could see his eyes, and judging from the faraway look in them, what he saw was pure possibility. Anna squinted and tried to imagine the same thing. She *wanted* to see it, for his sake. But it was hard. All she saw were the grungy remnants of all things automotive. She hoped that being here would bring Ben back to reality.

"Over there, by the hydraulic lifts?" Ben's finger stabbed the air. "That's where we'll put the dance floor. But when we get the lifts working, we can have dancers up on the risers. Where the customer waiting area was? How about a mini-theater? Tiny stage, seats for five or ten people to watch the actors, poets, rappers, performing artists, up close and personal."

"And how about where the gas pumps are now?" Anna prompted. She couldn't help but be charmed by his enthusiasm, even if she didn't share it.

Ben thought a moment. "I'm not sure. Maybe we'd take them down altogether and put in an outdoor café." Then he smacked his palm against the clipboard he was holding. "I know! What if we do car washes for people as part of our valet service? No, wait, we have gorgeous girls in bikinis do the car wash. Clubgoers drop their cars there, see them washed—it's definite added value."

"Not to mention eye candy," Anna teased, though she realized it was actually a very creative idea. She wandered around the interior. Ben was seeing the club. She was seeing work. Lots of it. And money. Even more. "Do you have any idea what this will cost?"

He nodded vigorously. "I talked to my boss at Trieste. He doesn't see this as competition—too far away—so he ran some numbers for me. He figures two and a half million for renovations and licenses, plus another one point five mil for advertising, staffing, et cetera. I really need four mil to get this place open and make a splash while I'm doing it. I've been working on the proposal nonstop for two days."

Anna smiled sweetly. She'd never see Ben this excited about anything. It was invigorating, in a way. "Well, I must be a club kid at heart, since I found the place, huh?"

"Under the pearls and the pedigree, you mean. Maybe I should add a reading corner. Chekhov, Proust, Balzac, and Dickens. Just for you."

"Very funny." She beamed at him, in all his kid-on-Christmas-morning giddy excitement. It was the strangest thing—she hadn't thought once about Caine or their parting of ways since their conversation at the W Hotel bar. It was as though it had been her and Ben all along, and the Caine thing had never even happened. With Caine out of the picture, it suddenly seemed clear that he'd only been there in the first place to tell Anna what she really needed: a step back from her relationship with Ben. And now that she'd had it, she felt more ready to throw herself into it headlong than she ever had before. True, she wasn't a thousand percent behind his club idea. The upshot was clear, if it ever came to fruition: It would mean his dropping out of Princeton after only one year. The idea appalled Anna—not that she'd said as much to Ben. Oh sure, he could always go back and finish his degree later. But Anna felt certain that though people said such things, in reality, "later" never came.

Then there was the painful long-distance-romance piece of the equation. It would be one thing for them to travel a few hours every other weekend between his school in Princeton, New Jersey, and her school in New Haven, Connecticut. It would be quite another to keep their relationship going with her in college on the East Coast, and him in L.A. running his nightclub. How was *that* going to work? She'd seen plenty of kids at her high school with so-called long-distance relationships. There were girls with boyfriends at Choate, or Exeter, or St. Paul's. These relationships inevitably faltered.

She didn't say any of this to him though. For one thing, she was the one who had pulled back on their relationship, so she really didn't have the right to question how they'd handle . . . whatever. For another thing, she definitely didn't want to dampen his enthusiasm.

"How long do you think it'll take you to get the place open?" Anna asked. There was a roll of blue paper work towels in the middle of the floor. She tore off three squares and wiped her hands, though she'd been careful not to touch anything.

Before Ben could reply, his cell rang.

"Yeah?" he answered. "Be right there," he said gruffly, then hung up. "We've got a visitor."

"Who?"

"My dad. Also known as the Bank of Birnbaum. Come on, let's let him in."

As they moved to the front door—avoiding several piles of debris along the way—Anna marveled that Dr. Birnbaum was buying into his only son's plans so easily. Ben had explained that he'd need a hefty loan—or even an outright gift—from his father to make the club happen. And if it was going to cost four mil, well . . . Anna couldn't imagine asking her own father for that sum to get a risky new venture off the ground. It simply was not Jonathan Percy's style to do such a thing, though he habitually bet millions of dollars on hedge funds, stock options, and initial public offerings. And should she ask her mother, Anna knew she'd be greeted by a look that said, *Did the dog just soil the carpet?*

Still, Anna knew that nepotism was as common in Hollywood as anywhere else—if not more so. Recently a major movie star from the 1980s who'd starred in just about every seminal teen film of that era had gotten her daughter the role of *her* daughter in a huge movie. The girl, who went to Beverly Hills High, hadn't even been able to snag a walk-on in the school play, but now she had a supporting role in a studio picture. As Sam had dryly explained once to her, buying your offspring a career was commonplace. Though Anna wasn't sure if the children of plastic surgeons to the stars qualified, Ben certainly seemed to think they did.

He opened the door to reveal Dr. Daniel Birnbaum. Anna hadn't seen him in months—not since the Academy Awards, in fact, where Dr. Birnbaum had taken her aside to remark on how hung up Ben was on her. She remembered him as being tall, with swept-back silver hair and chiseled features, and in excellent physical condition. The hair and the features were the same, but the physique had been bench-pressed, ab-crunched, and squatted into shape that would make Mr. Universe proud. Dr. Birnbaum wore faded jeans and a red Lacoste tennis shirt, the better to show off his hard body.

"Anna!" he boomed as he hugged her. "Great to see you again! Always knew you two were meant for each other."

She returned the hug as best she could. Even after almost eight months in Los Angeles, she still wasn't used to the idea that people you hardly knew would hug and kiss you as a greeting. Or tell you the most intimate details of their lives. It was just so . . . so L.A.

"Nice to see you too, Dr. Birnbaum." She smiled politely as he unhanded her and gave Ben a warm hug.

"Dan, please," he corrected.

"I'm glad you're here, Dad," Ben told him.

"You asked, I'm here. But I've got a rhinoplasty and tummy tuck in an hour and fifteen at Cedars-Sinai. Why don't you show me around this amazing discovery of yours?"

With Anna in tow, Ben played tour guide, painting a picture of how he saw the club taking shape as he walked his father through the various areas of the abandoned body shop. Dr. Birnbaum hung on every word, quizzing his son about things that Anna hadn't even considered: parking, security, marketing and advertising, bookkeeping and accounting. But for every question, Ben seemed to have a ready answer. When he didn't, he consulted his clipboard and found the answer there.

"Where can we sit down and talk?" Dr. Birnbaum asked, after a tour that had stretched for twenty minutes.

"I got that covered too. Come on out back."

Ben motioned to the back door. Outside, Anna was surprised to see three wooden folding chairs around a metal card table. On that card table was a red cooler full of ice-cold soft drinks, bottled water, and beer.

"No alcohol for me." Dr. Birnbaum patted his taut stomach. "Never before I cut."

"So, what do you think?" Ben asked as he took the seat across from his father, with Anna in between them. He gave Anna a bottle of pomegranate juice and cracked open a can of Guinness for himself.

Dr. Birnbaum took a long swallow of Fiji water before he responded. "You know that since I started my program, I live a life of complete honesty."

If this preamble fazed Ben, he didn't show it. Anna realized he probably heard it all the time, now that his father was a twelve-stepper. In fact, she remembered hearing the same thing from him at the Academy Awards.

"Good," Ben replied. He nodded enthusiastically, urging his father to continue. "I like you better when you're honest."

"I like me better too, son. How much are you estimating you need to make this club work?"

Ben gave him the clipboard. "Budget's on the third page. At least, it starts there."

Dr. Birnbaum studied the numbers there as if they were some kind of oracle. Then he turned to Anna.

"What do you think of this venture?"

"I think it has . . . potential." She thought that was the right note to strike, not wanting to speak out of turn about something she knew virtually nothing about.

"You have good judgment. I agree." Dr. Birnbaum checked out the figures in the budget again.

"That's great, Dad!" Ben couldn't contain his enthusiasm. "We can go to your attorney tomorrow and draw up the—"

Dr. Birnbaum held up one cautioning hand to his son. "Hold on! I didn't say I was in. It has potential, for someone who knows what they're doing. That could be you, Ben. Someday. But not now."

Ben looked incredulous. "We talked. You said you wanted to back my dreams because your father never backed yours."

"And I will," Dr. Birnbaum agreed. "But you've been in the club business for what—part of a summer? At someone else's club? That doesn't qualify you to run one on your own."

Anna looked over at Ben, who just seemed to wilt. "You're not going to be my backer then. I can't count on you."

"You've only finished one year of college. You know how many years of school I did? Undergrad and then medical school and then my surgical specialty training. And then I trained in someone else's practice before I went out on my own fifteen years ago. Look what you're trying to do—go into the operating room and start cutting without that training, so to speak."

"Maybe you failed to notice"—Ben's voice was tight with anger—"I'm not you. And maybe you failed to notice that a nightclub is not an operating room!"

Dr. Birnbaum shook his head lightly and took another swallow from his water bottle. "I noticed. Especially that you're not me. And yes, I have the money. But Ben, money is not lighter fluid. I don't intend to burn it. And I would be burning it if I invested in this half-baked insanity." He turned to Anna. "Help me talk some sense into my kid!"

"Um . . ." They were both looking at her. Anna had no idea what to say. "Maybe finishing college first really is a good idea, Ben," she ventured awkwardly.

"Exactly!" Dr. Birnbaum exclaimed, clapping her knee with a hand. "Smart girl. She knows this plan is nuts. I know you're disappointed, but in the long run, son, you'll thank me."

"No problem, Dad." Ben smiled coldly. "Can you see yourself out?"

Dr. Birnbaum rose, shaking his head sadly as he did. "I love you, Ben. And I believe in you—"

"Dad?"

"Yes?"

"Just go. If you follow the alley, you'll get to your car.'"

"It was lovely to see you, Anna," Dr. Birnbaum said finally, giving her a quick peck on the cheek and then making his way out of the club.

As soon as he was out of sight, Ben whirled around.

"Potential?" His voice was dripping with sarcasm. "He likes you. He thinks you have good judgment. And all you could say was that you think the place has *potential*?" The emphasis he put on the word *potential* made it sound like the Ebola virus.

Anna was taken aback by his anger. All that she'd been doing was trying to help. When they'd arrived at the shop, she'd been totally skeptical. By the time they'd sat down with his father, she'd felt something close to supportive, even if she didn't think his opening this club right now was a good idea. "But I *do* think it has potential!"

"You made it sound like you agreed with him. Like I'm just some overindulged child who wants to play in a bigger sandbox."

Anna's heart was pounding. "That's not fair."

"I asked you to be here because I wanted to have someone backing me up," he said quietly, his eyes focused on the hard ground of the alley behind the shop.

Anna's heart began to sink. She knew Ben was overreacting, but at least now she knew why. She'd been so carefully buttoned-up about her true opinions when he'd first voiced his plan to her, and then she'd only let her hesitation show in front of his father. He must have felt utterly betrayed.

"Ben, just . . . listen to me a minute." She touched his arm lightly. "I'm sorry I didn't back you up the way you wanted me to. Very sorry. But you have to admit it's possible that your dad is right. Sure, you could drop out of Princeton. But to turn your back on your education to open a nightclub—"

"My God. You sound just like him!" Ben muttered, tugging his arm out from under her fingers.

She moved her folding chair closer to his. "I know this might be what you want right now, but who's to say what you're going to want in five years? What if what you want then requires a college education? It might not even be that long—if the club isn't a success, you might find yourself—"

"Don't go there, Anna," Ben cut her off, his tone warning.

"What are you—?"

"Don't start lecturing me on not knowing myself, not knowing what I want." His voice was low, almost forboding. His piercing blue eyes suddenly had a dangerous glint to them. "Not when you don't even know if you want Caine or me."

"Is that what this is really about?" Anna sat up straighter in her hard chair, surprised. "You're still angry about Caine? You don't need to be. Caine told me—"

"You know, I don't want to hear about that asshole. Save it." He stood abruptly and chucked his father's empty Fiji water bottle toward the black metal trash can by the door. It bounced off the side, but he made no effort to retrieve it. Instead, Anna saw his shoulders sag in defeat. Then he turned and regarded her. "The thing that kills me is, for all your talk about a five-year plan, you don't even know what *you* want or who *you* are— you're just doing what was set out for you." His tone was icy and had an edge to it she'd never heard before. The glint in his eyes was still there.

She felt her cheeks redden. "That's not fair," she said

quietly, almost in a whisper. "Don't take your anger at your father out on me."

Ben grabbed his full beer bottle from the table, took an angry swig, and then threw it into the trash can too. It landed with a loud, reverberating clang. "No, really Anna. Tell me. Are you the New York intellectual I met on the plane, or are you the West Coast party chick? You came to L.A. to get to know your dad better. Did you do that? Or did you give up on him as quickly as I'm watching you give up on me? Don't talk to me about consistency, about knowing what I want. You want me, then you don't want me; then you want me again. You set up these impossible standards and when I don't live up to them—when I don't even know what they *are*—you get all disappointed in my lack of perfection."

"I don't deserve this, Ben." She was trying desperately to control the tremor in her voice. It didn't work. Tears came to her eyes.

"It's easy to take the path everyone expects of you, Anna." He started folding up the chairs one by one. Each closed with a hard clang. "So you played around in L.A. for a few months. But then you're going right back to the path that was laid out for you the day you were born. I bet you tested into the right preschool when you were four and just kept moving up the ladder from there. The next notch is Yale, so that's where you'll go, just like your mother and everyone else expects you to."

Anna stood and kept her voice cool. "You're taking your anger out on me when you're really pissed off at your father." She could feel her fingernails digging into the palms of her hands. No matter how much he was taking his anger out on her, she wasn't going to sink to his level. And she wasn't going to let him see how much he'd rattled her, taken the snow globe that was her life and shaken it so thoroughly that the pieces were falling from the heavens to the floor.

"Maybe," Ben allowed. He'd folded the other two chairs and now reached for the one she'd just abandoned. "Or maybe I'm just finally saying what needs to be said. You came to L.A. to shake things up in your life. Then you met me, a guy who was still acceptable because I had the Ivy stamp of approval. Because when you first saw me, I was wearing a Princeton sweatshirt. And now what—you can't stand the thought of being with a dropout, a guy whose dream is a nightclub rather than passing the bar? The truth is, for all your talk of mixing things up, you're too afraid to make a mistake. You're too afraid to go off the beaten path. You're always going to do what you were born and bred to do." With that, he grabbed her chair and closed it with a swift, final motion.

I won't cry. I won't cry. I won't cry, Anna vowed to herself. She gulped hard so that she could at least make an effort to speak without her voice shaking. "If you think so little of me, why do you even want to be with me?"

"Good point. I guess I don't. You know where the exit is—it's the way my father went." Ben rubbed a weary hand over his face. Then he headed back inside, leaving Anna by herself in the alley. She was alone, in a way she hadn't been in a very long time.

Bye, Bye Love

S am awoke to the sound of house finches chirping outside the open bedroom window of Eduardo's condo
on the Wilshire corridor between the 405 and the ocean.
She felt so fabulous that she thought she might just chirp
along with them if she could do so in tune, which she
definitely could not. Singing was not her talent. Hopefully,
film directing was; she was still on the lookout for a script
that would be her first full-length (if low-budget) feature.

With the pesky falling-in-love-with-the-right-guy thing
out of the way, she figured the script search would be a snap.
Everyone and his brother or sister was a writer in Los Angeles. You just had to shovel through a lot of shit to find the
hidden jewel.

Speaking of shit. Holy shit. She was *engaged*. She nearly
laughed with joy as she turned to study Eduardo's profile.
He was still asleep, one hand flung overhead, the muscles
in his shoulder and upper arm golden and defined. The
covers had slid down to his waist. She took in his torso,
the lean six-pack, the sheer beauty of him. This dashing,
fantastic, smart, sweet, wonderful guy loved her. Really,
really loved her, exactly as she was.

Damn. The ring was on her finger. She lifted it and
let the morning sun bounce though the diamond's fac-
ets. Brilliant. The guy had great taste in bling. If only her
friends could be so lucky.

It was ironic even for the town that had invented the
Age of Irony. Anna, who'd been so tight with Ben, had
called her late yesterday after her terrible argument with
him. Then Cammie had sent a text to mark the end of
her relationship with Adam Flood: ADAM CIAO ON 2 THE
NXT . . . Out of Sam, Cammie, Dee, and Anna, Sam had
always figured herself to be the least likely to end up
romantically happy, mostly because she only attracted
guys with an agenda: get next to the daughter of America's Most Beloved Action Hero. And yet, here she was.
Next to *him*. With *this* on her left ring finger.

She hadn't shared her news with Cammie or Anna
yet—or with anyone, for that matter. Normally Sam was
as much a part of the Tinseltown gossip mill as everyone
else. But about this? It felt delicious to keep the secret
for herself. For just a little while. The conference call
could wait.

Eduardo stirred, stretched like a panther, and opened
his eyes.

She smiled at him. "I was watching you sleep."

On the nightstand next to his bed, his cell phone
rang. He ignored it, slinked an arm around her, and
curled her into him, kissing her forehead. "Very boring,
I imagine."

"Better than most of what's on TV, actually," Sam
quipped, even as she wondered if she had morning mouth.
If she did, he certainly didn't seem to mind as he kissed

her, raising himself on one flat palm to peer at her in the bright morning sunlight.

For a moment she felt her usual panic—that her face wasn't pretty enough, that her body wasn't good enough, that her calves were the size of a thousand-year-old redwood's trunk. But Eduardo's eyes only got that lusty look she loved.

"Such a beauty." He nibbled at her neck, her collarbone, and then between the tops of her breasts. Then his cell sounded again. This time he checked caller ID.

"Sorry, I have to take this. *Hola.*" He answered the phone as he swung his legs out of bed, cradling it between his ear and his shoulder as he pulled on his red silk boxers and walked through the archway into the living room to continue the conversation. Sam strained to hear. Whatever he was talking about was entirely in Spanish. She could only make out a few words. *Nuevo York*—New York—was one of them. Then he was in a part of the apartment where she couldn't hear at all.

A few minutes later, he returned to the bedroom. She had been dearly hoping they'd pick up where they had left off, but now Eduardo sat on the edge of the bed, looking very serious. "I have to go to New York."

Damn.

"When?"

"This afternoon. The president of Peru is coming to speak at a special conference at the United Nations in a few days. The guy who was supposed to do the prep work at our mission to the UN had to go home to Lima because of some medical crisis in his family—I don't know all the details and frankly I don't want to know. So they've got me on a flight out of LAX in three hours."

"Need a ride to the airport?" Sam offered, trying to be understanding. Eduardo didn't have an ordinary job. He was an official representative of his country's government here in America. If the president of Peru needed him, he needed to be there, recent engagement or not.

He shook his head. "They're picking me up from the consulate here. They want to do some kind of briefing. Please put some coffee on, okay?"

"Okay." Geez, he was all business. But she put on one of his dress shirts, dropped two English muffins into his toaster, and brewed a pot of strong coffee while he showered, shaved, dressed, and packed in under thirty minutes. The coffee was in a mug on the table when he came into the kitchen with a garment bag. He was wearing a white shirt similar to the one he'd had on yesterday, a yellow silk tie in a double Windsor, and a charcoal gray business suit with black Bruno Maglis.

"When will you be back?"

"As soon as I can. I've got a bride-to-be waiting for me. That means I'm highly motivated."

She grinned happily, loving to hear him say it. "Don't forget your passport."

He tapped his back pocket. "Got it. But thanks for reminding me. I've forgotten it before."

"I miss you already."

"Me, too," he said, but he seemed distracted, as if this trip had already started for him. Well, that was fine. It was business, which was a far cry from lolling in bed together. But Sam was a big believer in mixing business with pleasure whenever possible. And while he'd been showering and packing, she'd gotten a terrific idea. In fact, she'd already made a few phone calls to put that idea into action.

"You know, I'm not doing much over the next few days," Sam said casually. She hoped he'd invite her to go with him. She hadn't been in Manhattan since the previous fall for a film festival at Lincoln Center, and she loved it there. What fun that would be, and so romantic: in New York City with her new fiancé. And if she booked a suite at the Hotel Gansevoort down in the old Meatpacking District, there'd be plenty of opportunity for pleasure.

"Well, hang out with your friends," Eduardo suggested. "And work on finding the right script for your sensational movie."

Either he hadn't gotten her hint or he hadn't *wanted* to get her hint. No, that was impossible. It was the former, not the latter. Either one had the same operative effect: He was going alone. Then he gave her a quick kiss goodbye, said he'd call when he could, and was out the door. Sam padded back into the bedroom with his untouched coffee and sprawled out on Eduardo's bed. She felt disappointed, slightly ticked, and—okay, she had to admit—somewhat anxious. Her brand-spanking-new fiancé had just taken off for the other side of the country, and he hadn't even thought of inviting her to go along.

"Me? I am the last person in the world who should give you guy advice. Because if someone were grading me, I'd flunk."

Anna stirred some milk into her pot of English

Breakfast tea as she spoke. She and Sam were sitting at an outdoor table at the City Bean coffee emporium, on Lindbrook Drive near UCLA. Each of them had chosen a jeans/T-shirt combo. Even though it was early August, the Westwood district was bustling with students— almost as bustling, Anna thought, as Bleecker Street back home in New York. Sam had called an hour earlier with the news that Eduardo had had to leave on a last-minute business trip to New York, and hadn't even considered inviting her along. She needed help figuring out what it meant.

But that hadn't been the shocking news. No, the shocker was the late morning sun sending glimmers of refracted light off the rock on her left ring finger. Anna had already said the requisite "I'm so happy for you." And she certainly was happy that Sam was happy, especially because Anna really liked Eduardo.

But *engaged*? Sam? It seemed so out there, so . . . so premature. Anna wondered—though she didn't dare say it—if Sam hadn't said yes because she was afraid of losing Eduardo. If that was the case, it seemed like the wrong way to be betrothed.

Betrothed. Was that even a word that anyone used anymore? And what insight could she possibly offer into the Eduardo-asked-me-to-marry-him-one-day-and-took-off-for-New-York-without-me-the-next crisis? She herself had barely slept the night before because of her fight with Ben. They'd argued before, but this was different. He'd said horrible things designed to cut her. She felt as if she'd been bled out; used up, empty, and fragile. She was the last person on the planet who could help a friend figure out the mind of her newly minted fiancé. Wasn't that supposed to happen *before* two people got engaged?

They were sitting close to the low-slung redbrick building, behind a short red wooden fence that separated the café seating from the sidewalk. Anna looked around. Every table was taken—didn't anyone in Los Angeles work during the day? To Anna's left was a young woman who carried a small white Pomeranian with an emerald collar. She was bellowing into her cell phone at a volume that could be heard in San Diego, ignoring the older woman—her mother, most likely—with whom she sat. To their right was a twentysomething couple who were clearly in the throes of lust. They had matching short punk hairdos and matching nose rings. As they held hands across the table, they had eyes only for each other. Their full cappuccinos sat untouched.

She and Ben had been that way once.

"When I asked Ben and Caine to date me . . . at the same time," Anna began, "was that when I wrecked everything? I really want to know."

"Maybe." Sam sighed. "Of course, if Cammie were here, she'd say definitely. But what I wanna know is, would Eduardo have invited me to New York if I'd said no to his marriage proposal? Let me answer that. Maybe. Maybe now he doesn't even think he needs to make an effort?"

"Maybe." Anna sighed. A lot of maybes. At least Sam wasn't sugarcoating the bad news for her, so she wasn't about to sugarcoat it for Sam. She'd felt so strong when she'd asked Ben and Caine to take a step back and date her. It had seemed like such an independent, powerful notion. Something that an active heroine would do. But look where it had led. The truth was self-evident: Both guys had dropped her.

Sam said she was hungry, and a waitress with butt-length platinum blond hair, whose fat-injected lips were spackled with strawberry lip gloss, came to take their lunch order. They both ordered chicken Caesar salads. Not that Anna had any kind of an appetite—she could never eat when she was upset, even though she knew Sam was just the opposite. As if to illustrate that, Sam called the Donatella Versace lookalike waitress back and added a side of fries.

"The Caine thing doesn't really hurt," Anna mused aloud when the waitress had gone inside to place their order. "Except for my ego, I mean. But Ben—"

"I don't get why you did what you did. You're in love with the boy and you pushed him away."

"Because it all happened so fast—"

"Oh, please." Sam waved a dismissive hand. "Look how fast it happened between me and Eduardo. When it's right, it's right." She downed the café Americano she'd ordered when they arrived. "God. Sometimes I wish I smoked. This would be a great time for a cigarette. Of course, you can't smoke in public anymore, anyway. Where was I? Oh yeah. Maybe I don't get this little New York wrinkle, but I'm wearing his engagement ring. I must be doing something right."

Anna didn't necessarily agree, but there was no point in saying so. Nothing felt right anymore; not the California sun slanting down, not the crystalline blue sky, not the smell of the salty ocean just a few miles away, not the pouty-lipped waitress or the movie-star-handsome valet she saw getting into the cherry red Lamborghini as its balding fiftysomething owner flipped him the keys.

She recalled Caine telling her that she didn't belong with Ben, that he was a Beverly Hills kid and "that's just not you." Maybe it was West Coast Ben who hadn't fit with East Coast her. Maybe this whole experiment was a failure. Maybe she didn't belong here at all.

"I'm ready to go home." Anna felt the words spill out of her.

"I hear ya," Sam agreed with a brisk nod, dumping a packet of Equal into her steaming coffee. "But stay with me. If I eat french fries alone, I'll never forgive myself. And I'll never forgive you if you don't eat half of them."

"I don't mean home to my father's place," Anna said slowly, stirring her tea as the idea began to form itself more fully in her mind. "I mean . . . home to New York." She looked up into Sam's surprised eyes. "Yale starts in three weeks anyway. What's the point in hanging out here now?" She shrugged and put her spoon back down on the table. "I should just pack my stuff and go back to Manhattan."

"Um . . . me?" There was a palpable edge to Sam's voice. "You've got a job with my dad's company helping me read scripts, remember? We're looking for one for me to direct too?"

"I can do that from New York. You can just FedEx me scripts and—"

"How about a little thing called friendship?"

Anna saw the hurt in Sam's eyes and felt bad that she'd carelessly blurted out her feelings.

"Sam, listen to me. Maybe it's not so much that I want to be in New York as it is that I want to be far from Ben. Besides, there's a cocktail party for incoming freshmen at the Yale Club in a couple of days."

"And the Yale Club is in Manhattan?"

Anna nodded. "Near Grand Central Station."

Sam held up a palm. "Speak no further—brilliance is breeding and multiplying in my great brain. We go to New York *together*. Just for a few days."

Anna looked at her friend thoughtfully for a moment. Actually, that really *was* appealing. Several days of shopping, seeing Cyn and some of her other old friends, maybe some real New York culture like MoMA or the ballet—she didn't know if she could drag Sam to Mostly Mozart, but it was certainly worth a try. Sam knew Cyn from their trip to Las Vegas in the spring. The three of them could hang together. It was the perfect thing to make her forget all about her never-ending tragicomedy with Ben Birnbaum and her L.A. experiment gone awry.

"We should stay at the Gansevoort hotel downtown," Sam went on, her eyes lighting up with enthusiasm. "We'll get a suite. We'll party our asses off. And I'll surprise Eduardo."

Anna looked at her friend with a knowing smile. There it was. Of course Sam wanted to go to New York. She wanted to find out what the hell Eduardo was up to.

Well, Anna didn't blame her for having ulterior motives—especially not when they dovetailed so perfectly with what she herself was craving so strongly right now. She hoped things would work out for Sam and Eduardo better than they had worked out for her and Ben. Because losing him this time hurt so much that Anna didn't think even three thousand miles between them could begin to heal the wound.

"You've got a deal," she said finally, moving her glass over as Sam's french fries arrived. "And I'll do you one better than the Gansevoort—we can stay at my house."

"How amazing would this have been?" Ben asked Cammie as they wandered past the row of long-abandoned hydraulic car lifts. She looked around at the layers of dust and grime, wondering which "amazing" part he was referring to. "I mean, sure, new clubs open in this town all the time. But my ideas are fresh, and this space . . ." He shook his head. "Culver City is cutting edge. There's nothing here now, which means we could establish something, the way the Meatpacking District became the spot for clubbing in New York. The space is off the hook. I have a million ideas." He leaned against a support pillar, seemingly not caring whether the accumulated filth rubbed off on his weathered denim jacket.

"So you're saying first your dad said he'd finance you, and then he changed his mind?" Cammie wanted clarification. When she'd called Ben for a friendly "Hey, want to get a drink?" he'd brought her here first, to show her the place of his dreams that had died on the vine.

Not that Cammie was seeing "successful club" in this piece-of-crap, covered-with-filth abandoned auto body repair shop. Hello—Culver City? Sure, the area could become the next big thing. But so could Cincinnati.

She herself was careful not to brush up against anything, lest the Nanette Lepore pink-and-white tartan
plaid strapless wool dress she wore be sullied: The dress
was brand-spanking-new. Its hem landed a mere two
inches past the bottom of her creamy La Perla thong.
Her impressive cleavage was on display too. Cammie
knew she looked fabulous. Just because this was a "casual,
friendly" outing didn't mean it couldn't turn into more.
Adam deserved to have his nose rubbed in his betrayal of
her. Without going into details, Ben had mentioned that
he and Anna were less than cozy these days as well.

It was almost as if fate were *begging* her to step into
the breach. And . . . okay, if she was going to be perfectly
honest with herself—a great rarity—the fact that Adam
hadn't tried harder to win her back hurt. Wasn't he supposed to be so madly in love with her? Was he really the
kind of guy to give up that easily? Or did he think *she*
wasn't the kind of girl worth fighting for?

"My father makes me nuts," Ben growled, bringing
Cammie back to the present. "He pretended to be all
interested in supporting my dreams, but he was against
it from the start. Then he told me later that he'd talked it
over with his step-sponsor from Gamblers Anonymous.
I never even met this asshole, you understand. My father
is so under this guy's thumb . . . it makes me sick."

"Well, that sucks," Cammie sympathized. She wasn't
big on college herself. In fact, she didn't plan to go at all.
What would be the point? She was already filthy rich,
and smarter about the things that really mattered than

pretty much anyone she knew. Besides, it wasn't like she didn't have plans. She was ready to launch her career in model management, and already had her first model, Champagne Jones, who at five-foot six was never going to make the runway. She'd talked a top new designer, Martin Rittenhouse—he was utterly corrupt but just as talented—into designing a line of petite clothing around Champagne. Now she was just waiting for Rittenhouse to finish his designs so she could begin to get Champagne showcased.

Then there was her father's business. If Cammie wanted to become a talent agent, she could walk into a gig at her father's firm tomorrow. There was nothing that college would teach her that she didn't already know or couldn't learn on the job. Hell, she'd learned most of it just from being under the same roof as the relentless Clark Sheppard.

The idea of spending four years stuck in lecture halls getting writer's cramp while some dopey professor with a comb-over and dandruff on the shoulders of his drip-dry shirt droned on about . . . *whatever* . . . was *not* Cammie's idea of a good time. She didn't really think it suited Ben, either.

"I even have a name for the place," Ben went on, that wistful tone still coloring his words. "Bye, Bye Love."

God. If he'd picked a name, he *was* serious.

"I love that," Cammie agreed. "This wouldn't be a club for love. It would be a club for fun, right? Check anything heavier at the door."

"That's exactly it. You know, even after my dad said no, I'm still getting ideas. I see vintage car seats instead of banquettes. Maybe an old-fashioned drive-in movie screen on one wall, showing nothing but party scenes."

"Or sex scenes," Cammie elaborated.

"No fucking *Casablanca*," Ben went on. "I don't care if Sam's dad does want to remake it."

"Or *Sleepless in Seattle*. In fact, no chick flicks at all."

He grinned. "You're seeing it like I'm seeing it."

"I am." She lifted the curls off her neck and saw Ben glance at the swell of her breasts. Underneath those curls, the well-oiled wheels were turning. When Adam did come crawling back—because in her heart of hearts, Cammie still believed he would—wouldn't it make him nuts if she was involved with Ben's new club? Heavily involved? *Very* heavily involved?

And then there was the joy she would get watching Anna's face when she heard the news. Not to mention the flexing of Cammie's guy-magnet muscles. At the party after the fashion show a few weeks ago, she had told Anna in no uncertain terms that if she and Adam were over, she and Ben would follow closely on that relationship's haute couture coattails. The idea held great appeal for Cammie. What better way to prove that both guys she'd loved hadn't dumped her than by proving she could make the second jealous by getting the first one back?

"So . . . how much did you need to finance this baby?" she asked casually, twirling one strawberry blond lock around her pinky finger. She liked how it looked against her bubble-gum pink manicure.

"Well, I've got half a mil I can put in without my father, but I'd need at least two more to get the place in shape, hire the right people, yada, yada. I've taken it down a bit from my first budget, but I still think it'll work."

Cammie shrugged. "That's all?"

Ben laughed. "Cam, to most people, two million is *a lot*."

"Ben, Ben, Ben," she purred in her sexiest voice. "Surely you know by now that I'm not most people."

"What does that mean?" he asked curiously, his face slightly perplexed.

"It means," she continued slowly, leaning the slightest bit forward to reveal her sexy décolletage, "I'm in."

He looked at her, momentarily speechless. "Wait, you're . . . ?"

"In," Cammie repeated. "I have twenty times the money you need in my trust. That trust came due when I turned eighteen. I control it completely. I love the idea of your club. I think I could help you make it spectacular. Deal?"

She extended one perfectly manicured hand.

Ben looked at her outstretched fingers, clearly tempted, and then slowly shook his head. "No."

"No?"

"No. This isn't some little whim, Cammie. We're talking about a hell of a lot of money and hard work, with no guarantees."

She shrugged prettily. "So what else is new in this town?"

"I want you to be sure," he cautioned.

"Nothing is sure, Ben," she pointed out. "Isn't the whole idea of this club to have fun? So fuck sure. Let's do it anyway."

She held out her hand again for him to shake. Instead, Ben wrapped his large hands around her waist and lifted her up so high that her pink strappy Joan & Davids were a good five inches off the ground.

"Oh yeah!" he crowed. "There is no one else like you in the universe, Cammie Sheppard."

As he put her back down again, she lowered her eyes to half-mast, knowing exactly how sexy she looked when she did it. "Well, well, Ben Birnbaum. It's about time you realized it."

Baguettes, Caviar, and Champagne

"Ladies and gentlemen!" The announcer, a DJ from a leading New York rock-and-roll station, boomed his resonant voice into the microphone. "Thanks for coming out to Central Park's famed Sheep Meadow for what I'm sure will be an amazing concert, being simulcast to eighteen countries. I'd like to give a big shout-out to our brave soldiers stationed in Afghanistan, Iraq, and around the world!"

At the mention of the American servicemen and women, a deafening roar erupted from the crowd of a hundred thousand people assembled on the soft grass of the celebrated meadow. Anna had been here many times before, to hang out with her friends from the Upper West Side on beautiful spring or fall days. But she'd never been here for a free rock show, and the sight of Sheep Meadow packed with wall-to-wall concertgoers was an image she'd never forget.

It was the strangest thing. She'd been back in Manhattan for all of a few hours, but it felt instantly like home. The big buildings, the babble of languages from all over the world, even the orange glow of the sky as the city lights bounced against low clouds—it was all familiar and even comforting.

"Now, let's give a New York City welcome to the reason you're all here on this fabulous New York night. Ladies and gentlemen . . . John Mayer!"

As the cleft-chinned, bushy-haired rock star walked shyly out from the other side of the wooden stage—it was guarded by a chain-link fence and a score of New York's finest with police dogs for security—the crowd took its enthusiasm to another level. All around the grassy expanse were drive-in-movie-sized screens, so that those too far from the stage could get a good look at what was going on.

"Better than the Hollywood Bowl?" Anna asked Sam with a grin. They were standing backstage together, behind and to the right of center stage. But there was a huge plasma screen monitor that had been erected so those backstage could watch the concert perfectly.

"Different," Sam allowed. "Fewer stilettos, more Birkenstocks."

Anna laughed as Mayer started his first song—the acoustic "Love Soon" from his *Inside Wants Out* CD. Cheers and shouting obliterated the first lines after the intro. Anna, Sam, and Cyn were standing with a clump of others with backstage passes at a ninety-degree angle to Mayer, and they saw him give a "What can you do?" grin and shrug, even as he played and sang. He was obviously enjoying the moment as much as the audience.

Anna was enjoying it, too, which amazed her, considering that she and Sam had just arrived from L.A. that day and that she was still reeling from the fact that things were over with Ben. Again.

Remembering the Ben debacle made her feel like puking, so she forced her mind onto other things. She and Sam had planned to take a commercial flight from LAX. But when Jackson heard that they were planning their trip, he insisted that they take his private jet. The day was crystal clear from coast to coast with the exception of some cloud cover over Nebraska and Kansas. They passed the time on Jackson's luxurious buttery-soft white leather Italian couches watching Louis Malle's *Au Revoir Les Enfants*, followed by a lunch of baguettes, caviar, champagne, and hand-churned French vanilla bean ice cream surrounded by Chocopologie by Knipschildt chocolates.

With each mile that was put between her and Los Angeles, Anna felt just a little better, even as Ben's stinging indictment of all her faults rang in her ears. Yes, she'd come to Beverly Hills to challenge herself. But maybe Ben was right. Maybe it was all sound and fury, signifying absolutely nothing at all. When you came right down to it, she was a New Yorker, born and bred on the sheltered Upper East Side to be exactly the person she was.

What was it that someone once said to her? No matter where you go, there you are. If her time in L.A. hadn't changed her at all, then she had to question every choice she'd made since the day before New Year's Eve, when she'd boarded a plane with the deliberate intent of shaking up her life. It felt now as if the only thing she'd shaken up was her heart, and her faith in her own decisions.

Well, at least for now she could lick her wounds at

home. And at least Sam would be with her. After their lunch at the coffeehouse near UCLA, she and Sam had gone back to Jackson's Bel Air estate and done some quick Internet research. The president of Peru was indeed coming to New York. He had an extraordinarily busy schedule—at least according to the Peruvian newspaper article that they ran through Babelfish to translate. So now Sam knew that Eduardo's business trip to New York was legit. But why he hadn't invited her to tag along remained a mystery, one that Sam promised Anna she would unravel during their weeklong stay.

The first call Anna made after they decided to come back east was to her best friend, Cynthia Baltres, whom she'd known since they were both preschoolers. Cyn had always been slightly off-kilter, both in looks and attitude. More striking and sexy than conventionally beautiful, with choppy dark hair, dark round eyes, and a definite tendency toward downtown East Village dark clothes, Cyn was the kind of girl who'd meet a guy at the Washington Square drum circle on Saturday and decide to go with him to Europe on Sunday. In fact, earlier in the summer, she'd done exactly that. Anna had found out when she'd gotten an e-mail from Cyn sent from an Internet café in Amsterdam.

Cyn had been thrilled to hear from Anna. She said she had two extra backstage passes to the Mayer concert and wouldn't take no for an answer. Which is how they found themselves, less than eight hours after boarding Jackson's jet at the Van Nuys airport, gazing out at the crowd on a hot New York night in August, with John Mayer running through his famous repertoire—"Daughters," "Gravity," and "Clarity" among the hits that Anna had actually heard before.

"You suck so hard, Anna—you never even call me," Cyn groused as the singer launched into an emo ballad. She was wearing one of her patented Cyn outfits—skinny black Joe jeans with sky-high emerald green Gucci platform sandals. The only thing between her beige mesh Mark Posner tank top and her flesh were a set of twin belly-button piercings and the new red peace symbol tattoo below the small of her back.

"That's not fair. I talked to you just last week!" Anna protested.

"Please, I've had two boyfriends and made out with an extremely handsome older gentleman at a loft party in SoHo since then." At Anna's widened eyes, Cyn added. "I'm kidding. Sort of. Who wants drinks? I'll be right back."

Cyn headed toward the open backstage bars, roadies' heads turning as she walked past them. Mayer's band had just started a slow blues instrumental when Anna spotted a familiar face. Olivia Macklow, a classmate of Anna's from Trinity, sidled up next to her. With her was cherubic Molly Burton, who spoke five languages and whose father worked for the World Bank. She had straight black hair down her back.

"Well, well. Who said 'You can't go home again'?" Olivia asked rhetorically, appraising Anna with a smile. Anna knew she was deliberately quoting Thomas Wolfe, a novelist Anna quite liked and Olivia quite loved. Olivia lived a block away from the Percys in a classic Upper East Side town house with gabled windows and a mahogany door. They'd purchased it from Truman Capote, and Olivia liked to claim that the famous writer haunted it. Their families used to give a joint Christmas party to which their friends and family flew in from all over the world. "Can you believe it, Molly? It's Anna! Back from the dead."

"I'm not dead yet." Anna grinned, hugging the two girls warmly, and then motioned to Sam. "Sam, I want you to meet two of my friends." She quickly made the introductions.

"So, Anna," Molly began, "it's still Yale, right?" Anna thought she looked great in a ruffled yellow blouse and herringbone shorts.

"She's only been planning on it since her zygote stage," Olivia joked.

"Still Yale," Anna confirmed. "How about you two?"

"Carnegie-Mellon," Olivia told her. "Western history. I'm going to set myself up for a Watson so I can go to Eastern Europe. And Molly—"

"Molly can speak for herself, thank you very much," her friend chimed in. "I got accepted to Dartmouth and Johns Hopkins, but decided I want to study Joyce in Dublin. So I'm going to Trinity College. Guess I can keep my old Trinity T-shirts and wear them around there," she added with a laugh. "Maybe it was fate."

"I'm going to USC," Sam declared. "To film school."

"Oh, right!" Molly exclaimed, understanding washing over her face. "Sam *Sharpe*. Your dad is in all those testosterone flicks." Her eyes flickered in a subtle way that spoke volumes about what she thought about the genre.

"Yes, which gross billions worldwide," Sam added, through what Anna knew to be a fake smile.

"Overseas," Olivia corrected. "That's why the writing is always so simplistic. They can't depend on a plot, so they depend on blowing things up, lots of gore, and it sells internationally to the masses."

Anna bristled on Sam's behalf. "Have you ever even seen any of Jackson Sharpe's movies?"

"Please," Olivia scoffed. She leaned back against one of the cargo-sized blue boxes that the roadies used to transport speakers. "I don't do testosterone flicks."

"Well, then, how would you know?" A breeze pushed some hair into Anna's face, and she brushed it away.

Olivia simply changed the subject. "So where are you staying? Your place, Anna?"

Anna nodded, moving a couple of feet to her right to let a roadie in shorts and a grungy T-shirt pass by. He was carrying two guitars for the star. "My mom's away in Florence, so there's no one there."

Olivia waved an ostentatious finger at Anna and then winked at Sam. "Unless you count the live-ins. They've got the best cook in Manhattan."

"She's in Barbados, visiting her kids," Anna informed her. "We're cook-free."

"Sounds fine to me. I'm psyched I finally get to see where you grew up." Sam tossed her hair back and rubbed her chin thoughtfully. "Maybe I'll find some geeky old class pictures, or better yet, unearth your diary—find out about some of your embarrassing crushes past."

"Oh, hey, did you hear that Penelope Stanhope's father got a MacArthur Genius Grant?" Molly asked Anna.

"He's writing a cycle of tone poems for the Brooklyn Academy of Music with John Adams. Her family is in India now. She sent me an e-mail—she's studying Sanskrit while she's there."

Sam laughed. "This is really funny. It's name-dropping, East Coast–snob style."

Anna smiled, because she'd never thought of it that way. "I suppose it is."

"I'm dying for some champagne," Molly groused. "Where's the bar?"

"I think it's behind us," Sam pointed.

"Great. We're off. Should we bring back a bottle?"

"No, because I'm coming with you. I'll bring it."

Molly and Olivia laughed as they started to thread their way back to the bar with Sam. For the moment Anna was alone, with John Mayer rocking and the crowd swaying to "Your Body Is a Wonderland."

There were so many reasons she could feel disquieted, starting with all the horrible things that Ben had said to her two days before. But as Mayer rocked on, and the crowd rocked with him, she actually felt at ease. This was New York. Her New York, where the name-dropping was, as Sam had pointed out, just as plentiful as in its West Coast show business equivalent. But it was name-dropping she understood.

Tonight, she'd be sleeping in her very own four-poster bed. She'd breathe in and smell not bougainvillea, but the faintest lingering of the clothes in her own closet. It had been so long since that had happened.

After eight months as a stranger in a strange land, she was home.

How the Other Half Lives

"So now I finally get to see how the other half lives," Sam teased, as she and Anna climbed the steps to Anna's bow-front Georgian brownstone on Seventy-eighth Street between Fifth and Madison. The front façade was brick and limestone, the double front doors slate gray granite. "And by 'other half,' I mean the East Coast version of filthy-rich me."

Anna rolled her eyes and used her key to let them in, then flipped on a hallway light. "You're incorrigible," she teased, smiling.

"So, this is where you grew up." Sam found herself standing in a portico entranceway tiled in black and white. The ceiling above her was easily eighteen feet high, and all the walls were exposed brick. A crystal chandelier provided all the lighting. On the wall to her right hung a Picasso from his Cubist period. To her left hung a Degas depiction of several ballet students in rehearsal. Two grand staircases with oak banisters spiraled upward.

"My mother inherited the Picasso," Anna explained. "Wait till we get to the atrium; you'll see her 'private collection' if you'd like."

"I'd like," Sam agreed.

"Great, come on. No need for the stairs. We can take the elevator."

"How many floors are there in this place?" Sam wondered aloud.

"Six. Five, not counting the service level, where the full-time help lives. They've got their own elevator in the back. Follow me." The elevator door opened immediately when Anna pushed a discreet recessed button—the cabin was easily big enough for six people when they stepped on. "You want the grand tour or the quickie version?"

"Let's go quickie," Sam decided, though she was curious to see the entire space. Sam was used to the sprawling mansions of Beverly Hills and Bel Air, where square footage was in direct correlation to status. How did a privileged family like Anna's live in a city like New York, where space was at such a premium?

Evidently, in certain residences at least, space wasn't such a premium after all.

Anna's brownstone was twelve thousand square feet, which meant that it was not nearly as big as the Sharpe estate in Bel Air, but about the same size as Dee's home in Beverly Hills. The difference was, the space ran vertically instead of horizontally. Anna explained that the place had once been two separate nineteenth-century town houses, but her grandmother had purchased both, gutted both, and rebuilt and combined them into the family home.

The tour started on the top floor, whose walls were burnished mahogany, the floors polished wood covered in centuries-old tapestry rugs from Morocco and Turkey, and there were wood-burning fireplaces in just about every room. The very top floor was a twelve-hundred-square-foot duplex atrium with four enormous skylights. Sparsely furnished, mid-twentieth-century Abstract Expressionist paintings hung not on the walls but from the ceiling, on slender, nearly invisible wires. White figurine sculptures rested on marble pedestals, or—as was the case with a huge white marble piece of two nudes entwined—on the floor itself.

"Welcome to the Jane Cabot Percy gallery," Anna pronounced, though there was something dry and ironic in her tone.

"Who are the artists?" Sam peered at a massive abstract in fire engine red and canary yellow.

"That one? Clyfford Still. The others? Mostly men she has known," Anna replied flatly. "I probably should add the word *intimately*."

"Wait—most of these were done by your mother's *boyfriends*?"

"I suppose you could call them that. Some people collect art. She collects young artists. Mostly Italian, with a smattering of French and German. It's like she has a golden touch, too. She meets them, and a year later their stuff sells at Sotheby's for seven figures. It's uncanny."

Sam laughed as she wandered around the huge space, then followed Anna back to the elevator. "I still can't believe your mom does these guys."

"I don't ask for details." Anna shuddered as they got back into the elevator. The mental images were obviously too much to contemplate. "But suffice it to say I can read between the lines."

"I'm just surprised you never told me this about her."

What *had* Anna told her? Sam tried to remember. That her mother was so old-money upper crust that she never showed emotion. Because if you were "well bred" it was simply "not done." Totally ironic, really, because Sam's whole life was about emotion. That was the film business. Not that any of the emotions on display were necessarily real, of course. But emoting believably was what got an actor—say, her father, for example—the big bucks. Maybe that was why Hollywood people would hug you when they first met you.

"You can use one of the bedrooms on this floor," Anna pointed out, as they got off on the fourth floor. "The one next door to my room."

"Works for me," Sam agreed.

Sam followed Anna down a long, brightly lit white hallway. On both sides of the hall, at regular intervals, were framed photographs of family members past and present. She recognized Anna's older sister, Susan, and stopped for a moment to admire a black-and-white of the family together posed on a beach.

"That's by Diane Arbus," Anna pointed out. "She knew my grandmother. Anyway, when are you planning to call Eduardo?" Anna pushed open a door.

"I sent him a text during the concert," Sam confessed. She looked around at the surroundings. "I think he's staying at the consulate. And I haven't heard back from—holy shit. Do you own every book ever written?"

The room they'd just entered was obviously Anna's bedroom. The schoolbooks still neatly stacked on the antique rolltop desk were the dead giveaway. The room was just as simple as Anna's room at her father's place in

Beverly Hills, furnished with an antique queen-size four-poster bed, an early American dresser that Sam suspected dated back to the original Ethan Allen, and a couple of expansive landscape paintings from the Hudson River school that were probably originals. There was a small bulletin board over the desk, to which was pinned a row of small photos of Anna and Cyn, taken in one of those el-cheapo photo booths, a program from an all-Bach New York Philharmonic program, and a small blue Yale pennant.

"How long has the Yale pennant been up there?" Sam leaned toward it for inspection. The print on the pennant was old-fashioned, from the 1950s or even before.

"Since I was eight," Anna confessed. "It used to belong to my grandfather."

"Wow. So you always knew what you wanted."

"According to Ben, that means I'm living out a pre-programmed existence."

Sam raised eyebrows that had been shaped and trimmed by Valerie on Rodeo Drive. "He said that?"

"More or less."

Sam wandered over to the built-in bookshelves—they were eight shelves high, made of teak, and covered two complete walls floor to ceiling. And they were jammed with hardbound books. Sam looked at some of the titles at random. Molière. Dostoyevsky. Willa Cather. Balzac. She considered herself a good reader, and she'd read at least one book by most of these authors. But she wasn't allergic to James Patterson or Jennifer Weiner either. This? This was wall-to-wall highbrow. It was impressive.

"Don't tell me you've read all of these."

"Oh, you know . . ." Anna vaguely waved a hand.

"You have," Sam surmised. "Just admit it."

It was one thing to know how smart and well-read Anna was in theory, and quite another to be staring at the hundreds of books she'd obviously pored through—probably right there on that brown teak four-poster bed.

"I have this thing about keeping the books I read. I suppose I collect them the way my mother collects art."

"Hardly the same, unless you've fooled around with all the authors." Sam smirked. "And most of them are dead. Plus, you can reread a book anytime you want." Her stomach growled. "Can we get some food? I'm starving."

"Up for Chinese? I'll find a delivery menu," Anna suggested. "Or if you want to go back out we could go for a walk. There's a great all-night Greek place on Lexington and Seventy-second."

"How about a diner? I'm thinking burger and onion rings. Or a Reuben. This is New York, after all. I'm texting him again." She fished her cell out of the back pocket of her dark Citizens jeans.

Anna shook her head. "Maybe you shouldn't. It's after midnight, Sam."

Sam felt her stomach turn over with anxiety. What was going on with Eduardo, anyway?

"All the more reason," she finally decided. "It's just a text. And if my new fiancé is otherwise engaged after midnight, he's going to find himself unengaged to me pretty damn fast."

Hello, Stranger

Anna and Sam were just about to step out the front door when Sam's Razr V3 sounded her familiar ringtone—Blondie's classic "One Way or Another." Sam dug it out of her black hand-tooled leather purse.

"Who's calling at this hour?" Anna asked.

"That's what I want . . ." Sam's voice trailed off as she checked the number. "Oh yeah. It's him."

"Eduardo?"

Sam nodded vigorously as she answered. "Hey! What's going on?"

"Tell him we're here," Anna hissed, but Sam shook her head no as Anna listened to Sam's side of the conversation.

"Uh-huh . . . Uh-huh . . . Well, it's only a little after nine, so I'm not doing much of anything. . . . Anna and I are going to the movies later at the ArcLight. . . . I wish you could come too."

A little after nine? That's right, Anna thought. Sam's cell was a California number. For all Eduardo knew, she was still in Los Angeles. And Sam was doing everything she could to continue the ruse. From the huge grin on her friend's face as she talked, the deception was working.

"I could still get on a plane and get to New York," Anna heard Sam offer. "Oh. No, of course I understand. . . . Okay. I love you too. Talk to you tomorrow."

Sam clicked off. "Eduardo says hi." Her voice was downbeat.

"You're bummed that he didn't want you come here," Anna observed.

"At least he called me. I was getting worried. Well, maybe a little worried." Then Sam brightened. "When I surprise him tomorrow, it's going to be deeply satisfying. He'll remember who it is he chose to marry."

"There's no one like you, Sam."

Sam opened the door to Anna's place. "I'll take that as a compliment. Come on. Let's eat. I'm starving."

Seventy-eighth Street was exactly as Anna had left it at the end of the year. The sidewalk—scrubbed every day by employees of the block association—was as clean as the sand on the most private beaches at Malibu. There wasn't a speck of litter or even an overflowing trash can. Brownstone abutted brownstone, each in immaculate condition.

Anna and Sam hadn't taken more than ten steps east on their trek to the Olympia Diner when Anna heard someone softly call her name.

"Anna Percy? Is that you?"

She turned around and saw a blond, preppy-looking guy with deep-set, serious eyes staring at her expectantly from the top step of the brownstone next door. He wore

an open light blue shirt over a T-shirt, khakis, and black
Gucci loafers without socks. He looked, Anna thought,
like he could be Daniel Craig's son. Same startling blue
eyes. Same slightly sticky-out ears. Same sandy hair and
jutting jaw.

Anna mentally smiled at her own thought process.
Before she'd moved to Los Angeles, she would never
have made a what-famous-movie-star-does-he-look-like?
comparison. Nor would she even have known who
Daniel Craig was, because she never would have gone to
see a James Bond movie. But she'd seen the latest one
with Sam, and liked it. For a split second, she studied
Daniel Craig Junior and tried to place him. He did look
vaguely familiar.

"Logan," she said softly. Now that she took a good
look at him, he didn't look all that different from the boy
she'd grown up with. She and Logan Cresswell had gone
to preschool together at the Y. And following that, they'd
sat next to each other in grade school. He was the first
boy she'd ever kissed—on the cheek, in the cloakroom,
in second grade—though she could no longer remember
why. She hadn't seen him in forever. He was one of those
kids whose parents sent them to boarding school.

"My parents still live here." He cocked his head
toward the brownstone. "But they're in East Hampton
for the summer. I'm here, though."

Memories flooded Anna. She remembered holding
hands with him on a third-grade school trip to the Metropolitan Museum of Art. And also how smart he'd been
back in grade school. One year they'd tied for first place
in the school spelling bee, because the staff became too

weary to go on any longer when the two of them continued to spell every word they were given correctly.

"Logan, of course. Hi!"

She started toward the stoop; he bounded down
the stairs, and she found herself enveloped in a not-
unwelcome hug under Sam's curious gaze. He held her at
arm's length afterward, grinning wildly.

"You know I went to St. Paul's, right?"

"Yes, I heard." Anna did recall. St. Paul's was a prep
school in Concord, New Hampshire, about as exclusive
as they came. He'd started there in fifth grade, and Anna
tried to remember if she'd seen him since. She didn't
think so. That really wasn't so surprising. On school
vacations, her own family invariably went away on vacation. During the summer, they went to their retreat on
Martha's Vineyard.

"You look great. Anyway, my parents bought a place
in Ireland—on the Dingle Peninsula. It's fantastic, so I've
been spending a lot of time there during the summer. But
whenever I came home—which wasn't often—I'd pass
by your house and wonder where you were. I hoped I'd
run into you one of these days. I've been here all summer.
But I heard you were out in Los Angeles."

Logan yielded the sidewalk to a passing woman of a
certain age wrapped head to toe in tasteful summer black
Chanel, accompanied by two equally regal Labradoodles.
Walking the dogs after midnight dressed to kill was just
so New York.

"I have been. For the last eight months," she explained.

"Which would account for the Los Angeles accessory,
also known as me," Sam put in. She stepped forward and

extended a hand; Anna was embarrassed that she hadn't yet made the introduction. That wasn't like her.

"Oh, sorry, Sam." Anna quickly introduced them. "So, what have you been doing with yourself, Logan?"

"Tonight? Just got back from a party. A guy I know from St. Paul's just came into his trust fund. Be glad you weren't there. He was trying to do a Jell-O shot for each million he just inherited—not the brightest idea when twelve million bucks is involved." Logan paused as Anna bit her lip. She *was* glad she hadn't been there. She would have been appalled.

"Are you working for the summer?" Sam queried. "Or just leading the lifestyle of the rich and infamous?"

"Working. I'm a writer's assistant. With Danforth Marsh? He—"

"Won the Pulitzer Prize three years ago," Anna filled in. "I loved his last short-story collection. *Tree Rings*. I read it four times."

"Well, I'll pass along your enthusiasm. He's doing a reading of his new novel at the Ninety-second Street Y later in the week. You should come."

"I'd love to!" Anna found herself saying. She couldn't help but notice that Logan's childhood cuteness had turned into eighteen-year-old hotness. But what also impressed her was the kindness that seemed to be emanating from those deep-set eyes. Standing here on their shared block, talking under a streetlight, just felt so comfortable.

"If we're still here next week," Sam clarified. "We've got to go back to L.A."

At the mention of those two little letters Anna's

stomach twisted like taffy. The thought of returning in a week seemed way too soon. Now that she was standing on familiar cracked concrete, hearing the never-ending traffic roll north on one-way Madison Avenue, and breathing the late summer Upper East Side evening air, she never wanted to leave.

"So how about you?" Logan asked. He sat down on the front step and beckoned for Anna and Sam to join him. They did. "Where are you headed for school in the fall?"

"Yale. And yourself?"

"Harvard. I thought about Yale, because I want to study creative writing. But my parents both went to Harvard, so it's really a legacy thing. . . ."

"Excuse me, I hate to interrupt the reunion of the mental titans," Sam said sweetly. "But we were on our way to get something to eat, remember?"

Anna winced. She knew she was being a bit rude by talking about East Coast things, places, and people that Sam wouldn't know. "Right, sorry. Logan, we're on our way to the Olympia. Want to come with us?"

Logan shook his head solemnly. "It's crazy, but I can't. Danforth is an early riser. He likes to work from six in the morning till two in the afternoon."

"He'd never survive in Los Angeles," Sam quipped.

"Don't get him started on that subject. He hates L.A. When Ned Tanen was running one of the studios, he once tried to buy one of his short stories. When it turned out Tanen hadn't read it, Danforth threw a pencil at him. I heard it stuck in his chest. Anyway," he said, standing, "do you have plans for tomorrow night? Can I take you two to dinner?" Logan asked hopefully.

"I'd love that," Sam told him. "As long as it's just you and Anna. My boyfriend is here in New York. I'll be busy."

He looked at Sam quizzically for a moment, then laughed. "Well, alrighty then. Dinner with Anna. If Anna is willing to be seen alone with me?"

"Sounds good," Anna grinned. He handed her his cell phone, and Anna input her number.

"Great, so I'll call you during the day, we'll plan something truly exciting. Nice to meet you, Sam. See you tomorrow, Anna." He bounded up the steps to his brownstone two at a time, waving to them once more before the door closed behind him.

"Very cute," Sam mused.

"You could say that," Anna agreed, as they started out toward Lexington Avenue again. "I must admit, it's nice to run into him after all these years."

"And by that you mean, right after Ben kicked you to the curb and stomped your heart into the sewage grate," Sam translated.

"Maybe so," Anna admitted as they stopped at the corner to wait for a light. Traffic zoomed by, making it impossible to jaywalk.

"A cute guy to hang with till we go back to Los Angeles?" Sam looped an arm through Anna's as the light changed. They started across Madison. "I'd call it perfect timing."

The Most Exclusive Ticket in Town

The noise inside the old auto repair shop was deafening. The sounds of jackhammering, sawing, pipe-cutting, and drywall-sledgehammering filled the air. Ben cupped his hands and shouted so loudly that Cammie was tempted to cover her ears.

"Okay, everyone! Hold it down!"

His bellowed words had their intended effect. All work that was under way suddenly ceased.

"Nice one," Cammie quipped, as a couple dozen workmen put down their tools and looked at her and Ben dubiously. Evidently they weren't used to bosses who were a decade or more younger than they were. "If you can do that with the traffic on the 405, you're hired."

Ben grinned, then cupped his hands again. "Okay, lunch break! See you in an hour. And thanks for your hard work, everyone."

Cammie watched as Ben's crew—upward of twenty-five or thirty workmen—shuffled noisily toward the doors, some of them with old-fashioned lunch pails and Thermoses or classic brown paper sacks. It was the strangest thing. She'd gotten involved in this project out of her pique with Adam, to make him jealous and to prove to herself that she had bigger and better things awaiting her when everyone scattered off to college. But the more she worked on the club with Ben, the more excited she got. If they were going to do it, it *was* going to be a success. Cammie Sheppard never failed at anything, and she wasn't about to start.

And then there was the B.F. Ben Factor. Being around him again reminded her of all the reasons she'd been into him in the first place. And now that he was an aspiring club owner, his appeal had been upped exponentially. He was always three places at once, giving orders, pitching in with drywalling, on the phone with one regulatory authority or another, checking out marketing materials— the list went on and on. Assertive and active guys were hot. The fact that the building was as yet un-air-conditioned, and he'd taken to wearing wife-beaters and his most battered jeans, didn't hurt either.

Being warmed by Ben's heat factor, even if nothing was going on between then except work—yet—made losing Adam feel a little less cold. He still hadn't called, texted, or e-mailed her. She was beginning to resign herself to the fact that he never would. And that hurt. Much more than she'd ever admit to anyone. From time to time, she wondered what he was doing, whether he was even in Los Angeles. Maybe he'd gone back to the walleyes in Michigan. But she always cut off that line of thinking.

Ben turned to her. "You aren't exactly dressed for manual labor."

True. Cammie had selected her outfit with even more than her usual care. She wanted to look hot for Ben, but she didn't want to look as if she'd tried very hard to do it. She wore a YA-YA beaded lavender silk halter top with Miss Sixty dark distressed cropped jeans, and her newest Ferre gold-foiled strappy sandals with the narrow three-inch heel.

"Bosses don't labor—they delegate," Cammie pointed out slyly. "Although I see you're taking a more hands-on approach."

As usual, Ben had dressed to work in scruffy jeans with holes in the knees and one of his new supply of wife-beaters. Both were now covered in sawdust. There was a tool belt around his waist, and he wore a red bandanna pirate-style over mussed brown hair that protruded sex-ily from beneath the cloth. There were beads of sweat on his forehead. He still looked yummy. Hot-carpenter yummy, to be more specific. Cammie had never done a hot carpenter.

"We're still in the clean-it-out phase, not the renovate-it-and-get-it-ready phase," he explained, glancing around his now-deserted workspace. "There are two full Dumpsters in the back, and we've got two more to fill. Should be ready to start real construction in a couple of days, though."

"You know what you're going to build?"

Ben grinned, and motioned to the back door. "I thought you'd never ask. Come on out back. I've got something to show you. It's where my dad told me he wouldn't back me. Before my angel—better known as Cammie Sheppard—came along."

"Hey. You know me better than that. Never call me an angel—it tarnishes my image. Besides, the papers my dad's lawyer drew up make *me* the majority owner. So I'm not exactly a philanthropist," she pointed out, raising one perfectly arched eyebrow.

"Thanks for reminding me, majority owner." Ben led her out the back door of the building into an alley that was cramped by the aforementioned Dumpsters. But just outside the door, an open card table and four folding chairs stood in a small area that faced the rear alley. On that table was a large three-dimensional model.

"Cammie, meet Bye, Bye Love." He pointed to the mock-up. "How I see it, anyway."

She marveled, taking in the model of the club. It was roughly the size of a dollhouse she'd played with when she was younger. Ben's model was painted sky blue and silver, with the name of the club on one of those low-rent yellow changeable letter signs that you saw so often in front of auto repair shops advertising the latest oil change and tune-up specials.

"Let me give you the grand tour."

As Cammie watched, Ben removed the roof from the model and showed her his vision of the club, getting more excited as he spoke. He envisioned it as three separate spaces, much like Trieste was laid out. One area would have its own bar, serving unlimited Taittinger champagne to VIPs and other select people on the list. Those people would get temporary silver-and-blue tattoos of the Bye, Bye Love logo on the backs of their hands. Cammie knew this would be wildly sought-after. Another would house a small stage, with only enough seating for ten or fifteen people.

"The idea is, we'd put on short plays or have comedians

do their acts on the stage—very short, maybe fifteen minutes max. People would come in to be entertained, to get away from the noise, and of course because it's the most exclusive ticket in town. Speaking of, did you talk to your dad about the liquor license?"

Cammie nodded. "How ridiculous is that? Every kid in Beverly Hills gets a fake ID at fourteen, but whatever. I talked to my father. He'll sign for it."

"More than my dad did," Ben commented as he replaced the roof on the model.

Frankly, Cammie had been surprised at her father's immediate yes. It seemed to her, though, that ever since she'd signed sixteen-year-old Champagne to a modeling management contract and convinced Martin Rittenhouse to design a new line of petite clothing around the girl, her father's attitude toward her had changed. It was as if now that Cammie was taking some initiative for her future, Clark Sheppard decided that she was worthy of support. Talk about conditional love. But she made a mental note anyway to invite Champagne and Martin to the opening—models and hot-shit designers always carried a certain cachet, even if Rittenhouse was little short of a felon, albeit a talented one.

"You're a go-getter," her dad had told her with admiration in the deep, commanding voice that had scared many a studio head to death. "Chip off the old block."

Cammie had been pleased by his reaction, and, at the same time, irritated with herself for wanting or needing his approval.

Ben gestured to the model. "I'd say this is it. So what do you think of the performance space?"

"I think it's a fabulous idea," Cammie told him. "But you need something more to make it really special. First, charge more. A lot more, to get in there. A hundred bucks, with unlimited champagne."

"I kind of wanted to stay away from the only-the-rich-can-afford-to-get-in thing."

Cammie shook her blond curls out of her blue eyes. "The less you charge, the less prestige you have, and the less success," she decreed. "You want to be overrun with kids from the Valley, also known as the Kiss of Death?"

"No . . ."

"So charge big. You can always put the hip-but-poor on the guest list. In fact, you should, so the place gets talked about."

"Good point." Ben folded his arms thoughtfully. "How about we do entertainment each night by themes, with a different subject each night. Politics, or the battle of the sexes?"

"Asshole former boyfriends and girlfriends," Cammie suggested.

Ben regarded her. "Did you have anyone particular in mind?"

"Both names start with an *A*."

"Anna's not an asshole," Ben insisted, his voice low, "if that's who you're referring to. And neither is Adam, for that matter."

Cammie raised a well-plucked eyebrow. Having Ben defend Anna was definitely not in her game plan. "She didn't support your dream, did she?"

Ben sighed. "No, she didn't. Not like I wanted her to, anyway."

"And Adam . . . he dissed me."

"Dissed you how?"

Cammie didn't want to go into the details. Not here, not now. She suspected that if she told Ben she'd given Adam an ultimatum about getting his ass back to Los Angeles, he would take Adam's side.

"It's private," she finally declared.

Ben whistled. "You, not spilling details? I'm impressed."

"People grow up, Ben. Are you the same guy you were back when we were together?"

"Nope," he confirmed.

"Well, I'm not the same girl I was then, either. So let's just leave it at that. Now, how about if you finish the tour?"

Ben turned his attention back to the model, taking the top off once again and pointing to what used to be the main repair area of the shop. "My idea here was that this space—it's the main nightclub area—could be transformed every week into something new. You know that club people have the attention span of gnats. I've already talked to the Los Angeles Art Institute, and they've got a senior industrial design class whose professor swears they can come in on a Sunday and have a whole new look in place for the following Monday night."

"Great!" Cammie exclaimed. "We just have to be careful. One bad design could kill you."

"I can have them do models like this."

"But it's all in the execut—hey, I've got an idea. How about Trash It Night?"

"Excuse me?"

"Call it Trash It Night. If you hate the design that goes up, let people pay to come in, give them sledgehammers, and let them bash the shit out of it. "

A slow smile spread across Ben's face. "That's genius."

Ben Birnbaum, Princeton student—well, *former* Princeton student if he really stayed in L.A. with this club—calling her, not-college-bound-at-all, a genius? Cammie smiled sweetly. "Why, thank you. It took you long enough to figure that out."

Ben replaced the model's roof again, then took Cammie's hand in a gesture that Cammie hoped was slightly more than friendly. "Let me take you back inside and show you what I've got in mind for music."

"After you, fearless leader."

"I thought you owned the majority share," Ben reminded her.

"True. But this is your dream, all the way. I just want to help you make it come true."

He touched her cheek. "Thank you."

She could see how much this meant to him. *Score ten points and a big shot at getting Ben back.*

"The sound system will be outrageous," Ben exulted as he opened the rear door for her. "I've got the guy who designed Rain at the Palm in Las Vegas designing it."

Cammie looked around the interior of the dilapidated space. And though it was still decrepit, without a single fixture, speaker, or clubgoer, she could actually see the club in her mind's eye. Filled wall to wall with actors, singers, and models, the chef from L.A. Farm making his famous feuilleté of salmon mousse in the kitchen, and Sarah Silverman performing for exactly fifteen people who'd paid a hundred dollars apiece for fifteen minutes of comedy. Sarah wouldn't be performing because of the money, either. She'd be doing it because Bye, Bye Love was so cool that performing in the little theater was worth *more* than money.

That is, if the music was good. If the music sucked, or even if the music was ordinary, it was over.

"Who's our DJ going to be?" she asked suddenly.

Ben furrowed his brow. "I haven't given that a lot of thought. I'm not sure."

There was a workbench next to the door to what would be the club kitchen. Ben sat, and indicated that Cammie should sit too.

Cammie nibbled on her lower lip so long that she could taste her own MAC lip gloss. They were going to charge a hefty cover, but the club couldn't hold that many people. They had to go for exclusivity. Which meant their music had to be better than anyone else's. She snapped her fingers. "I know just the guy."

"Who?"

The week before, she and Sam had gone to the Montmartre Lounge in West Hollywood, at the top of the hill where La Cienega met Sunset Boulevard. It was currently the second-hottest place in the city, other than Trieste. The line to get in had been interminable. Naturally, they hadn't waited. The DJ was a guy in from New York for one night only, an incredibly charismatic and strikingly handsome, tall, thin, blond dude named John Carlos who worked absolute magic on a sophisticated Hollywood crowd. When they got inside at eleven, the place was a seething mass of sweaty, dancing bodies, and everyone knew that no one ever got moving before midnight. The music was a heady mix of trance, techno, and rock from the sixties. The segues were immaculate, the build in the beat infectious. It was impossible not to want to dance.

John Carlos was their guy. There was only one problem, and Cammie knew it. Club owner Fred Kahlilian had offered him a contract at fifty thousand dollars a week. It had made the *Los Angeles Times*, in fact. John Carlos was one hundred percent completely and totally locked up.

Ha. If there was one thing Clark Sheppard had taught his daughter it was that no contract was ironclad, no deal airtight.

"Let me take care of it," she told Ben, her mind already racing.

"We don't have a whole lot of time."

"But we do have a whole lot of tricks up our collective sleeves."

Ben looked at her bare arms. "No sleeves, Camilla."

"Aren't you observant. How about you get two beers and we toast the most popular new club in Los Angeles, and maybe the entire universe?"

"That's a bit premature."

"I see it, Ben," Cammie insisted. "And I feel it. Your dream is about to become reality."

He flashed a smile that made all the money she'd invested in his club seem worthless in comparison.

She was going to see that smile again. And she was going to get him back.

Wild Amazon Monkey Love

Sam was nervous. She'd already tried on five outfits that morning, surveying her reflection in the antique full-length gold-gilded mirror in Anna's room. Anna had liked the Chloé black trousers and black sleeveless cashmere shell, but Sam had tossed that outfit on her tall wooden bed with all the others. Nothing she'd brought with her looked right for ambushing Eduardo. So she'd coaxed Anna into a quick trip to Bergdorf's, where she'd found the Melissa Masse wrap dress in cherry red that emphasized her curvy breasts and camouflaged her even curvier ass. It was one thing for Eduardo to say he loved the curves below her waist. It was quite another to believe him when he'd blown off the chance for her to join him here in Manhattan. Twice.

By the time she was dressed, made up, and shoed up it was midafternoon. She'd called the Peruvian mission to the United Nations just to make sure he was in. The chirpy receptionist with a charming accent confirmed that he was indeed on the premises, which made her feel a little better. He was also in a meeting that was expected to go on for another hour. Would Sam like Eduardo to return the call?

She demurred. Instead, she hopped in a cab and headed for the mission, located on the sixteenth floor of an office building on Second Avenue between Forty-second and Forty-third Streets. Not that she planned to burst into his meeting—unless, of course, she found out that he was ensconced with whom she now thought of as That Bitch Gisella. She couldn't help it. Even if he'd professed his love to her last night, she wondered whether the reason he didn't want her here in New York was tall, dark, sexy, and one hundred percent Peruvian female.

In some tiny corner of Sam's mind, where rationality and sanity still reigned, she told herself that she was being paranoid. Why in the world would Gisella be in New York? If Eduardo wanted to cheat on her while he was here, he could do so with any number of girls. Thinner girls. Cuter girls.

She sighed and let her head loll back against the seat before she rethought that position—God only knew who or what had rested their head in that spot previously. She sat up again and rubbed her neck. She had no *real* reason to suspect that Eduardo was unfaithful. Maybe all of this had to do with the getting-engaged thing. Maybe she was still uncomfortable with it, maybe she wasn't ready. . . .

But no. That was stupid. You didn't turn down the greatest thing that had ever happened to you just because it had happened to you when you were too young.

She shook her perfectly-streaked-by-Raymond hair off her face and folded her creamy white arms. Stay on track, she told herself. When Eduardo's meeting ended, she'd be waiting for him. And his reaction would tell her everything.

With luck, it would be a good surprise. If it was a bad surprise, she'd throw his gleaming engagement ring in his face, turn on her Beverly Feldmans, stomp down to some dive in the East Village, and get completely plastered.

God, she couldn't help thinking, as the taxi stopped in front of the consulate building. *Please, please, please don't let him be with That Bitch Gisella.*

Sam paid the driver, who had a photo of his wife and TV-cute little girl taped to his dashboard, and got out. The building was like any other—tall, glass, home to a dozen corporations, law offices, and advertising agencies. Just a few blocks from the United Nations, it also held the missions of six or seven other small nations. Security was tight. She had to show identification and go through a metal detector before she could even enter the elevator. Upstairs, a desk blocked the way to the mission itself.

"Hello," she told the guard behind the kidney-shaped black marble desk. He was built like a football tight end—tall, wide, and muscular all at once. "I'm here to see Eduardo Muñoz."

He lifted the multibuttoned phone on his desk. "Is he expecting you?"

"Not exactly."

"Your name please, miss?"

Damn. She did not want to be announced. That would give Eduardo time to stash his mistress in the ladies' room. She took a deep breath; she knew she was being ridiculous. Even if he and That Bitch Gisella were hanging from the chandeliers singing the Peruvian national anthem while making wild Amazon monkey love, that would happen *after* hours. Eduardo was the son of a high government official. He wouldn't risk it at work.

"On second thought, I'm a little early," Sam said with what she hoped was a radiant grin. "I'll just wait a little while." She could feel the guard's eyes on her as she took a seat on one of two low-slung white leather chairs in the entry area. There was a black onyx coffee table with some magazines. *Vogue. Sports Illustrated. Time.* Evidently the whole South American thing didn't extend to reading material.

Sam pulled out her new Razr V3 and speed-dialed Anna. "I'm here. What are you doing?"

"I'm at MoMA. I still can't get used to the Monet water lilies straight across the wall. How about you? Did you find him?"

"I'm still outside the main office." Sam kept her voice low so that the guard wouldn't hear her. "I can't get in without getting announced and—"

She stopped midsentence. One of the elevators at the end of the hall had just opened, and Eduardo himself had stepped out. He wasn't alone. Instead, he was chatting with a swarthy man in a double-breasted charcoal gray Ralph Lauren suit. As for Eduardo, he wore taupe trousers, a yellow shirt and patterned tie, and a sports jacket Sam had never seen before.

"Gotta go," she told Anna quickly, then stashed her cell phone and rose awkwardly from the damn low-slung chair. Whoever had designed it clearly hated women whose center of gravity was south of their navels. By the time she was on her feet, Eduardo was staring at her. He didn't look thrilled, either.

"Sam? What are you doing here?"

She slapped a smile onto her Lipfusion cherry-glossed lips. "Waiting for you. Surprise!"

This was the moment where, in her fantasy, he would take her into his arms and give her a passionate kiss, so thrilled was he to see her. Evidently her fantasies were much better than real life, because he didn't try to approach her at all. Of course, the fact that there was some bizarre-looking rotund colleague with him could have had something to do with it.

"Ah, here is the address of the restaurant," the other man said, holding out a business card he had been fishing for in his wallet. In contrast to that of the security guard, his accent was quite thick. For a moment, Sam wondered why they were even speaking in English. Maybe it was some sort of consular protocol. "This is supposed to be the best Thai food in the city. Call and arrange for the president to eat there this evening. Representatives from Paraguay, Canada, and Jamaica will join him. Plus a security detail, of course." He smiled politely at Sam. "Hello. Are you a friend of Eduardo's?"

Eduardo plastered a smile on his face. "Joaquin, this is Samantha Sharpe. Samantha, this is Joaquin Loyo-Mayo. He's the consul-general here in New York."

"Lovely to meet you." Joaquin took Sam's hand and gave a formal little bow.

"Would you excuse us just a moment, Joaquin?" Eduardo asked politely. "I need to speak with Samantha."

"I'll see you inside," the consul-general said. After telling Sam again that it was nice to meet her, he bustled past the guard desk.

The moment that Joaquin was gone, Eduardo hugged
Sam warmly.

"How wonderful to see you!"

"Love that this-is-Samantha-Sharpe-my-*fiancée* intro,"
Sam blurted. It was impossible to keep the edge out of her
voice.

He kept her in his arms. "This is not the time or
the place to inform a colleague that I recently became
engaged. But seeing you is a lovely surprise."

"Yeah," she agreed sarcastically. "You're oozing joy."

"Are you angry about something?" He stepped back;
a quizzical look darkened his face.

Sam sighed. Acting like a bitch was *not* going to fix
anything.

"I guess I just expected a more enthusiastic greeting,"
she admitted. She gave his hand a little squeeze. "You
know what I mean?"

"I think so. Follow me."

Eduardo led her to the elevator and then pushed the
down button. The doors opened immediately. He got in,
pushed the button for the lobby, and then hit the emergency stop button. Then came the softest, most gentle
kiss in the world.

"Like this?"

"Much better." She grinned from ear to ear.

"Kissing is frowned upon in front of the consul-general,
Samantha. So how is it that you're in New York?"

He hit the emergency stop button again, releasing the
car; it started smoothly toward the lobby.

"Well, I was—"

Before she could finish her answer, his PalmPilot

sounded. He answered it in English, then switched over to Spanish. Eduardo's half of the conversation consisted of two lines of Spanish, which even Sam could translate: *That sounds fantastic, but I can't talk now. Call me later.*

Who the hell was he talking to?

The elevator doors opened; they stepped out into the building lobby, and Eduardo pocketed his PalmPilot. "I would love to take you to dinner, but as you could see, I have an embassy affair tonight. That was one of my colleagues at our mission to the United Nations. It wouldn't be good for you; everything will be in Spanish. I'd neglect you terribly."

"I already have plans," Sam assured him, though she felt a little disappointed. "I flew in with Anna. We're going to this fantastic new club tonight called Europa. Have you heard of it?"

"I have. It's supposed to be impossible to get into. But I'm sure you and Anna will find a way." Eduardo nodded and looked pleased.

Did he have to look so happy? He should be *unhappy* that she was going to a club without him. What about that stereotype—that Latin men were hot-blooded and extremely proprietary about their women? Well, okay, he was hot-blooded enough. But where was the proprietary part?

His PalmPilot sounded again. Every fiber of her being wanted to ask him who was calling. But that would make her sound like an insecure, jealous cow. Just because she *felt* like an insecure, jealous cow did not mean she had to advertise the fact.

Eduardo clicked it off, then pulled her close again. "I

wish we could go right back to my hotel. Did I tell you how gorgeous you look in that dress? It's new, no?"

This was much more like it.

"It *is* new. So are you mentally undressing me?" Sam teased. She loved the feel of his arms around her.

"Actually, I am mentally doing this."

He lifted her hair and whispered something very specific in her ear that made her blush.

"And then this."

He whispered in her ear again.

"Get food poisoning during dinner," she whispered suggestively. "We can go back to your hotel and you can show me."

"I can't. I am here to work. It will go very late tonight, so I cannot even promise to meet you later. And in the morning, there's a seven-thirty breakfast for the president with the Spanish ambassador to the United Nations. All the staff will be there. Me included."

Sam nodded slowly and tried to look understanding, which was the last thing she actually felt.

"How long will you and Anna be in New York?" Eduardo asked.

"A few days. Till the weekend, at least. Maybe even a week. I'm not sure."

"Then I have an excellent idea. You two must come to the embassy dinner on Friday night." It felt like more of an order than a suggestion. "It's actually at the consulate, but it should be quite the affair. The president is speaking that day at the UN; there'll be a lot to celebrate. I'll introduce him to you." He winked slyly. "Maybe he'll want your autograph."

"Maybe he'll want my father's autograph. I'm good at signing his name." Sam smirked, but she was happy he'd invited her. People who were engaged were supposed to invite their partners to occasions like this. And now the invitation had been issued.

But even as Eduardo gave her one last kiss goodbye, she couldn't help wondering if That Bitch Gisella would be at the embassy party, too.

Fourth-Generation Legacy

"Wo Hop?" Anna said with delight as she and Logan got out of the taxi on Mott Street in Chinatown. "I haven't been here since I was a little girl."

Chinatown had always been one of her favorite neighborhoods in Manhattan. Teeming with people who spoke in rapid-fire Mandarin, full of open-air markets that sold fish, shellfish, and exotic vegetables, with strange music wafting from shop stalls and every second doorway seeming to lead to a tiny, family-owned restaurant, Chinatown had a vibrancy and excitement that she knew her Upper East Side neighborhood lacked. Back when she lived in Manhattan, she and her friends would come here often, just to walk around or to eat. As far as she knew, her mother had *never* been here. Which said something significant both about the area and about Jane Cabot Percy.

"With your nanny, my nanny, and me. I think we were eight. Something like that," Logan recalled.

Memories flooded Anna as she stood with him at the busy corner of Mott and Canal Street. At the time, her nanny had been a wonderful young woman from Taiwan, who'd ordered for them in perfect Mandarin.

"Lian," she remembered. "That was my nanny. She was going to Hunter College at night."

"At which time the night nanny took over. Lian told us her name meant 'graceful willow.' I think she's the reason I ended up studying Chinese at St. Paul's, actually." Logan led the way down to the basement level restaurant. "Can I make a true confession?" he asked as he opened the glass door, a bright, honest look in his soft blue eyes.

"Of course," Anna allowed, trying to conceal her curiosity.

"That nanny Lian? She was my first crush."

Anna laughed. She was happy to be here. Logan had called to confirm their plans earlier in the day, while she'd been at Bergdorf Goodman with Sam. He'd suggested dinner, and told her that he'd pick the place, but that she should dress casually. Anna had asked Sam again whether she wanted to come along—she'd cleared the possibility with Logan, even—but Sam again insisted that it just be the two of them. She'd go to Lincoln Square to see the new Gus Van Sant film. Anna deserved some positive male attention after the fiasco with Ben. Some *solo* positive male attention.

Anna was dressed casually, in white cotton vintage ripstop roll-up shorts and a simple Proenza Schouler white eyelet cotton blouse with pearl buttons, her grandmother's antique diamond stud earrings, and black Chanel ballet flats. Her hair was pulled back in a casual low ponytail, while her only makeup was pale pink Stila lip gloss and dark brown Christian Dior Snow mascara.

When Logan had rung the doorbell exactly on time,

Anna was waiting for him. He wore khakis with a pale blue linen shirt with a white sport coat. He looked devastatingly handsome, especially when he grinned and handed her a single white rose.

Anna was delightfully surprised. And, she had to admit, impressed. She hadn't thought it would be that kind of a date, and probably it wasn't. But no one had given her flowers in forever. She was even more impressed when she learned that he recalled from grade school that white was her favorite color. "We were studying abstract art in second grade, and we were supposed to draw our own. You spilled white paint on a white sheet of paper. The teacher hung it on the bulletin board and said you were the next Frank Stella."

"How do you remember all these things?" she asked him now, still charmed by his admission of his nanny-crush.

"The curse of a great memory," he answered lightly, holding the door open for her. Anna walked in, their arms lightly brushing as she passed. "Besides," he added with an impish grin, "you never forget your first crush."

Inside, the restaurant was as noisy and crowded as she remembered, the air fragrant from the food being served by graceful men who could carry several plates at once balanced up and down their arms. They only had to wait ten minutes before a table for two opened up, something of a feat in a popular place that didn't take reservations. Logan ordered in English—squid with black bean sauce, eggplant stuffed with shrimp—and the waiter scurried off.

"I'm surprised you didn't order in Mandarin," Anna

remarked, sipping aromatic green tea from a tiny white bone-china cup.

He shrugged. "Somehow that screams 'pretentious.' When I was in Beijing last summer I forced myself to speak Mandarin, even with Chinese people who spoke English, because I was there to improve my language skills. But to do it here? In Chinatown? It would be so that other people could overhear me and so the waiter could be impressed, not so I could order what we wanted."

"I see your point." She studied him, trying to remember exactly the last time she'd seen him. Fourth grade? Fifth grade? "Your eyes are the same," she decided.

He sipped from his tea. "So are yours."

She wrapped her fingers around the fragile teacup. "So, I want to hear everything—The Life of Logan."

He cocked a furrowed eyebrow. "Everything, huh? Well, there's boarding school, or as it is not-so-fondly called by the inmates, boring school."

"Really?" Anna asked, somewhat surprised. "You hated it?"

"Sometime yes, sometimes no. I had two amazing English lit teachers my junior and senior year—that helped. And friends I've known forever. And I traveled with my parents a lot—that's been great."

"Where did you go with them?"

"Europe, Asia, Africa. I loved Tanzania. The people are amazing. Their national poet, Shaaban Robert—do you know his work?"

Anna shook her head.

"I'll get you a book of his poems," Logan promised. "He writes about the savannah, about native tribes, about how even a Masai tribesman has the same hopes and dreams as anyone else. Really amazing stuff."

Logan's story continued. He was, as he'd told her, going to Harvard. That had been his choice since sixth grade, and he'd planned his schooling to that end, graduating second in his class at St. Paul's, captaining the soccer team, and volunteering as a literacy-in-schools worker three afternoons a week. It had worked. He got the same early-decision letter from Harvard that Anna had received from Yale. The fact was, she thought, he probably would have gotten it even if he wasn't a fourth-generation legacy.

At least two hours later, the waiter brought the check. This time, Logan said thank you in Mandarin, which earned him a happy grin.

"You up for a surprise?" Logan plunked his black AmEx card down by the check.

"Sure."

"Fair warning—it's another walk down memory lane. So if you've had your fill of that . . ."

"No, no, it's fine." Anna was charmed that he'd put so much thought into their date. She was curious to see what he had in mind.

It was a long taxi ride away—all the way uptown to Fort Washington Park, at Lafayette Place and West 181st Street—and Anna still didn't know the ultimate destination. In fact, she didn't figure it out until he led her down the footpath to the bridge over the West Side highway, then down across Riverside near the George Washington Bridge and south to . . .

"The Little Red Lighthouse!" she exclaimed.

This was amazing. The red lighthouse was located just south of the bridge on the New York side of the Hudson. Back before the bridge had been built, the lighthouse kept the tugboats on the river from foundering on the rocks. After the bridge went up, it didn't have much of a purpose. Yet New Yorkers always loved it.

More memories came flooding back. The yearly school outings to the autumn Little Red Schoolhouse Festival, where an Urban Park Ranger would take kids and their parents or nannies (for Logan and Anna both, it had always been nannies) on a tour of the historical lighthouse, where an elderly gentleman—Anna found out later it was the folksinger Pete Seeger—would read the children's book *The Little Red Lighthouse* to the enchanted students.

They made their way to the red balcony at the base of the tower and rested their hands on the railing. The Hudson River stretched out in front of them, the air coming off the water just cool enough for Logan to offer his coat, a gesture Anna gratefully accepted. Although the lighthouse was out of commission, the ambient light from the George Washington Bridge made the ripples in the water shine and wave.

"Once the bridge was built, they were going to tear down the lighthouse," Anna recalled. "But children wrote to the government and got it saved."

"Because of the book," Logan added. "The little red lighthouse feels small and insignificant, and the great gray bridge tells the lighthouse how much it's needed to guide ships along the river—"

"'Because even if you are small, boys and girls,'" Anna

began, quoting the man who read the book to them every year, "'you're still—'"

"'Very important,'" Logan finished with her.

They ascended to the top of the lighthouse now, looking out at the Hudson River, and up at the great gray bridge. A full moon brought out the water's purple hue; the rumble of traffic on the bridge overhead was like distant summer thunder.

"I love that you brought me here," Anna said softly.

"Full disclosure—I considered and rejected about a hundred first-date options before coming up with Wo Hop and this. I have this bad habit of overthinking things...."

Anna chuckled. "Me too. It's like I have this running loop in my head, second-guessing myself, analyzing everything—"

"Until you just want to scream," Logan concluded.

"Exactly. It's exactly like that."

They were the only ones on the red deck, gazing out at the water in companionable silence. Anna felt Logan put a light hand on her back. If felt normal, natural. But she couldn't help thinking how a friendly touch could lead to a significant touch, how the touch could lead to a soft kiss and then a different kind of kiss. She stiffened.

"What?" he asked softly.

"Do you want to hear my mental loop, or should I cut to the chase?" Anna asked ruefully.

"Oh, give me the loop. It will make me feel so much better about my own."

Anna hesitated. It was not in her nature to discuss her personal life. Back in New York, she'd been the only girl not to have a blog on MySpace. Other girls would call their friends and gossip endlessly about their latest crushes, but Anna was not one of those girls. There had been a few good lessons in the *This Is How We Do Things* Big Book. The chapter called "Public Is Public and Private Is Private" had always been one of her favorites. Besides, her friend Cyn had done enough oversharing for both of them; Anna had never minded being on the listening end.

"Well, first there's a loop running about us. This . . . date, I guess."

"What about it?"

"I wasn't planning for it to be a date," she admitted.

"It's not a date. Or maybe it is. Or maybe we can figure that out later." He reached down and picked up a pebble, then dropped it over the side of the lighthouse. It was so far down to the cold waters of the Hudson that Anna didn't even hear it hit the water. "We can decide when we find that pebble again. How's that?"

"Sounds good to me."

"But somehow, I don't think that's the only loop," Logan prompted. He leaned back against the circular windows of the lighthouse. "And I'm not in any hurry."

She knew he was right. But to tell him about Ben now felt . . . odd. Her instinct was to change the subject. But then she realized: that was exactly what her mother would do. Anna decided to do the opposite.

"It goes something like this: I had a boyfriend in Los Angeles. A serious boyfriend. We had so many ups and downs and misunderstandings that I never felt sure of anything, and—"

She stopped abruptly, lest she get into oversharing territory that even her newfound resolve wouldn't allow her to stomach. "Anyway, he broke up with me two days ago; it's what prompted this trip to New York. And here I am with you, having a really great time. But the last thing I want to do is to pretend he—Ben—isn't still in my heart and on my mind and . . . I'll stop there." She took a deep breath. "Did I utterly confuse you?"

Logan shook his head lightly. He didn't look at all stressed or upset by her confession. "Not at all. What you just said made me think about my former girlfriend, actually. She just finished her freshman year at Haverford. We broke up at the start of the summer. It was just one of those things. I'm not so sure I'm over her, either."

This made Anna sigh with relief. Though she couldn't help wondering about Logan's former girlfriend. What did she look like? Where was she from? How long had they been together? How was the—

No. She was not going there.

"So, then you *do* understand—"

"And that's why we'll leave it at that for now. Okay?"

"Okay," Anna agreed. Though she was pleased, in some small way, that he didn't have a girlfriend.

Happily, Logan changed the subject. "Are you planning on going to that thing at the Yale Club the night after next?"

Anna nodded. "That's one of the reasons I came home. How do you know about it?"

"Ivy League planning. Yale, Harvard, Brown, and Dartmouth are all on the same nights, at their respective clubs. Want to go out someplace afterward? We could compare war stories. I'd ask you to bring Sam, but I just think she'd be totally bored."

"You're right. She would be. And I'd love to."

Logan smiled. "You know, I remember one other thing about you and me and this lighthouse."

Anna thought she remembered too. But she wasn't sure if he had the same memory, until he leaned over and kissed her . . . on the right cheek.

"I did *that*." A slow smile of remembrance crossed his face. "It took all my nerve. I thought maybe you'd punch me or stomp on my foot or run crying to Mrs. Posner."

"But I didn't run to the teacher," Anna recalled. "I did *this*."

She leaned forward and kissed him back. Not on the cheek.

A Hetero Guy in Fashion

"Wow. This is . . . this is amazing."
Cammie smiled knowingly as sixteen-year-old Champagne Jones gazed around the enormous downtown loft space a block from the Staples Center that the fashion designer Martin Rittenhouse had transformed into one of the most exclusive clothing design ateliers on the West Coast. Rittenhouse was a rising young designer, with an uncanny knack for creating clothes in a variety of genres, from high fashion to sportswear. His designs had been featured a couple of weeks before at an L.A. County Museum of Art show to benefit the New Visions organization, a foundation that assisted at-risk teenagers in the Los Angeles area.

Cammie, Anna, and Champagne had modeled in that show as part of some volunteer work they'd done. Champagne was one of the girls in the New Visions program, and her tale of a married-divorced-remarried-redivorced family structure sounded like that of lots of families Cammie knew. But two things were different about Champagne. One was that with her combination of classic, platinum blond, high-cheekboned beauty and darling, emerald-eyed, unpretentious sweetness, even Anna paled in comparison. The other thing was that Champagne was poor. Not middle-class. Not even lower-middle-class poor. Poor-poor. Cammie knew it wasn't politically correct to even think in these terms, but facts were facts. If she was going to help Champagne in any way, the first thing that had to be done was to face facts.

Though Champagne was a good student, she had one goal in life, which she'd been all too eager to share with Cammie: She wanted to be a model. She certainly had the looks and the body type—long, coltlike legs and a lithe, slender body. What she didn't have was height. Five-foot six did not a model make. Oh sure, Cammie had taught her how to do the necessary straight-line model walk in three-inch heels. The problem was that the five-foot-ten models were also wearing three-inch heels, meaning that stilettos still gave Champagne no advantage in the modeling world.

Cammie wasn't sure why she wanted to help Champagne as much as she did; *altruism* was not a word usually associated with her. There was just something about the girl. Yes, she was smart. And yes, she was disadvantaged. But there were plenty of smart and disadvantaged girls in Los Angeles. Cammie had sparked to something else. Maybe it was the hunger in her eyes to *be* somebody, to be the best. That kind of hunger was something that Cammie understood. Didn't she feel the need to be the hottest, most stylish girl in any room? And didn't she usually succeed? There was a certain validation in that; that the world understood how special you really were.

It wasn't that Cammie had ever pined for a future as

a model's manager, yet she had become one for Champagne. That she'd managed to get Martin Rittenhouse to create a new line of petite fashions for which her first client would be the print model was quite satisfying. It hadn't occurred via any conventional route: it had taken Rittenhouse making a criminal mistake and Cammie essentially blackmailing him. But outsmarting the designer was another kind of validation for Cammie. She was definitely her father's daughter.

She'd brought Champagne here on a dual-pronged mission. One—see how the new clothing line was coming along. Two—manipulate Rittenhouse into using his contacts to ensure that the guest list for the Bye, Bye Love opening would be star-studded with the highest-profile fashionistas.

There was a simple Los Angeles club calculus. Fashion designers brought their models. Models—as much as celebrities, maybe even more—brought paparazzi and hot, well-heeled guys. Cammie had the celebrity thing covered, both through herself and Sam. But a dozen big-name designers and at least as many big-name models would be better than an insurance policy. With the right DJ spinning the right music plus the right people in a new and utterly unique club, she and Ben couldn't fail.

"So, what do all these people do?" Champagne asked Cammie. They stood just inside the entrance of Rittenhouse's third-floor-loft atelier. Directly in front of them, dozens of seamstresses worked furiously at a long line of sewing machines. Further back were other workers.

Cammie didn't really feel like explaining. They were already a half-hour behind the schedule she'd mentally set for this little outing, because when she went to pick Champagne up, the girl had on a short, tight denim skirt and a cheap hot pink tank top, cosmetics spackled on her face, and her hair back-combed to make her look taller. She was trying to look "hot," she explained.

Cammie had her scrub her face and put on the outfit she had purchased for her: casual Ralph Lauren black linen capris and a simple but well-fitted white T-shirt—and brushed the hairspray out of her hair. Real models, Cammie had advised, never wore makeup when making rounds. They dressed simply and let their natural beauty and shape shine. Trying too hard, she had told the enraptured girl, was the modeling kiss of death. Champagne hung on every word and swore never to make the same mistake again.

Now Cammie looked around; the loft space was a crowded, almost frenetic environment, with Eric Clapton's *Timepieces* pounding over the sound system and Rittenhouse's crew busy with their assigned jobs. She pointed to the left. "It's organized chaos, I know. Over there are the fabric-cutters. Behind them are the sewers. He has measuring blocks and three-way mirrors in the center, and an area marked off like a fashion catwalk down the middle. Over to the right are his storage racks, and an office for paperwork."

"Cammie! Champagne! Welcome to the center of everything!"

Martin's familiar voice boomed out as he bounded across the glossy parquet floor to them. Cammie hadn't seen him since the fashion show, and he looked very much as she remembered. Martin was a metrosexual's metrosexual, built correctly for his medium height, with thick, glossy black hair, and not a thread misplaced or a wrinkle noticeable on the black Kim Jones rib-panel crew shirt and Zegna trousers that he wore. With him was a young man in his early twenties whom Cammie immediately nicknamed in her mind Mini-Martin. He was a younger, shorter, but no less meticulously put together version of Martin. They were even wearing variations on the exact same outfit.

"This is my nephew Seth," Martin introduced Mini-Martin. "He's here from Texas for a couple of weeks to learn the business from the inside."

"I go to FIT in New York. I love clothes. Always did. Must be in the gene pool." He smiled at Champagne and it was definitely a hetero grin, because Cammie simply knew these things. Hmmm. A hetero guy in fashion. The way Seth was beaming at Champagne gave Cammie the perfect opening, since she was to be alone with Martin for ten or fifteen minutes.

"So Martin," she began, "have you got any roughs of the new petite line?"

"I just finished one yesterday." Martin flashed pearly white veneers. "Seth helped. I'm very proud of him for his contributions."

"Mini—uh, Seth, why don't you give Champagne a tour and then have her try on the prototype," Cammie suggested. "I'd love to see it."

"And I suspect Seth would love to show it to her. Off you go, you two. See you on the runway. Champagne, what music would you like?"

"Excuse me?" The young girl was uncomprehending, but clearly exhilarated by the surroundings.

"The runway down the center of my loft. You're going to model the new dress. What music would you like? We have everything on Rhapsody piped through."

"Wow," Champagne breathed. "How about . . . Rush? Quiet Riot? Ozzy?"

Cammie saw Martin try to cover his wince, then rally. "Quiet Riot it is. Seth, pull it up on the Bose deck and bring me the remote."

"You got it, Uncle Martin. Come on, Champagne, I'll give the tour, and then show you *our* creation."

Mini-Martin boldly extended the crook of his elbow, and Champagne just as boldly took it. Even before they'd sauntered off, Rittenhouse's nephew had begun a spiel about the inner workings of the fashion design business. Cammie could see that Champagne was hanging on every word.

"Cute," Martin observed. "He's a good kid, my nephew. Talented, too. So I understand that you're branching out into the world of nightclubs. Fashion model management isn't enough for you?"

Cammie was taken aback. How could he possibly know? She and Ben hadn't done any publicity yet.

"Oh, don't be so surprised." Martin waved a dismissive hand. "If you're in the know, word travels fast. And Culver City? Aren't you an edgy pioneer."

"Thanks."

"What's the name of the place again? Bye, Bye something . . ."

"Love," Cammie filled in, as she tapped her feet a bit

impatiently. She and Ben had been trying to keep the news about their club under wraps, so they could make a bigger publicity splash when the time was right. "Who told you?"

Martin grinned. "I was at a Bebe show the other day. One of the models is dating the owner of Trieste. Your partner works at Trieste—"

"Worked."

"Works, worked, whatever." He fiddled with a pinky ring that contained a ruby the size of one of Cammie's knuckles. "Anyway, word's out. Break a leg and all that."

"Actually, Martin, I'm counting on you to help me break it," Cammie replied.

Martin's eyebrows rose toward his hairline. "How so?"

"You and your fashionista friends at the club opening."

Martin touched her arm to move her back toward the door, as two of his assistants swiftly moved by, pushing an overstuffed garment rack. "And when would that opening be?"

"Two weeks from tonight. Exactly."

He took out his Sidekick and touched a few keys, then peered at the screen. "No can do—I'll be in San Diego. I've a four o'clock flight from Burbank, dinner meeting at eight. Much as I'd like to help you. Perhaps Seth can come in my stead."

Across the room, Cammie saw Mini-Martin shepherding Champagne behind a white curtain into what was evidently the makeshift changing area. Champagne stood there, patiently and politely waiting for him to take the hint and leave her alone to change, but the clueless boy didn't seem to register and just stood there staring back at her.

"I don't want your nephew," Cammie told Martin. "I want you."

"Can't do it."

"Of course you can." She stayed utterly cool. Moments like this, when others would get upset, were her strong suit. "Don't forget why we're here."

Martin's nostrils flared in protest. Cammie had caught him stealing his own couture gowns at the volunteer fashion show, then reporting them stolen so that he'd get publicity for it. Instead of pressing charges, Cammie had cut a deal with him. In three words, Martin owed her.

"You fucked up royally," she added in a husky whisper. "I'm the only reason you're not in jail right now."

"How could I be prosecuted for stealing from myself?" he asked, his shrill voice belying his confidence.

"Fraud, perjury," she ticked off. "You seem to forget that you blamed others. That's a no-no."

"But you're blackmailing me!"

Cammie winced. "That's such an ugly word. I prefer to think we have a mutually beneficial arrangement."

"You remind me of a guppy," Martin sniped as he smoothed some nonexistent wrinkles on his starched white shirt.

"A gay urban professional? How so?"

"Aquarium fish. They devour their young."

Cammie smiled. "I don't ever plan to breed, but thanks for the compliment. Glad we've had this little chat. So you'll make your meeting a breakfast meeting, and I can count on you to be at the opening of my club, with a couple dozen of your closest big-name friends. Right?"

"I really do resent your attitude," he muttered huffily.

"And I resent that you tried to pin your little scam on my friend and client Champagne," she pointed out. "You could have ruined that girl's life, so you'll understand if compassion isn't exactly what I'm feeling for you."

"Well . . ."

Before Martin could finish his answer, "Cum On Feel the Noize" blasted over the sound system so loudly that all work in the Rittenhouse loft stopped. Suddenly, the lighting changed too—from the all-points-over bright fluorescents to three pin-spotlights focused at the top of the fashion runway.

Then, Mini-Martin's El Paso twang suddenly boomed out over the speaker system. "Presenting for your viewing pleasure, a Martin Rittenhouse/Seth Rittenhouse Petite Couture original, modeled by Miss Champagne Jones!"

Champagne struck a model's haughty pose at the top of the runway, and then did the famous one-foot-directly-in-front-of-the-other walk. She looked like she'd been doing it her whole life instead of at a single charity show at the county art museum.

"Go, Champagne!" Mini-Martin shouted. "You are fierce!"

Cammie was impressed; not just with Champagne's modeling, but with what she was modeling. Martin and Seth had fashioned a flowing, ruby-colored, off-the-shoulder calf-length dress for her that draped perfectly around her body with every confident step she took.

"That's gorgeous," Cammie told Martin, raising her voice to be heard over the blasting heavy metal music.

"Thank you." He nodded in agreement. "I told you I'd fulfill my end of our bargain. I promise you the whole Petite Couture by Rittenhouse line will be equally fabulous. What I'd like to know is, for how long can I expect you to hold one little self-serving error in judgment against me?"

"Come through on the petite line and use Champagne in all your print ads, show up at my opening with your hot-shit fashionista friends, and we'll call it even," she decided.

"And just how do I know you'll stick to that agreement?"

Cammie smiled benignly. "You don't." She held out a hand whose nails had just been manicured that morning at the spa at the Beverly Hills Hotel. The Japanese nail artist Kumiko had done her usual stellar job. "Deal?"

"Deal." Martin sighed

"Fabulous." Which, Cammie decided, described both her deal with Martin and her life. Yes, she was still smarting over losing Adam. And yes, when she allowed herself to think about him, which was as rarely as possible, she still missed him. But now that she was working with Ben, who was suddenly and wonderfully single, she found herself obsessing about Adam and where he might be a hell of a lot less. He could be in Michigan, he could be home in Beverly Hills twiddling his thumbs in front of pictures of her that he had stored on his MacBook. Frankly, it didn't make a particle of difference. She'd just helped guarantee that the opening of Bye, Bye Love would be a monster success. Ben would undoubtedly be very grateful. And Cammie was pretty sure she could get him to show it.

Fuck Adam. Still, she couldn't stop the lyrics to "Bye, Bye Love" from suddenly flying into her mind. *Bye, bye, love. Bye bye, happiness. Hello, loneliness.*

Cammie banished the ghost of Buddy Holly, shook her strawberry blond curls, and marched determinedly to the catwalk to congratulate her first modeling client. Her life was goddamn *fabulous*, and nothing was going to convince her otherwise.

Skin Like a Relief Map

F ounded in 1989 by Robert DeNiro, the Tribeca Film
Center was a large redbrick commercial building in
lower Manhattan that had been converted into office and
production space for a slew of media-related companies.
Sam was here to meet Joe Jeffrey, the writer of *Ass Man,*
a script she'd read and instantly fallen in love with. Joe
lived out in Sheepshead Bay, Brooklyn—he told Sam he'd
been focusing for the last couple of years on "legit" work
in New York theater—but suggested that they meet for
lunch on the film center's garden roof deck.

Joe Jeffrey was truly talented; that much Sam knew.
She'd read his screenplay three times. The first time,
she'd been struck by its humor—she was still laughing
aloud at many of the lines. The second time, by its dia-
logue. The third time, it was its surprising sensitivity
that really came through. *Ass Man* was the story of an
unsung Hollywood actor, who, after kicking around for
years and getting nowhere, gets cast in a national commercial for a popular hemorrhoid cream. America falls in
love with the commercial and with him, and the actor is
quickly catapulted to fame and fortune.

Sam loved the intelligent way in which Joe had skewered all things Hollywood, especially the way that the same managers and agents who'd ignored the hero precommercial battled for his attentions postcommercial. It was clear that he knew of what he wrote. Since she likewise knew of what he wrote, she figured she was the perfect director for the movie. And since he'd admitted during their phone conversation that no one else was coming after him to produce and direct his script, he'd readily agreed to meet Sam for lunch.

"How will I recognize you?" she had asked.

"I'm bald," he'd declared without a hint of embarrassment. "And I don't wear one of those weenie Hollywood baseball caps to cover it up."

It was the day after Sam had ambushed Eduardo at work, and she arrived first for the meeting. The roof deck was exactly that—a rooftop restaurant that overlooked the Hudson River to the west and much of lower Manhattan to the south. There were fifteen or twenty old-fashioned round redwood picnic tables with red-and-white Film Center umbrellas shading them from the noonday sun, but the planks on the deck were set close enough so that women didn't have to worry about having their Gucci heels breaking in the cracks. Dressed in New York black despite the warm summer sunshine, a waitress showed her to the table farthest from the entrance, with the best view on the roof. Sam could actually see the Statue of Liberty off in the distance, as ferry boats chugged back and forth beween Battery Park and Staten Island.

"Can I get you anything while you're waiting?" the

waitress asked politely. That she was both beautiful—
with short, choppy black hair and almond-shaped amber
eyes—and attitude-free struck Sam as refreshing.

Sam asked for an iced cappuccino, which arrived
almost instantly, and looked around at the other tables.
Kate Winslet was sitting with Quentin Tarantino a few
tables away; they had a movie script open between
them. She knew Quentin from a dinner party her father
had given but had never met Kate. She was more petite
than she looked on-screen, which was always the case.
She looked lovelier, too; fine-boned and animated, with
a huge smile and a ready laugh that peeled across the
terrace.

Sam made a mental note: *Work with her as soon as possible.*

"Sam Sharpe?"

She looked up. Standing before her was an exception-
ally short man, his eyes hidden behind oversize black
sunglasses. His face was round and pale—he clearly spent
a lot of time indoors with the shades drawn—and he was,
as advertised, entirely hair-free, save for a wispy blond
goatee on his dimpled chin. He wore old Levi's 501 jeans
and ratty brown Birkenstock sandals that displayed fat
pink toes. His scruffy, brown silk-screened T-shirt loudly
proclaimed WAR SUCKS ASS.

Funny how he hadn't described himself on the phone
as short. Really, really short. Like that wasn't the first
thing anyone would notice about him.

"Hi, you must be Joe," Sam rose, and found herself
towering over him. She was five-foot four on a good day,
and he barely reached her chin. For this meeting, she was

wearing her favorite Imitation of Christ jeans, with a black—after all, she was in New York—top and Joan & David sandals with a medium stacked heel. Even with the heels taken into account, Joe had to be four inches shorter than she was. Fair enough. There were plenty of short people in Hollywood. Marty Scorsese. Danny Devito. Mary-Kate and Ashley.

"I must be," he agreed, taking a seat opposite her, not bothering to offer Sam a hand. He did, however, carry a stack of scripts. He had told her he was a character actor when he wasn't writing. Sam guessed that was true, since she couldn't imagine any other roles in which he'd be cast. Except maybe *Shrek IV*.

"So. Sam Sharpe." Joe folded his diminutive hands on the redwood tabletop. "You want to direct."

"Possibly," she hedged. Not because what he said wasn't so, but because a lifetime in Hollywood had taught her to never, ever come to the point unless it was absolutely necessary, lest the point turn out to be wrong and someone blamed it on you.

Joe leaned forward. Well, as far forward as his torso could lean. "This is New York, sweetheart. No need to do the West Coast shuffle here. I did my homework. You want to direct; daddy wants to finance; you're looking for a script to be your first. Tell Joe he did he his homework."

Sam sipped her cappuccino. "Do you always carry on a conversation with yourself?"

"Even though I lived in Studio City for ten years, I'm a New Yorker. I cut to the chase."

The waitress reappeared. Sam ordered a Cobb salad

with Bac-Os instead of bacon. Joe ordered a burger and asked the waitress to put Sam's salad bacon on it.

"Don't overcook it. I want it like ten seconds from raw," he instructed the waitress, in a voice that could have been issuing orders for the start of World War III. "Not rare. Rare sucks. I want it singed on the outside. That's it. I want the cow to still be mooing on my plate. And some fries. And a Budweiser. Don't need the glass."

Before their waitress—she'd been unfazed by Joe's brusqueness—was halfway to the kitchen, he whipped off his sunglasses. His deep-set blue eyes were surprisingly bright, almost hypnotic, under thick, bushy brows. "So, Sam Sharpe. You didn't tell me I was wrong with what I said. Talk to me. Talk to Joe."

"You are a terrific writer—"

He raised a stubby hand. "Please. Cut the foreplay. We've both got better things to do and the food isn't gonna be that great. Where are we going with this?"

"We're not going anywhere unless we can actually have a discussion. That means you don't interrupt me, and I try not to interrupt you."

Joe nodded approvingly, then spread his arms wide. The wingspan was nothing to write home about. "I'm laying it out there for you, Sam. Here's what I believe in: betting on myself. *Ass Man* is comic genius. I'm holding out to direct it myself."

Sam felt an instant letdown. Not that she was enjoying her time with this grumpy screenwriter, and she wasn't convinced that she even wanted to direct *Ass Man.* But if anyone was going to be the one to say no, she felt that someone should be her.

"Ever directed anything?" she asked, wrapping her hands around the cappuccino glass, enjoying the icy cold against her fingers.

"Have you?"

Sam opened her mouth. She was not about to say the two terrible words—or at least they were terrible when put together—*student film*. The only kind of film she had directed. Admitting that her only feature was a documentary about some of Beverly Hills high school friends for which Anna had written a short but decent script would be the kiss of death. Instead, she nodded and took a long sip of her cappuccino.

Joe didn't seem to mind that she had dodged his question. "Listen to me, Sam. Comedy is what I do, because I'm great at it. But it's not what gets my blood pumping. Guess what my genre really is."

Sam arched a brow. She'd IMDB'd the guy—he'd done juvenile comedy after juvenile comedy, mostly in the role of the guy who ends up falling into a Porta Potty. But she decided to flatter him. "Porn?"

"Ha! Wrong kind of hard-core action. I'm a blood-and-guts guy. High body count. Realist nihilism. The next Sam Peckinpah—hell, the next Scorsese—if someone will just give me a fucking break. Which is why I got a deal thing going around in my head. I let you do *Ass Man* in return for a deal with your father, action with a capital fucking *A*."

Sam wasn't surprised. But she was, again, disappointed. "You want to use me to get to my father? Wow. *That's* fresh."

The waitress brought Sam her Cobb salad, ranch

dressing in a silver dish on the side, and Joe a burger that made Sam grateful for the bun, so she wouldn't have to think of it as half-dead cow. Sam added fries to her order. And a black-and-white milk shake. If she was going to get through a meal with Joe Jeffrey, she was going to have to indulge in carb loading. Of course, if Joe didn't come around reasonably quickly to her point of view, she'd end this luncheon before the fries and milk shake arrived.

"Maybe you want to reconsider. The carbs will go right to your ass. Give you a big ass, man. Get it? Ass man!" he hooted. She looked away as blood oozed from his burger even before he bit into it.

"I'm not getting you a deal with my father," Sam said bluntly. "And you might want to change the title of your spec script from *Ass Man* to *Ass Hole*."

Joe's tiny hands flew to his heart. "Ouch!" he barked; then he laughed. "Okay, I deserved that. Listen, who says I can't compromise? Make your case. Convince Joe." He popped a fry into his mouth.

There was nothing more annoying than a guy who referred to himself in the third person. Suddenly Sam knew there would be no compromise with this cretin. Even if there was, she'd have to *work* with him.

She took her white linen napkin from her lap and put it next to her untouched salad. "Enjoy your meal. Eat my salad too, if you want. You've got my cell number. And when you change your mind about your script—I won't even take it on without giving it to someone for a top-to-bottom rewrite—give me a call."

As she rose, Joe seemed genuinely shocked. "You're leaving?"

"I am." She hoisted the strap of her black Prada bag over her shoulder and tossed a hundred-dollar bill on the table. "Have a pleasant life."

"Your father is on the way down, I hope you know that!" Joe called after her as she made her way across the deck to the entrance.

God. How could a person be so funny on the page and such a wanker in person?

"Come on, man. Call upstairs!"

Seven hours later, Sam stood with Anna and Logan outside the main doors of the residence of the Peruvian ambassador to the United Nations, an elegant brownstone on East Sixty-eighth Street between Second and Third Avenues, easy walking distance from Anna's place. They were already a half hour late to the party for President Alan García of Peru, but the guard manning the front door obviously didn't care. He had dull eyes and skin like a relief map, and even though Sam had dropped her name not once but twice, he still insisted there was a little problem with their admission to the party.

As in, their names weren't on the list. And no amount of appealing to the fame of America's greatest action hero—one Jackson Sharpe—was having an impact. Neither were her and Anna's stunning new outfits.

Sam had been so frustrated and depressed after her aborted lunch with the little Ass Man that she'd sought succor with retail therapy. She'd cabbed over to Horatio and Eighth Avenue to shop at Darling, a small boutique that was owned by Broadway costume designer Ann French Emonts, who'd also done costumes for two of her father's movies. One of them, *Buzz Bomb,* about a simultaneous worldwide assault by genetically altered killer bees, had been the number-two grossing film of its year, second only to a Mel Gibson–directed gorefest. Sam adored her, and always tried to shop at Darling when she came to Manhattan.

Anna had told Sam she was planning to wear a simple black Chanel shift that had been handed down from her exceedingly fashionable maternal grandmother. Sam convinced her otherwise. Wouldn't she like Logan—who they'd quickly included in their invitation to the party after his and Anna's date had gone so well—to see her in something drop-dead gorgeous and new at the embassy party? Besides, Sam needed company. With the help of Ann French's "darling girls," as the assistants were known, Sam ended up buying a low-cut red chiffon Christy Long that floated over her hips. Because it was only fitted above the waist, she'd been able to squeeze into a size eight, which brightened her mood considerably. Anna had chosen a Lotta Stensson nude vintage slip gown covered in delicate hand-embroidered lace. In addition—Sam was incapable of leaving the store without buying just a few other things to be shipped back to Los Angeles—she had added a Fix burnt orange velvet camisole, a Hank Vintage Threads lace skirt, and a half dozen triple-ply cashmere tank tops to her fashion repertoire.

She and Anna stood outside the front door in their finery, with Logan in an elegant Ted Lapidus tuxedo that wouldn't have looked any better on Daniel Craig, and the low-two-digit-IQ guard was not allowing them in because they weren't on the list.

Sam tapped an impatient black patent-leather stiletto-toed heel against the tiled entrance. "Can you please check one more time?" she asked in her best fake-sweet voice. "We're guests of Eduardo Muñoz. My fiancé."

The guard shook his head, but then his eye caught something on the desk. He held up a sheet of paper sheepishly. Sam sighed. He had misplaced a supplemental sheet of late-registered guests. After he quickly found their names and crossed them off methodically with a black marking pen, they were quickly ushered into the brownstone, directly to an elevator to the penthouse.

The penthouse was obviously designed as a party and reception space, with large murals of native Peruvian scenes covering two walls, a stylized map of Peru on a third wall, and the fourth wall of entirely glass looking out over East Sixty-eighth Street. The room was jammed with dignitaries and UN representatives—Sam recognized the mayor and governor of New York, the secretary of state, and the conductor of the New York Philharmonic amongst the partygoers. In one corner of the room, a beautiful blonde with a swanlike neck played a white grand piano. Discreet Peruvian waiters snaked amongst the throng, offering hot and cold hors d'oeuvres and flutes filled with Cristal.

"Sam!"

Even before the elevator door closed behind them, she heard her name called and saw Eduardo waving over the head of a svelte, middle-aged woman with whom he'd been speaking. Anna and Logan joined her as she eased through the crowd to her gorgeous new fiancé. She was looking forward to him seeing her in the new red chiffon gown.

ZOEY DEAN

"Samantha. *Qué guapa!*"

How beautiful. Nice.

Eduardo happily greeted Anna, who quickly introduced Logan; then he introduced them all to his compan-
ion. "Samantha, Anna, Logan, I'd like you to meet Masha
Bereskova, who is the wife of the Russian ambassador to
the United Nations."

"Lovely to meet you all," Masha said in her lush
accent. She had short, spiky, platinum blond hair, a figure
that would make Angelina Jolie envious, and puffy red
lips. She wore a dazzling white-and-amber Chloé gown.
It made Sam think that the Russian ambassador to the
UN had to be well compensated.

Sam said the usual thing you said when you were
introduced to someone at a party—blah, blah, blah—but
her mind was still on Eduardo's introduction. Once
again, there'd been no mention that she was his fiancée.
Was this more diplomatic protocol, or was it something
more? She couldn't see how it could be the former. It
wasn't like Russians didn't get engaged or married.

"So Anna, how do you and Logan know each other?"
Eduardo asked. If he was sensitive to Sam's disquiet, his
smile didn't reveal it. They weren't far from the entrance
to the room, and had to edge toward the picture window at
the south end of the room to let arriving guests pass by.

"We grew up together, actually." Anna sipped champagne from the crystal flute one of the waiters had
brought.

Sam saw the smile that passed between Logan and
Anna. They'd spent some time with Logan at Anna's
place before leaving for the party, and Sam liked him.

A lot. He was one of the few old-money richies she had ever met who didn't seem full of himself, as if somehow having wealth that went back many generations made him superior to anyone who'd acquired it more recently.

"The funny thing is, she hasn't changed at all," Logan observed as he leaned against one of the white beams that supported the high ceiling of the reception room. "I could have picked her out of this crowd even after all these years."

Sweet.

A moment later, Eduardo was introducing them to someone else, a swarthy middle-aged man in a fabulous dashiki. He was Dirago Biagne, the distinguished representative to the United Nations from Senegal. Even as Anna chatted easily with the man in French, Sam had a hard time concentrating. Once again, Eduardo had neglected to introduce her as his fiancée. Instead, he'd merely stated her name.

She was obsessing, and she knew it. Reality-check time.

"Anna, come to the ladies' room with me?" she murmured, once the Senegalese guy had moved off and Eduardo had taken Logan to meet one of Peru's best soccer players.

"Sure."

They made their way across the expansive room, threading past well-dressed party guests who chattered away in a plethora of languages. An international sign above one of the heavy oak doors pointed the way to the bathrooms, which they found at the end of a narrow, wood-paneled hallway behind a heavy gilded door labeled MUJERES. The ladies' lounge was all black marble and gold, with black leather high-back stools in front of the vanity.

Sam took in her image in the vanity mirror. Sure, the dress was fabulous. But it was so apparent to anyone—especially herself—that she was less than fabulous in it. Compared to Anna's, her hips looked like red-chiffon-swathed ham hocks. Not that she'd ever seen a ham hock, or even knew what one was, for that matter. But she could imagine.

"Are you okay?" Anna asked.

Sam deliberately turned away from the vanity, all the better to avoid her own image. "Am I acting weird?"

"You just don't seem . . . happy. You're at a glamorous international party in New York City with your new fiancé—"

Sam pointed at her. "Ha. Stop right there."

"Sorry?"

"Fiancée," she repeated. "Did you once hear Eduardo call me his fiancée?"

"No, but—"

"No 'but' is involved. Being engaged and not telling anyone is like winning an Oscar and keeping it a secret. What's the point?" She opened her Hermès Birkin evening bag, took out her So Chaud cherry red MAC lipstick, and slicked it over her pouting lips.

Anna looked at her closely. "Have you even had the discussion?"

"What discussion?"

"Talked about whether or not you're going public yet?"

"Why would we need to do that?" Sam asked.

"Because maybe they don't do things the same way in Peru that they do them here," Anna reasoned. She eased herself into a red brocade chair and stretched her legs. "I mean, you haven't told your dad yet, have you?"

"No, but that's different."

"Maybe it isn't. Maybe in Peru, you don't make a public announcement of an engagement until your family knows." Anna smiled. "Anything wrong with my logic?"

"No," Sam admitted, a little embarrassed. She was right. It was so obvious. It made her feel dumb. "And no, he hasn't told his parents yet, either."

"That's probably it, then. He doesn't want to tell the world before you tell your families. Wouldn't they feel terrible if they heard about it from someone else instead of the two of you?"

Sam sighed, a little ashamed of herself. "I knew there was a reason I wanted to talk to you. Thank you for your usual brilliant analysis and logic. Let's go back to the party. No, wait."

"What?" Anna had already started for the bathroom door again.

"Before we go back out there and pretend that I'm grown-up enough to get married, what's up with you and Logan?"

Sam watched her friend's face soften. "I like him."

"This is like saying that Cammie likes boys," Sam pointed out. The bathroom door opened, and Masha swung in. Wordlessly, she moved between them and into one of the stalls. Sam lowered her voice just a touch. "Less than revelatory. I just always thought you and Ben—"

Uncharacteristically, Anna interrupted her. "Can we not talk about Ben? Talking about Ben hurts. Thinking about Ben hurts."

But Sam couldn't resist.

"So Logan is, what? Rebound guy?"

"I don't know what he is, except my friend."

"Friend as in, Pass me the rose petals so I can spread them on the bed, or friend as in, Pass the popcorn?"

Anna thought about that a moment; her face as pensive as if she were recalling a tough vocabulary word for the SATs. "I guess I don't know yet. But I'm not over Ben—it's only been a few days. And I'm not about to get involved with Logan while I'm still licking my wounds."

Sam fluffed her hair and snapped shut the little ruby clasp on her evening bag. "I hate it that you're so much more grown-up than I am, you know."

"Or maybe I just know how to hide a broken heart better than you do. Sam, Eduardo loves you. And you love him. You don't have anything to worry about." Anna smiled sadly. "Let's go back so I can see you hug him."

As they made their way back to the party, Sam thought about how amazing it was that Anna could put things in perspective for her. Why was she herself making everything so complicated when it really didn't have to—

If it was possible to stop midthought, then that is exactly what Sam did.

Directly across the densely packed room, over by the wall-to-wall glass window that fronted on Sixty-eighth Street, she saw a young woman hug Eduardo. Long, dark glossy hair, burnished copper skin and deep-set eyes, curvaceous body thinly covered in a pale blue, off-the-shoulder taffeta gown cut down to the small of her magnificent tawny back.

No. It couldn't be. Sam had been so sure it was only her own paranoia that had led her to think . . .

Only there she was. Hugging Eduardo.

Shit. Shit, shit, shit.

But by the time Sam crossed the room to Eduardo—dodging around the gray-haired, distinguished-looking president of Peru in his presidential sash, and the president's entourage—her fiancé was entirely alone. In fact, Eduardo grinned broadly when he saw her, and even took her hand.

What would Anna do? Anna would stay cool. So cool.

"What was Gisella doing here?" Sam asked, trying not to add the words *That Bitch* to her name.

"Who?"

What nerve. Sam shook her Bumble and bumble blown-out hair off her face. "Do you know more than one girl named Gisella?"

"You mean Gisella Santa Maria?"

"Yes," Sam replied easily.

"Gisella wasn't here."

"Oh, come on, Eduardo. Don't bullshit a bullshitter. I *saw* her. She was hugging you!"

"Or maybe you just think all Peruvian women look alike," he teased with a twinkle in his eye. "They are about to serve dinner downstairs. The finest Peruvian meal you'll ever eat. Better even than my cooking. Shall we?" He offered her his arm.

She took it, but she was not at all convinced. She was almost positive that Eduardo was lying to her. And she could not for the life of her figure out why.

Sophisticated Laughter of the Upper Ten Percent

"Ladies and gentlemen, look to your right."

Anna dutifully turned to her right. Sitting on the folding chair next to her was a hirsute guy—bushy red hair on his head along with a thick, wiry beard, and flip-flops on his feet. He wore black pants and a white shirt flecked with hot pink and black paint. She noticed that his thatch of hair traveled into the collar of his shirt, both in front and in back. She wondered idly if it mingled with chest and back hair in a sort of pelt. It was an odd thing to wonder, but then, she was feeling particularly odd at that moment.

"And now, to your left."

Anna turned again. To her left was a girl so slender and pale she was nearly opaque. Her face was tightly pinched, with close-cropped, boyish dark hair, and she wore red tights under black walking shorts and layers of baggy tops, which had to have been designed to disguise her alarming boniness. Anna peeked at her seatmates' name tags. The guy had a first and last name of so many syllables that it barely fit on the tag. The young woman's name was Abernathy Hathaway-Birch. Anna guessed she came from an East Coast WASP family of the type with which she herself was all too familiar. Who else would name their daughter Abernathy?

All around the room—an impressive, wood-paneled meeting area in the venerable Yale Club in New York City—incoming freshmen from the New York metropolitan area were doing the same thing, following the instructions of the Yale dean of students, a slightly built thirtysomething man in wire-rimmed glasses with short brown hair, who wore a light brown sport coat over a white Oxford shirt and navy blue tie. Anna would have bet anything that he was wearing corduroy pants, though an official Yale podium blocked the view.

"Okay." The dean began in the confident voice of a man who was used to being treated with respect. "I don't want to scare you, but statistics prove the following: one out of three of Yale's entering students end up married to each other. So the person to your left or right could end up as your husband or wife. Or, since we're in the twenty-first century, it might not be going too far to say perhaps both."

There were chuckles around the room, the sophisticated laughter of the upper ten percent. It was laughter that Anna knew well; the laughter of the living room when her mother held dinner parties, the laughter she heard in her AP classes at Trinity when a teacher made a clever joke. It was laughter she hadn't heard in eight months, since she'd moved to California. Not that the West Coast didn't have its own brand of elitism, because it definitely did. But somehow she couldn't help but feel it seemed too trivial to seem important. She didn't *care* how much Universal or Paramount was paying Angelina or Meg for her next movie, or whose boobs were real and whose weren't.

But as the laughter continued, Anna realized that this kind of elitism—the intellectual, sophisticated, it-takes-an-education-to-understand-the-context kind of snobbery—had colored her thinking for her entire life. It was the water in which she swam. But now that she'd been out of it for months, in the designer-clad shark-infested waters of Beverly Hills, coming back to it didn't feel quite like home.

The California club Anna had just found kind of silly. But this particular club—the properly bred, old-school New Englander club, made her feel sort of sad. It was all about intellectual sparring, and nothing at all about who people really were.

Anna noticed Abernathy's eyes flit nervously around the room. Then she turned toward Anna. "Ancient civilizations," she declared. "And I'm never getting married. You?"

It took Anna a beat to figure out how these two statements might relate. When she realized they didn't, she said, "I'm probably going to be an English major."

Abernathy scowled. "I couldn't care less about your major. Where are you on marriage?"

What kind of a question was that? She'd known this girl for what, three point two seconds, and she was asking about her stance on marriage?

"It's . . . been popular for a few millennia of recorded history," Anna replied. She figured that a joke was the best way to respond.

"Dodging the question," Abernathy said. "You'll never last at Yale. Next." She turned away.

Whoa. What was that about?

Fortunately, the dean of students was engaging and distracting enough to hold Anna's attention. This mixer—he used the old-fashioned term to describe it—would be an opportunity for students to get to know one another and some of the faculty before official freshman orientation began in two and a half weeks up in New Haven.

"Some of you will be able to meet your roommates tonight," the dean went on. "There's a list posted by the bar that you can check; it also has your dorm assignments in the event that you didn't receive the orientation packet. Of course, if you didn't, you've already called the admissions office at least five times. You're coming to Yale, after all."

Again, the two hundred or so New York–area freshmen laughed at the joke at their own expense; the laugh of the few, the proud, the overachieving. Anna wondered whether the same jokes were being made at the Yale cocktail parties that were simultaneously taking place in Boston, New Haven, and Washington, D.C., this same night . . . and whether Logan was hearing a variation on the theme at his own Harvard event just a few blocks away.

Anna had thought long and hard about what to wear tonight. "We are what we pretend to be." Kurt Vonnegut, one of the few popular writers she enjoyed reading, and whose recent death she'd mourned, had said this, and it had stuck with her. Clothing in Los Angeles was all about the sizzle and not necessarily the steak. Appearance was everything. Looking hot, hip, and trendy was considered a worthy goal. In New York, Anna and her friends had treated fashion differently. No one put anywhere near the same effort into looking rich that they did in Los Angeles, where designer tags were a badge of honor. This protective coloration was stated in ancient khakis and triple-ply cashmere sweaters with frayed hems or holes in the elbows. Dressing down *was* dressing up. Even to a cocktail party or a gallery opening, people generally wore something simple and black.

She sighed at her own predictability. She wore a perfectly cut black Chanel skirt that fell to just below the knee, and a House of Hsu white silk boat-neck shirt with tiny pearl buttons down the side. She'd had it made on a trip to London years ago with her mother and her sister, Susan (who had been between rehab stints, as Anna recalled), by one of the best silk couture houses in the world.

The Yale Club was located in midtown, across from Grand Central Station, and was more like an extension of the university in New York City than a clubhouse. The twenty-three-story building had been recently renovated to the tune of ten million dollars, and contained a number of restaurants, guest rooms for club members visiting from out of town, banquet facilities, and a spectacular library, as well as squash courts and a small gym. In addition to the reception, there was a classical guitar recital taking place in another of the function rooms, plus a cocktail party for French-speaking alumni in the rooftop garden.

The reception had opened with speakers, some of

whom had been engaging. A well-known historian on the faculty gave a preview of his upcoming book about the Civil War. A composer played a new sonata she'd written on a Steinway grand. And a past star of *Saturday Night Live* who'd graduated from Yale drew a standing ovation for a politically charged address where he took a liberal number of very funny shots at the current White House occupants.

And then there were—did she dare even think it?— the disappointments. Mostly, they had to do with the incoming freshmen she'd met before the formal program began. So many of them reminded her too much of the kids she'd grown up with, vacationed with, competed against, and partied with. There were even several people she knew, either from Trinity or from East Hampton or Edgartown. Oh sure, there were the few who stood out for one reason or another—the jocks, the math geniuses, the trying-way-too-hard-to-be-goth group, even the freaky hair-all-over guy who'd sat next to her. He probably fared better from his brag sheet than his alumni interview. But mostly, it was the same sandbox in which she'd always lived, with only the best and brightest sand.

Speaking of. She was not thrilled when she spotted a particularly noxious piece of glittering sand by the name of Stevens MacCall Richardson. He was editor of the literary journal at Trinity, and one of the most pompous individuals she'd ever met. Stevens, who looked a little like a young Nicolas Cage, with the same swept-back dark hair, broad shoulders, and prominent teeth, had been running the literary magazine for two years. Once upon a time, at the end of junior year, she'd made the mistake of submitting a short story to him about a scary nor'easter storm she'd experienced as a child on Martha's Vineyard. It had blown part of the widow's walk off their nineteenth-century home, and Anna had spent most of the blow cowering in the basement.

To say he hadn't liked her story was an understatement. The first half of the two thousand words had been marked in more red ink than the balance sheet of Enron in its entirety. The second half was untouched, as if Stevens MacCall (he insisted on being called by both names) had become so irritated by its content, or even worse, so bored, that he'd just given up. Across the top he'd scrawled, "REALLY NOT FOR US," in bright red caps.

And now, he was going to Yale, most likely to the English department. Gee. Big fun. He had the most annoying habit of saying, "Ah," after anyone said anything, giving the word an emphasis that implied a profundity Anna never understood. At the moment, he had one khaki-clad leg crossed over the other, hands clasped around his knee, and the most supercilious look on his face as he listened to the admissions dean. Anna could almost hear him saying, "Ah," and he was clear across the room.

"So we're pleased to welcome you to your first official Yale experience." The dean of students was finishing his remarks at the podium. "There's food, there's drink, there's no lack of fascinating people to talk to. You are at the threshold of a wonderful, life-altering adventure. Now's your chance to get to know each other and to size up the competition. Have fun."

The audience laughed one more time; then everyone

seemed to stand at once to mingle. Oh no. Stevens Mac-Call was making a beeline straight for her.

"Hello, Anna." He thrust his hands into the pockets of his Naldini navy blue sports jacket.

"Hello, Stevens." She simply couldn't bring herself to call him Stevens MacCall.

"Ah," he uttered, quite predictably. "So. You're going to Yale, too." His voice was as disdainful as ever.

"Yes. Early decision," she added, which was so petty, she knew, but what the hell. The way he'd dismissed her writing still stung after two years.

"Interesting. Your parents must have donated quite a bit of money. I heard through the grapevine you'd gone all West Coast on us. UCLA or some such."

"I've been living out there, but no, I'm going to Yale."

"Ah." He tented his fingers. "You're not planning on the creative writing program, are you?"

What an asshole. What if she was? What if she had talent and he had simply been too in love with his own prose to see the worth of hers? Anna doubted that was true, but considering the possibility made her feel better.

"Literature, I think," she replied. She sat back down in her seat, hoping he would go away. He didn't. Instead, he plopped down next to her. Anna hoped that Abernathy had kept the seat warm for him.

"You'll be fine, then." He patted her arm in a patronizing fashion. "Meet your roommate yet?"

"My roommate's here? I haven't checked the list." Anna was startled for no particular reason other than that she hadn't really thought about it.

"Ah." Stevens MacCall smiled. "I met her. Lovely girl. Beautiful. Contessa. I'll be seeing her. Which I suppose means I'll be seeing you."

He planned to date her new roommate? Oh dear God. Anna didn't want to spend any more time in his company than she had to.

"Ah, there's Joyce Maynard," Stevens MacCall noted as he glanced over his shoulder toward the back of the room. "She's teaching a creative writing seminar first semester, by invitation only." He patted Anna's arm again. "Don't feel badly. She only took twelve students. Gotta run. See you in New Haven." He stood and hurried off to join Joyce.

"Ah," Anna mumbled to no one in particular, then kicked herself for unwittingly parroting Stevens MacCall. The idea of spending another four years in his haughty, judgmental presence made Anna want to barf. Preferably on him. She would have liked to meet Joyce Maynard, though. She'd read Maynard's stories of her relationship with J.D. Salinger back when Maynard had barely graduated from high school, and her memoir *At Home in the World*. Instead, Anna got to watch Stevens MacCall practically barrel into the slender, brunette novelist.

Well, maybe she'd get to talk to her up in New Haven—if she wasn't surrounded there by huge groups of seniors and graduate students, as well as eight or ten Stevens MacCall Richardson clones.

But wait. She should find her roommate. They ought to talk about what they were each bringing up. No need to duplicate floor lamps and stuff like that. What was her name? Contessa? She started toward the back of the meeting room, edging around knots of people who all seemed to know one another, though Anna understood that most of them had never met before. It was like being in this room, being part of the next Yale freshman class, made them all part of a special society that conferred the blessing of instant rapport and camaraderie.

She'd swum in this water her entire life. So why did she have the unsettling feeling that she was sinking?

"Hi." A pert-nosed girl approximately the limited height of Dee Young, with flaming, obviously dyed red hair, stood in front of Anna, pointing to her name badge. "Contessa Weiss. I think we're roommates."

Contessa wore fingerless fishnet gloves on her hands. Her stubby nails were painted black. She had multiple piercings in each ear and a tiny skull-shaped stud in her nose. She wore a short red plaid pleated skirt, like something from a Catholic girl's school uniform, and a zebra-striped cardigan over a Hello Kitty T-shirt. Her huge eyes were lined in kohl black, and she was chewing some kind of green gum with her mouth open.

"Nice to meet you, Contessa," Anna said politely.

"What makes you say that?" she asked, looking perplexed.

"Well, we're going to be roommates. . . ." Anna's voice petered out. She was trying to be civil.

"But in fact you don't know if it's nice to meet me because in fact you know nothing about me except that the visual signals you and I choose to give out to the universe are diametrically opposed and utterly dissonant, correct?"

"Being pleasant to someone you've just met seems

like a gracious choice," Anna commented. She heard her mother's frosty tone in her own voice. But honestly, what was up with this girl?

"From your arcane sociological perspective. Point taken," Contessa allowed. "Although if we were debating, you would lose. So I met a friend of yours over a cappuccino. Stevens MacCall?"

Anna blanched. "Stevens isn't my friend," she couldn't help commenting.

Contessa cocked her head and regarded her. "Define 'friendship.' Give me specifics. Generalities are irritating."

No, you're *irritating*, Anna thought, but carefully kept her face in neutral.

"I don't want to define 'friendship,'" she said pleasantly. "My point was simply that while Stevens and I went to Trinity together, we were not, in fact, friends."

"He said your writing sucks," Contessa commented.

Anna clenched her hands into fists. "Evidently that's his opinion."

Contessa blew a bubble and popped it, then rechewed her gum. "I have two poems in the new anthology of *Tomorrow's Best Writers Today*. Stevens MacCall had a devastating short story about killing rats in the Bowery. He's going to be immense."

Anna resisted the biting remark that came into her head, which was, What the hell did Stevens MacCall know about the Bowery? Or about rats? He knew yachting. And his daddy's Range Rover. And how to show his passport to the customs officials in Bermuda, where his family had their third home. But rats in the Bowery?

"And of course I'm in Joyce's creative writing seminar," Contessa continued. She stretched lazily and rolled her head back and forth, working out some real or imagined crick. "You?"

"I didn't even know about it to apply," Anna admitted.

"Oh, it was by invitation only," Contessa explained. "Evidently you didn't even make the first cut."

"Oh," Anna said, and gulped hard.

"So, let's talk music. What we'll be listening to when we study," Contessa went on. "I'm a retro hair-metal girl. Give me Van Halen or give me death."

"I like silence," Anna answered directly. "Maybe you could use earbuds."

"Hate 'em. Never use 'em. I'll get you some noise-reduction headphones. They're not that uncomfortable. Okay, moving on." Contessa popped her gum. "I study. Seriously. I had the highest GPA at Horace Mann. I've never gotten less than an A plus, except once in elementary school, and the teacher made a mistake. He had to rescind it and write me a letter of apology, which is in my permanent file to this day."

"I study a lot, too," Anna added, latching on to the one thing they seemed to have in common besides, say, female genitalia.

A girl with a waterfall of white-blond hair laughing with a boy who looked a lot like Ben jostled Anna as she passed by.

"So, have you got a boyfriend?" Contessa asked bluntly.

That was definitely territory that Anna didn't want to explore with her future roommate. She certainly was not about to go into the details of either how much Ben had hurt her or her very new flirtation with her very old friend Logan. "No, I don't."

"I don't do boyfriends," Contessa declared.

"Oh, so you're gay," Anna clarified. Stevens Mac-Call was going to be terribly disappointed. She couldn't help thinking that if she were Cammie, she'd be doing everything she could to encourage their relationship. The notion made her smile for the first time since she and Contessa had started to talk. "That's fine."

"Please," Contessa scoffed. "I am totally a breeder. I love sex. I just don't do the guy. I expect the guy to do me, if you know what I mean. It takes the edge off all that tension you get from studying. Relationships are so twentieth century."

This girl is a horror.

Contessa pointed a stubby, fishnet-encased finger at Anna. "You're repressed. No loud animal noises, am I right?"

Anna's jaw fell open. Was this girl really asking her about whether or not she made noise when she . . . ? Who *asked* someone a question like that?

"I just think that to discuss such personal things with someone I just met is a bit . . ." Anna searched for a word to substitute for *insane.* "Odd," she finally concluded.

"'Odd,'" Contessa echoed. "You are too funny. Check out my new video on YouTube. It's the real me." Contessa looked past her. "Hey, I see a friend from Fieldston. E-mail me. I'll make you some metal DVDs and send 'em to you. I predict that by finals, you'll be in love with Sammy Hagar too. Ta!"

Contessa took off, which Anna was very glad about. Unfortunately, she left the headache she'd given Anna behind. Why, why, why had they saddled her with this girl as her first college roommate? She knew that part of the freshman experience was that you could not put in for a roommate change for six months. The idea was that you would learn to get to know someone quite different from yourself. She had expected to be matched with someone who was not from the East Coast, for example. Maybe someone who grew up in the suburbs, or who played sports. She had not expected to be matched with a confrontational, heavy-metal-loving sex addict.

Anna stood there with crowds of happy, excited, and undoubtedly brilliant people swirling around her. She was sure some of them were lovely, interesting—fascinating, even. She was sure she could make friends. But she'd be stuck living in a tiny dorm room with Contessa for at least six months, with the noxious Stevens MacCall dropping by for unexpected visits.

At the moment, all the energy swirling around her like a tornado made her feel as if she were in its eye: silent, separate, and very much alone.

Vintage Red "Like a Virgin" Madonna T-shirt

"This place is a madhouse!" Ben shouted over the pounding, distorted beat.

"Woo-hoo!" Cammie screamed, enjoying the rush of the party atmosphere. They sat on the tall risers that formed the north end of the Vermont Theater nightclub and disco, watching two thousand or more revelers rocking on what used to be the floor area of the theater. Overhead, suspended from the ceiling, an actual NASA space capsule emanated multicolor rays of light that danced over the partiers. Smoke machines poured out cold white fog. Every few minutes, vibrant balloons dropped from the ceiling, either to be popped by the dancers or batted overhead like beach balls at a concert.

The Vermont Theater, located on the east end of Hollywood near the Children's Hospital, was Los Angeles' hottest mega-dance venue. It accommodated more than two thousand partiers on any given night— far more than the maximum capacity of nine hundred at Ben's former club, Trieste—and got its name from

its convenient location on Vermont Avenue near Santa
Monica Boulevard. Once upon a time, it was a major
legitimate theater. That theater turned into the largest
burlesque house in the city in the 1930s, only to be converted into a movie theater in the 1940s.

In the past few years, though, the theater had fallen
on hard times with the rise of the megaplexes and sat
vacant for many years until a couple of San Fernando
Valley movie producers who'd made a fortune producing
the kind of salacious direct-to-DVDs that the valley was
famous for decided they wanted to be in the nightclub
business. They bought the theater, dropped five million
or so on the renovations, and opened to great fanfare at
the start of the summer.

Cammie had never been there. Most of the time, she
couldn't care less about the Vermont Theater, which
attracted a clientele that was obviously less exclusive than
the usual Beverly Hills A-list. But the club's egalitarian
door policy—they let in everyone, as long as the cover
charge was paid—had been ballyhooed in the press, and
it had developed an overnight stellar reputation for outstanding music and even more outstanding DJs.

If there was one thing that Bye, Bye Love needed,
it was an outstanding DJ. The DJ could make or break
a club. Cammie was determined that the right one was
going to make theirs. Tonight was the theater's battle
of the DJs, and John Carlos—of Montmartre Lounge
renown—had been listed as one of the competitors for
the fifty-thousand-dollar first prize posted by the Valley
movie producers. Cammie knew that if she and Ben were
to have a shot at him, it would have to be away from the

video surveillance cameras at Montmartre. Poaching DJs was considered beyond the pale.

This night would be their opportunity. It was turning out to be rather fun, and not only because she was with Ben. She glanced over at him. Ben had that thing that instantly attracted girls to him. Adam didn't have it; of that Cammie was aware. He was the kind of guy you thought of as a friend, and then one day you were surprised to find that you'd fallen madly in love with him.

Adam. She knew he was in town, because he'd texted her multiple times and left one message on her voice mail, asking if she'd be willing to meet him for a drink. She hadn't responded, and didn't intend to. If he couldn't be the kind of boyfriend she deserved, then he didn't deserve to be her boyfriend at all. It was simple: he'd go to Michigan in a few weeks, and she wouldn't ever see him again. Out of sight, out of mind. This decision was helped along by what—or rather who—was in her line of sight: Ben. Ben was *heat*. He'd been heat in high school, and now that he was—or at least had been—in college, he was heat squared. Plus, his enthusiasm for this project was contagious. The more time she spent working with him on his dream, the more excited she got about it herself. Of course, Cammie mused, if this dream had belonged to someone short and squat, but equally as fabulous as Ben on the inside, would she feel as enthusiastic? She laughed out loud at her own mental query. Looks mattered. Anyone who said they didn't either looked like a bag of dirt or was lying.

A tall, buff guy who seemed to be channeling Justin Timberlake walked by and gave Cammie The Look. She was glad she'd worn her new black Forplay silk halter top and matching micro skirt. She cut her eyes to see if Ben was watching Justin check her out. But Ben had his eyes glued to the DJ in the cage, an Asian girl with hair down to her ass who wore oversized khakis that fell around her hipbones, and a man's sleeveless T-shirt that showed her pierced nipples nearly poking through the material.

Okay. So Ben was looking. It didn't mean anything. Guys looked. It wasn't like he was looking at Anna. Cammie could deal with free-floating lust. Ben nudged her. "That chick is hot." He cocked his head toward the DJ.

"Girls don't really do it for me."

He nudged his hip playfully into hers. "We're looking for a DJ. I was talking about her talent." He looked right into her eyes, a bit more serious now. "Hey, thanks for hooking this up, Cammie. Really."

She smiled. "No prob." A quick phone call to the producers of the DJ Smackdown had been all that was necessary to get her and Ben comped, plus given plastic bracelets that made paying for drinks unnecessary. The waitstaff was keeping a careful eye on them, to make sure they had plenty of drinks and free food. And the battle of the DJs itself was interesting—each DJ was given a ten-minute set to show off his or her skills at scratching, MC'ing, and revving up the crowd. Since the club's DJ booth was a Plexiglas cage suspended over the dance floor, they could see the competing DJs in action, and each seemed to have brought their own cheering section, judging from the crowd reaction when a new competitor took over the booth.

Cammie consulted a small card that one of the

waitresses had given her when they'd arrived. "John Carlos is next," she declared. "Let him do his thing. Then
we'll meet him in the VIP Lounge."

Ben pointed. "Isn't that him?"

A huge roar went up from the crowd as John Carlos
climbed the short ladder from an overhead catwalk and
stepped into the booth. He was dressed in skinny black
jeans, a vintage red *Like a Virgin* Madonna T-shirt under
an open black-and-white bowling shirt, and a black pork-
pie hat. Even with his soul patch, he still looked younger
than his nineteen years. The dueling mix-stations ensured
that the music shift from DJ to DJ could be seamless,
and John Carlos wasted no time. Even as the hot Asian
girl was finishing her set, he started scratching.

"I am . . . John Carlos! I am . . . John Carlos!"

Cammie had no idea where he'd found vinyl tracks
with those words on them. Maybe he'd had it specially
recorded. But his fans on the dance floor—which seemed
like the size of a football field—knew how to respond, as
if they'd been cued along with the music.

"You are . . . John Carlos! You are . . . John Carlos!"

And then the beats started in earnest. A cool, eclectic
mix of hip-hop and techno, with some eighties Madonna
and rap mixed in just for fun. John's fingers flew around
the rack's sliders and pots, flipping vinyl as if he were
playing three-card monte, all without drawing a single
seam in the beat. But his concentration must have been
on the pulse of the dancing crush below him. For a kid,
he sure knew how to control a crowd.

"Check it out," Ben said, jutting his chin out with a
smile. "They're going nuts down there."

He was right. If the scene on the dance floor before John Carlos started his set was intense, now it was positively frenetic.

"You want to dance?" he asked, offering his hand.

Damn. Any other time, Cammie wouldn't have passed up the chance to dance with Ben. But tonight, she had to keep her eye on the prize, and the prize was John Carlos. Besides, Cammie knew Ben was not used to being turned down. That was a good thing. It was easy to play easy to get. Hard to get was harder, but better. Always.

She gave him her most flirtatious smile. "Maybe later. Let's go to the lounge. He's only got ten minutes in there."

He nodded, and they made their way down the three-story-high set of risers, cut along one edge of the club past a crowded bar, and reached a roped-off room guarded by three hefty security guys.

"Ben Birnbaum and Cammie Sheppard," Ben told the tallest, baldest, and beefiest of the security guys, the one who held the clipboard. "We're on the list."

Wordlessly, the guy scanned it and then moved the velvet rope aside and opened a thick black double door. A moment later, they were in the club's inner sanctum, which was a world away from the pulsing masses outside. Done in cool blues and blacks, with light emanating from cubes on the floor, the walls, and the low ceiling, the space featured an open bar area, comfortable conversation nooks set into the wall for maximum privacy, and several round-top Plexiglas tables and matching stools.

In contrast to the throbbing dance mix in the club, the music here was cool jazz. The crowd was thin, though, confirming Cammie's belief that this place would never catch on with Hollywood royalty. Still, she was pleasantly surprised at how nice this area was. She recognized a few of the earlier DJs from the competition at the bar, drinking beers together.

"You're sure John Carlos will show up here?" Ben queried.

"He's got to wait for the results to be announced. He'll be here."

"And how do you think you're going to persuade him?"

"This is me you're talking to, Ben."

He laughed. "Oh, you've got the golden ticket, huh? You gonna share it with me?"

"Can't," she demurred. "I need the shock value."

For a moment, Ben look puzzled. Then he laughed again. "Shock value. You need me to look surprised. I can pull it off."

"Cammie Sheppard? Ben Birnbaum? Welcome to the Vermont Theater." The VIP lounge waitress was Latina, about five-foot seven, extremely slender, with tendrils of auburn hair curling down her back. Cammie was impressed that she would know their names. Once again, the porn-producers-turned-club-owners were showing that they had their shit together. "Is there anything I can get you?"

Ben answered first. "I'll take a beer—Rolling Rock if you've got it. Cammie?"

Cammie looked closely at the girl. Her doe eyes were fringed with sooty lashes that appeared to be natural. She had the carriage of a ballet dancer, and while she was wearing makeup, it was so subtle that it looked as if her features were simply more perfectly defined than anyone else's. She wore oversized menswear plaid trousers, slung low, and the staff VERMONT THEATER T-shirt. Cammie noticed that her navel was not pierced and she had no visible tattoos.

"Sparkling water. Fiji," Cammie ordered. "And your phone number."

The waitress raised her eyebrows. "I'm flattered. But I'm straight and I have a boyfriend."

"There's a reason I'm asking. What's your name?" Cammie just had a feeling about this girl. Everything about her screamed "fresh-faced petite model." And she was going to need more than one client.

"I'm Roxanne," the waitress told her.

"Ever done any modeling?"

Roxanne's eyes shone. "No. But I'd love to!"

"When you bring our drinks, bring your number too," Cammie instructed. "I'd love to take you to lunch and talk."

"It's legit," Ben assured her.

Cammie pointed at Ben. "He's my type," she told Roxanne. "You're not."

Roxanne laughed. "Got it. I'll be back with your drinks." She headed for the bar.

"I like how you multitask," He commented.

"You'll like how—hold on." Cammie chucked her chin toward the doorway. "Here he comes. Go over to the bar, please. Wait for my signal."

Without waiting for Ben's response, she got up from the couch and crossed the lounge.

"John Carlos?" She tried to look inscrutable when he turned to check her out. "I'm Cammie Sheppard. My father owns Apex. Clark Sheppard?"

"Damn," John Carlos commented, obviously impressed. He shook the hand she offered. "Your father is the man."

Cammie did an instant assessment. Well spoken. No alcohol on his breath. No grille on his teeth. All good signs.

"Who handles you, John Carlos?" she asked.

"I make my own deals. Don't want to give up the ten percent to an agent. And to tell you the truth, I've never really been approached seriously."

"I can understand that," Cammie commiserated. For the first time, she smiled. "Your contracts must be pretty simple. The nights you're spinning, the length of your shifts, how much you're getting paid, blah, blah, blah. But what happens when the club you're working for changes ownership? It's been known to happen. Or shuts down? That's been known to happen. Or if you want to take a few weeks to work as a music supervisor on a movie? Something like that can come up. And believe me, if my father handles you, it will definitely come up. And for that, you will definitely want an agent."

John Carlos looked interested. "Talk to me."

"I'll put you in a room with my father, and you'll take it from there. Now, he's going to need to see your work. I know that there's a new club willing to pay you twenty grand a week more than you're making at Montmartre, and guarantee it for three months. I can ensure that Clark Sheppard will be at the club's opening to check you out."

"Who owns this new club?"

"Me," Cammie replied.

John Carlos laughed and studied her with that look she knew oh so well. It said, *You're hot.* It said, *I'm imagining you naked and I like what I see.*

"You do know how to work it, girl."

"Why thank you."

"The problem is, I'm under contract with Montmartre. I don't think I can get out of it."

"John Carlos . . ." Cammie put a flirty hand on his shoulder and leaned close. "Trust me on this. Contracts can *always* be broken. And I would *love* to work with you."

She handed him her father's business card; she'd already written her name and number on the back. "Call me. You'll be glad you did."

He looked at the card, then stuck it in the pocket of his bowling shirt. "Thanks."

"Don't wait too long to call," she cautioned. "I can't keep the other gig open indefinitely. And congratulations. I'm sure you won tonight."

With that, Cammie stepped away. Ben was waiting for her at the bar, where he'd been watching the encounter with interest. But rather than give John Carlos the impression that she was there with either a date or a business partner, she walked right past Ben and ordered a Flirtini from the tall Japanese bartender with a samurai-style band tied around his forehead. She could feel John Carlos's eyes on her from across the room.

Am I fucking good or what? Cammie thought. And speaking of good, John Carlos was as good as theirs.

Red Velvet Panels and Priceless Tapestries

"I'm in front of the building," Logan's welcome voice crackled through the phone. "And I'm holding the taxi. That is, if you're done 'mixing,'" he added with a laugh.

"More than. I'll be right there." Anna looked around for Contessa Weiss, her soon-to-be-roommate, to say goodbye—not because she wanted to, but because it was the right thing to do. But Contessa, Stevens MacCall, and a select group of freshmen were huddled around Joyce Maynard, and it was clear from their body language that outsiders were not encouraged. Anna regarded the large room still buzzing with self-aware erudite chatter. There was no one there she wanted to say goodbye to, so finally she just left.

"Eighty-sixth and Fifth, please," Logan told the dreadlocked taxi driver when Anna was safely in the backseat.

"A life-changing experience?" he asked, regarding her with a half smile on his face.

"Sure," she fibbed. She didn't want to admit that she felt even a little let down. It made no sense at all. This was one of the world's great universities. She'd been accepted, and she'd be starting there in less than three weeks. She should be flying.

"How about you and all things Harvard? Did it make you want to transfer to Yale?"

"The brilliance in the room made me squint," he joked. "Every incoming freshman had graduated number one in his or her class, or they were already a world-class violinist or something. You could literally *feel* people sussing each other out."

"As in, Who's my comp?" Anna asked. "I know the drill."

Logan regarded her thoughtfully. "Don't get me wrong. It was very cool, in a way. And stimulating, for sure. And, you know, pretty much everything you'd expect a Harvard thing like that to be."

"Right. Yale, too," she said quickly.

"We're both getting what we always wanted," he pointed out, then smiled wanly. "Which doesn't happen all that often."

"Right," Anna agreed. She turned to the window and saw a homeless woman clad in a polka-dot shower curtain rummaging through the garbage and talking to herself. "Lots of people never get what they want," she added quietly, and couldn't help but feel slightly ashamed. She had so much. So many people had so little.

She hadn't given any thought to where they were headed and was surprised when the driver pulled up in front of the Metropolitan Museum of Art. She glanced at her watch. It was nearly eleven. She loved this museum; it was her favorite in the world, tied only with the Louvre in Paris. But it had been closed for hours.

Logan was paying the driver.

"Are we going to a café?" Anna wondered aloud, because there were all kinds of cafés near the museum, and, this being New York, they were not only all open, but spilling with people on this warm summer night.

He smiled enigmatically as they slid out of the taxi, and the driver immediately got another fare. "Does that smile translate into actual words?" she asked curiously.

"A café of sorts," he finally answered, touching the small of her back to propel her down Fifth toward Eighty-sixth Street. "Hungry?"

"Starving," Anna admitted. She hadn't realized it until that moment. There had been various hors d'oeuvres at the party, but Anna hadn't eaten a thing, because she'd been too busy awkwardly trying to mingle with her future classmates and too anxious about what exactly that future would hold.

"This way." Logan led her down an alley to the museum's side entrance. He still had a funny little half smile on his face, like he was in on a joke that Anna would soon hear.

"Where are we—?"

"You are a hard girl to surprise." He held open the metal door marked SERVICE ENTRANCE. "This is supposed to be a go-with-the-flow moment."

A few feet inside the service entrance was a large desk, behind which sat an even larger uniformed guard. He had ruddy skin, a broad face, and sharp cheekbones, and a black braid shot with gray that went down his back.

"Logan!" His face broke into a huge smile. "Hey, you weren't kidding, she really *is* a beauty." He held a meaty hand out to Anna. "James Broadband. You must be Anna."

"Nice to meet you," she replied softly, blushing at the compliment. "I have no idea what's going on. So I'm just going with the flow."

"Well, you'll find out soon enough," James said with a broad smile. He picked up his walkie-talkie. "Charlie, you heading to the service desk?"

"Rounding the corner," a staticky voice replied. A moment later, an older man, bald, with a red nose that reminded Anna of the classic silent film star W. C. Fields, came into view. He wore the same uniform as James.

"I'm on my break for the next fifteen," James declared in his powerful voice, as Charlie stepped behind the desk. He made a follow-me gesture to Logan and Anna, and they headed down the narrow service hall. It opened into the main hall of the museum. Massive columns stood sentry to a grand staircase, which James led them down. "When's the last time you were at the Met?" he asked Anna.

She tried to remember. She and Cyn had been planning to go on a warm early evening last fall. But two guys at Caffe Grazie around the corner had started flirting with them, and they'd ended up going downtown with them to an East Village bar called Arlene's Grocery—it actually used to be a grocery store—to hear a punk band doing an afternoon set to try out new material. Anna had neither heard of nor liked the band. Fifteen minutes into their gig, Cyn was sitting on the carved wooden bar, making out with the cuter of the two guys they'd just met. Anna had sat there for two hours listening to music that gave her a headache. Why hadn't she simply left?

Because it wasn't nice to leave, that's why. God. Sometimes she just got so sick of being *nice.*

"You're frowning," Logan pointed out.

"Oh!" Anna remembered herself. "I just couldn't remember the last time I was here. And it's bugging me. Sorry, James."

"No big deal," he assured here. "You're here now."

Her stomach grumbled. Logan had said something about eating. But here they were at the Met, after hours, without a croissant in sight. They turned down another hall. James pushed open wide double doors.

"The Hart Room," he announced triumphantly.

Anna stepped in and gasped. The room was furnished with priceless seventeenth-century antiques. And she recognized them. Because they had once belonged to one of her great-great . . . well, she didn't exactly know how many greats—a *lot*—maternal grandmother, Mary Elizabeth Hart, who had hailed from Ipswich, Massachusetts.

"I remember," Anna breathed, looking around at the priceless antiques. She'd been little—eight years old, maybe? The Harts had donated the furnishings to the Met, but a lawsuit over a complicated will meant the furniture had sat in storage for years and years, being put on display shortly after the time Anna had seen it in the first place.

They had been studying the Founding Fathers in school. Her first-grade class had taken a special tour of the furniture—arranged by Anna's mother—which the public had not been allowed to see. The furniture looked like something from a princess's house. All the girls ooed and aahed over it. The boys, Anna remembered, had been bored to death.

They had all been told not to touch *anything*. But thinking that she was somehow entitled to enjoy the furniture that had belonged to her family more than the other children, Anna had climbed onto the ash-and-pine four-poster bed from which red velvet panels and price-less tapestries were hanging.

"Anna Percy, get off that bed this instant!" her teacher, Ms. Duke, had bellowed.

Anna remembered how humiliated she'd felt. Not that it was such a big deal. But she was always such a good girl that to be publicly reprimanded had made her cry in front of her entire class. Which had only humili-ated her even more. One did not show emotion in pub-lic. That was Jane Percy's motto. At age eight, Anna had already blown it.

And now here she stood, among that same furniture once more. The carved cupboard of pine and walnut, lined with blue-and-white tin-glazed earthenware, the white oak baby cradle.

"I'll just leave you two alone," James whispered. He stepped out the door and closed it behind him.

"The site of your grand humiliation." Logan pointed to the four-poster bed.

"I can't believe you remember that." Anna shook her head in disbelief. "How in the world did you get James to let us in here?"

"My aunt Clarissa was in charge of the Met's fund-raiser

this year. Plus my uncle Chester donated some of the money for a new school on James's reservation upstate."

"So you're just all-around connected," Anna teased.

"It has its perks," Logan admitted sheepishly. "I feel better when the money goes to good things. Anyway, this room isn't even open to the public yet. I seem to recall that you mentioned an appetite. Follow me."

He led her around the bed to a tarp covered by a red blanket. On it were an old-fashioned picnic basket and champagne chilling in an ice bucket.

How had he done this? When had he organized this? Who had he had to bribe to do this?

Anna grinned. "This is just . . . incredible of you."

They sat, and Logan opened the champagne. "I couldn't decide if it was a great idea or just crazy," he confessed. He poured champagne into two crystal flutes. "I was hoping it would remind you of how far you've come since that day. How happy you are, on the verge of starting Yale, all that."

He handed her a baguette glazed in Brie. She bit into it, feeling guilty. Now *there* was an emotion with which she was familiar. Yes, Ben had dumped her. But here she was with a handsome, brilliant, thoughtful guy she'd known since she was a kid, one who'd gone to a lot of effort just to put a smile on her face. She was on the verge of starting Yale, her lifelong dream. So how could she not be happy? How was it possible that she felt so . . .

She put down the baguette. "I am an ungrateful, horrible person."

"Wow, I was just thinking that myself," Logan teased.

"No, seriously. You are terrific. This—this is terrific. I have everything. So I can't figure out why I feel so bad." That wasn't honest. She should be honest. "Actually, I can."

He took a sip of champagne. "Do tell."

"I—I hate that I'm even saying this. I had a miserable time at the Yale Club."

Logan didn't respond right away. He just chewed a bite of sandwich and washed it down with some champagne. "How come?" His tone was completely nonjudgmental, which Anna appreciated.

"I don't know. That's what I mean. It's what I've always wanted and now that I have it, I don't know if it's what I want at all. . . ."

Damn. Had she really just said that out loud?

Logan didn't look shocked, though. He just waited, patiently, for her to elaborate.

"I went to L.A. to change my life," she explained, thinking this was an intimate thing to share with a guy she didn't know all that well. On the other hand, she'd known him longer than any of her Los Angeles friends, including Ben. "I thought I could—believe me, I know how ridiculous this sounds—reinvent myself. And then on the way there—on the plane—before I even set foot on West Coast turf, I met a guy. Ben."

Logan nodded. "The guy you just broke up with."

"Are you bored to death? Am I totally self-involved? I really should just shut up now." She winced, afraid she had overshared.

He reached for her hand. "I really do want to hear this."

Anna bit her lower lip pensively. "So . . . I feel like everything I've done since I went there has to do with him. That I've been . . . defined by him, somehow, which was not my plan at all." Her eyes met Logan's. "You know that expression, Wherever you go, there you are?"

"Yep." He reached for a grape and popped it into his mouth.

"I think I was the same me in L.A., just me with a boyfriend," she admitted. "I have had some adventures, but honestly? I don't feel like I've changed my life much at all. In L.A. I'm still the girl from New York. And here in New York . . . I'm still longing for something else. But I don't even know what that something else is."

She paused to take a breath, then plunged on. "I don't know why I told you all that. I'm sorry."

Anna realized that Logan was smiling at her. Why?

"I can't think of one thing I said that was remotely amusing." She sighed. "I'm surprised you're not asleep in the big canopy bed."

"I'm smiling because life is amazing and bizarre and crazy," he mused. "All the feelings you had at the Yale thing? That's how I felt at mine."

"You're kidding," Anna insisted.

He took her hand with one of his, then held up his other palm. "I swear. I didn't want to say anything, because I figured you were all psyched about your experience, so why put a damper on it?"

"Did you meet your future roommate?" she asked eagerly. "Was he—?"

"He smokes a pipe. He races sailboats. His other hobby is foxhunting. He name-dropped royal this and royal that. And I know the precise location of his family's three homes. Does that explain it?"

"Too well. My roommate was an entirely different kind of eccentric. It wasn't just her, though. It was the whole atmosphere. There's a creative writing workshop, and I guess some incoming students were handpicked for it. Evidently I wasn't even considered. And do you know how I felt? Crushed. Absolutely crushed. Which is ridiculous, I know. But that doesn't mean I didn't feel it." She drained her champagne.

Logan took a container of fresh strawberries drizzled in dark chocolate from the hamper and set it on the blanket. "There's also the legacy issue for a lot of them." He stopped himself. "A lot of us."

Anna nodded and popped a raspberry into her mouth. "Me included. My father went to Yale. So did my grandfather."

"And my dad went to Harvard, undergraduate and business school. Then he took over the hotel chain and built it into the monster it is today." Logan sighed. "I can't even blame my parents for all these second thoughts I'm having. They're fine with me not going into the family business. They could have asked me to go to the Cornell School of Hotel Management."

"And miss Harvard? Never. Which makes us equally insane," Anna surmised. "And now I'll be up all night, tossing and turning, trying to make sense of out it."

"Overthinking everything. You're a female me." He regarded her thoughtfully. "This guy you talked about, Ben. Do you love him?"

Once again, Anna was struck by how awkward it was to discuss this with Logan. And yet, in another way it just felt right. Sitting amidst her ancestors' antique furniture, in one of the world's most celebrated museums late at night, pouring her heart out to a long-lost childhood friend somehow couldn't be any stranger than her surroundings.

"I wish I knew, Logan." She exhaled. It hurt to even think about Ben. "I guess it doesn't matter anymore, though. He definitely doesn't love me."

Logan looked at her, sympathy etched into his eyes. "It's better to have loved and lost . . . all that."

"Sometimes it doesn't feel that way."

"Yeah." He leaned over and brushed some stray wisps of blond hair from her cheek. "If it makes you feel any better, I got my heart broken last year, too."

Anna smiled sadly. "It doesn't. I wouldn't wish it on anyone as nice as you."

"And on that note . . ." He gulped down the last of his champagne. "How about if we go down to SoHo? I know this great little blues club on Thompson Street. The musicians are killer. They show old movies on the walls and serve a French pastry version of dim sum."

"We just ate," Anna pointed out, putting the leftover fruit back in the picnic basket.

"We hardly ate anything. Besides, who cares?"

He was right. Who cared? When they'd packed up everything from their picnic, Logan tugged on the door so they could leave. It didn't budge. He put the picnic basket down and tried again.

"It's either stuck or locked." He took out his Razr but couldn't get service here in the bowels of the museum. Anna tried her cell. Same result.

"The guards must make rounds," Anna guessed, trying to think logically. "So one of them will come find us."

"Eventually," Logan said ominously.

"James knows we're down here. He's not going to just leave us here."

"Maybe he thinks he's doing us a favor." He scratched his chin. "So how about . . . we take advantage of it."

For a moment, Anna thought Logan meant they should tear off their clothes and have sex. And while she liked him, *a lot,* she was still stinging too much from Ben to do anything even remotely close to something like that.

"All clothing will stay on, Miss Percy," he joked, as if reading her mind. "I've got an even better idea."

"Better than sex?" she teased. "Guys never say that."

He leaned close and pointed to the bed. "Let's get in it. There's no teacher here this time to bust you."

"What if it hurts the bed or something?" Anna asked, her brow furrowed.

"Your great-great-great-whatever slept in that bed every night. I don't think you and me lying on it will suddenly destroy it. "

She eyed the bed, then turned to him with a smile. "Let's do it."

She climbed in first, and he followed right after her. She lay on her back, legs splayed, just as she remembered doing all those years ago.

"Fun?" Logan asked.

"Definitely." She rolled over and looked down at him. "Thanks for this." Then she leaned over and kissed him softly on the lips. The next thing she knew his arms were around her, and the kiss turned into something amazing and passionate that she hadn't expected or anticipated. But then, maybe that's what made it so special.

Vermilion Dreadlocks and a Nose Stud

I *Climb the Stairs.*
Anna read the name of the play off the playbill
she'd been handed by a black-clad usher with vermilion
dreadlocks and a nose stud. Finding seats was easier than
she'd expected—they were in the Westsider Theater, a
ninety-nine-seat house on West Twenty-eighth Street
in Chelsea, where there just weren't that many seats to
begin with. The stage had no curtain, just two sets of
wooden stairs leading to a white-painted wooden platform. Other than that, the playing area was just the bare
floorboards.

"Honestly, I never thought Tabitha could write worth
shit," Cyn confided. "But I promised her I'd come to
this, so whatever." She fished in her purse for a pack of
cinnamon Trident sugarless gum. "You want?"

Anna declined. Tabitha Matheson had been a year
ahead of them at Trinity, and had gone on to the creative
writing program at Columbia despite Cyn's doubts
about her talent. Her mother was an editor at the *New
York Review of Books* and her father was a New York
University literature professor and a poet who'd twice

been a winner of the Walt Whitman Award for Achievement in American Poetry. His teaching was a sinecure, and he spent all his time on poetry. Yet Tabitha lived in an Upper East Side town house even more lavish than where Anna had grown up, since Professor Matheson's great-grandfather had been a founding partner of Matheson and Matheson, the venerable Wall Street law firm.

As the theater filled with lots of young Brooklyn artist types and parents of actors, Anna tried to read the program, but she kept thinking about the Yale party and her date with Logan last night. The date was like the best dream—they'd lain in the ancient bed for what felt like hours, revealing the truth about what they'd thought of each other way back when. It turned out that Logan had been intimidated by Anna, because she was the only person in their third-grade class who read better than he did. She was astonished to recall that she'd thought exactly the same thing about him. By the time James came to unlock the door, with a wink that made Anna suspect he really *had* locked them in on purpose, she knew that whatever happened, she would feel close to Logan for a long time—even if they parted ways and didn't see each other again for years, the way they hadn't all this time. Shared history meant a lot.

But as much as she'd had the perfect end to a memorable evening, the early part of her night wasn't sitting well with her. She couldn't deny feelings of unease about Yale. All from one stupid get-to-know-you event, with just a fraction of her incoming class. What was wrong with her?

She felt Cyn nudge a shoulder into her own. "Where the hell are you?"

"Here." Anna smiled. "When's the last time you and I went to see a play together?"

"Sophomore year. The millionth revival of *Cat on a Hot Tin Roof* at Circle in the Square. Michael Flannery and I locked ourselves into the handicap john, smoked a bone, and made out for the entire second act."

Anna laughed. "Michael Flannery. I remember him!" He'd been an exchange student from Ireland with curly black hair, smoldering blue eyes, a perpetual three-day growth of beard, and the shoulders of a rugby superstar. Cyn had bet Anna she could bag him before any of the zillion other girls who'd been after him. Of course, Cyn being Cyn, she'd succeeded.

"It's so weird, isn't it?" Anna asked. She realized this was her first time back home as an actual high school graduate. "To think that high school is really over?"

"Yeah." Something flickered across Cyn's face. She blew a meager bubble with her gum, then popped it. "Hey, you'll come visit me in Paris, right? I promise I'll cook you an amazing welcome dinner," she added with a grin.

Anna nodded, but couldn't help her head from spinning a bit at the thought. Cyn in France at cooking school—it seemed so bizarre, because as far as Anna knew, Cyn had never shown an interest in cooking and was supposed to be starting at Middlebury College in Vermont. She'd decided to defer only a few weeks ago, as she'd explained on the cab ride downtown. But she didn't feel any ambivalence about it. Middlebury wasn't going anywhere, Cyn explained.

"You'll be too busy seducing every hot guy at your cooking school," Anna teased, even as she swallowed down a little lump in her throat. It was one thing to be in L.A. while Cyn was in New York, but quite another to think about her best friend leaving to go abroad. She'd miss her a lot. Even after all these years, Cyn hadn't changed much at all. She was the same outrageous hellion she'd been when they'd met in elementary school. Today she wore a white lace pinafore she'd found at Threads—their favorite East Village thrift store—over tattered Chip & Pepper jeans, and red-and-white polka-dot Marc Jacobs platform heels. Anna wore khakis and a pink Armani T-shirt that was cool in this hot weather.

"Just the guys?" Cyn cracked. "Do you think I'm slipping?"

"Not at all."

"Because I'm not. But there is more to life than seducing everyone around you just to prove you can. Which I can. At least that's what I've heard." Her eyes flicked to the back of the theater, and she groaned. "Oh gawd. Tabitha is back there."

Anna craned around and saw the skinny girl with the close-cropped hair that she remembered. Tabitha was dressed entirely in black, which was the only color she'd worn for as long as Anna had known her. She had shoulder-length thick dark hair, kohl-rimmed eyes, and the same pale skin that Anna remembered.

"Katie Prescott told me she comes to every performance and mouths the words with the actors, but I didn't believe her. Too bad we're not on her aisle to check it out.

Anyway, she'll see us and you'll have to say something nice afterwards."

"And you won't?" Anna asked, arching a honey-blond eyebrow.

Cyn guffawed. "Please, this is me we're talking about. I don't give a shit. Besides, that's what I've got you for," she added.

"Thanks," Anna replied dryly. "Besides, you gave a shit enough to come when she asked you to," she pointed out.

"Because she has a cousin in Paris by the name of Pierre, a junior at the Sorbonne. I checked him out on Facebook. All I can say is, well worth checking out. I am so on Air France."

Anna laughed. Suddenly the houselights dimmed and the audience hushed. A moment later, when the stage lights came up, the play began with a party sequence that had the Red Hot Chili Peppers' "Suck My Kiss" blasting from the sound system. The six actors looked like they were in high school, though Anna was certain they were actually older.

The lead actress, a gaunt girl with platinum blond hair and enormous eyes, had bandages around both wrists. Anna soon learned that this was because she was recovering from her latest suicide attempt. It was the last party of the season at her parents' summer house in Mattapoisett, Massachusetts. The girl had an unrequited crush on her father's best friend, a middle-aged, raging alcoholic who was only attracted to very young girls. The party went on and on, and thirty minutes in, Anna was bored out of her mind. *I Climb the Stairs*, she finally figured out, was a metaphor—although the main character, Charity, literally climbed the stairs onstage whenever she was going to have sex with the middle-aged guy. The final time, though, she kicked the guy in the testicles and ran away.

The lights dimmed. The audience erupted into thunderous applause as the cast took their curtain calls.

"Hated it," Anna whispered to Cyn.

"How many ways can you spell 'pretentious'? But Tabitha wrote it in high school, and Chilton Pennysworth at the *Times* gave it a rave, so she's the new hot flavor of the season. Come on. Let's suck up and then we're out of here."

The Westsider Theater was somewhat ramshackle, and by the time they reached Tabitha in the small lobby, a thick crowd surrounded her. Cyn tried to push their way inside, but the person now standing with Tabitha made Anna resist.

Scott Spencer, her first, achingly unrequited crush. With his Chad Michael Murray–esque good looks, and his easy, brainy insouciance, for years, seeing him had done things to Anna's internal organs—they spontaneously rearranged themselves. In fact, the fact that Scott and Cyn had become a serious item at the time was one of the main reasons she'd left New York for L.A.

But her reaction now was neutral. Because when she'd really had a chance to get to know Scott, she'd been less than impressed. When he and Cyn had come to surprise Anna and her L.A. friends several months ago in Vegas, Anna had realized then that her crush had been on an *idea* rather than on the guy, whom she hadn't really known at

all. He wasn't who she thought he was, and soon he and
Cyn were history too.

"I guess I forgot to tell you about that." Cyn's eyes
flitted from Anna to Scott and back to Anna again.

At that moment, Scott turned and his eyes met hers.
It was the strangest thing. She didn't blush. She didn't
even blink.

She was really and truly over him. When he went and
put his arm around Tabitha, she even smiled.

"I'll be back," Cyn announced.

Anna's waif-thin friend propelled herself through
the crowd and jumped on Scott, hands around his neck,
legs circling his waist. He didn't seem to mind, though
Tabitha was scowling. He laughed, gave her a kiss, and
set her down. Then he said, "Anna!" and held his arms
out to her.

Anna moved forward for a hug and noticed Tabitha's
scowl deepen. Then the playwright's attention was taken
by a middle-aged woman, with hair the color of burnt
coffee, who passed the knot of people in the center of
the lobby.

"Fabulous, just remarkable!" she called loudly.

"Thank you!" Tabitha called back, then turned her
attention to Cyn and Anna. "So, you loved my play,
right?"

"I've never seen anything quite like it before," Cyn
mused thoughtfully, taking a couple of steps away from
Scott . . . but not so many that she couldn't sling a friendly
arm over his shoulder.

"Exactly what I was going to say," Anna added, working very hard to keep a straight face.

Scott let Cyn's arm stay around his neck, but snaked an arm around Tabitha's black-cinched waist. "So, does my girl rock or what? She's a fucking literary genius."

"Oh, you," Tabitha demurred, leaning into him. But Anna could see that in fact she agreed with Scott; she *did* think she was a literary genius.

"Where are you going to school this fall?" Anna asked politely.

"Columbia," Tabitha replied matter-of-factly. "But I'm being offered a number of screenplay deals. TriStar, New Line, even Miramax. Every studio has sent a rep to see my play, and I just signed with Paradigm. It's wild. How about you, Anna?"

"Yale."

"Oh yeah, I remember you telling me that," Scott recalled, looking past her. "Damn, there's Fisher Stevens— heard he's got some killer Thai stick. I'll be right back." He crossed the lobby to a short guy with a scraggly soul patch.

Tabitha smiled at Anna. Her lips were painted glossy red, the only color amid her pale skin and dark clothing. "What do you want to study? Do you know?"

"Creative writing," Anna said instantly, without pausing to think. The words coming out of her mouth shocked her. She'd always said classic literature. Why had she *said* that? Was it Tabitha's success? Was it being shunned by the Joyce Maynard crowd at the party? Was she, in fact, simply jealous of everyone?

"*You?*" Tabitha asked, sounding incredulous.

"I write."

Tabitha cackled like the Wicked Witch of the West

and ran her fingers through her short-cropped hair. "Oh, I guess it's a hobby thing for you. That's kind of cute."

"It's not *cute*." Anna felt her fists start to clench, but willed herself to stop. "I really can write."

"If you say so," Tabitha chirped. "So how are the airheads on the West Coast? I heard you were out there."

Before she could reply, Cyn jumped in.

"I never realized what a patronizing little bitch you are, Tabitha. Also, your play sucks, so enjoy your abbreviated rocket ride while the public is delusional enough to provide the fuel."

"Fuck you, jealous cow." Tabitha snapped back.

"Oh, *that's* fresh," Cyn sneered. "And by the way, your boyfriend is horrible in bed. Of course, if you haven't figured that out yet, you're probably just as bad. Let's go, Anna."

"You can forget hooking up with Pierre in France, scag!" Tabitha yelled after them, her face scrunched as tightly as an artichoke heart.

They stepped out of the dim theater and hit the Chelsea sidewalk, where they were instantly assaulted by the heavy, humid night air. But Anna felt fantastic as they walked together toward Sixth Avenue, where they could easily catch a cab uptown. "You were amazing." She beamed at Cyn.

"Always have been. No one gets away with dissing you in front of me."

Anna felt a lump rise in her throat. She would never have another friend like Cyn, never. "I was just thinking . . . you're more of a sister to me than my sister."

"Oh gawd, you're going to get all maudlin on me," Cyn groaned. "Let's go to the Pyramid Club and get loaded. You've been there—you have fond memories, right?"

Anna laughed. "This is *me* you're talking to. I've never been there. And I don't drink. Much."

"Right. The I-don't-get-loaded queen. Okay, we'll just go flirt shamelessly, pick up a couple guys, and leave them wanting more. How's that?"

Anna hadn't told Cyn about what had happened at the Met with Logan, and she wasn't sure why, unless being in New York had returned her to form. She was a private person in an age when living an unedited life on MySpace and YouTube was the thing to do. She couldn't understand her friends who needed to broadcast everything about themselves to anyone who might possibly take an interest. Like the Big Book said, there were things that were public and there were things that were private. It made sense to know the difference. Of course, she'd tell Cyn eventually. Just not right now.

"I'm not really up for the Pyramid Club, either," Anna admitted. "I think I'm going to head home."

"You are so boring," Cyn joked, but even as she said it something that looked like sadness flitted across her perfect brow. "Hey, we'll always be best friends. Even when I'm tasting every vintage ever produced in France and you're in the Yale ivory tower being boring. Right?"

They stopped at Sixth Avenue and waited for the light to change. This was a part of town Anna rarely came to—a mix of hardware stores, supply shops, and the occasional restaurant praying desperately for gentrification to arrive. There was little pedestrian traffic, save for a woman with matted gray hair wheeling a shopping cart of her worldly goods—which included an iBook—who swerved around them.

"Always," Anna promised. "I'll be back in New York in a week and a half, remember. I'll see you before I leave for New Haven." She hugged Cyn hard. "Best friends forever," she whispered, feeling the whisper veer danger-ously toward a choke.

"Forever," Cyn whispered back. If she sounded like she was eight years old, Anna didn't care. And she was pretty sure her best friend didn't, either.

A cab pulled up, and she got in, leaving Cyn to go clubbing. When Anna got home, the place was empty. But she found a note from Sam on her desk. She and Eduardo had gone to dinner at Bouley and then to hear Keith Jar-rett perform a solo concert at the Beacon Theater. Anna smiled to herself. She was glad they were spending the evening together, and she'd given Sam a key. Besides, it might be good for her to spend the rest of the night alone. So she shed her clothes, took a hot shower, then put on her old navy blue Trinity sweats and climbed into bed.

But she wasn't tired. Something was niggling at her; she just couldn't figure out what it was.

Oh, I guess writing is a hobby thing for you. That's kind of cute.

Tabitha's condescending words rang in Anna's ears. They made her think about when she had tried writing—when they'd been at Veronique's Maison spa out in Palm Springs and Sam had asked her to write a script for a short film. That felt like a lifetime ago. Sam had said then that

Anna had talent. Who the hell was Tabitha to patronize her, anyway?

She threw the covers back and went to her silver iBook. Wouldn't it just kill Tabitha and Stevens MacCall and her new roommate if she wrote something not just good, but really good? Something that would prove all of them wrong?

No. That wasn't a good reason to write. Thackeray didn't write to prove that he was better than Dickens. Chekhov didn't write to prove he was better than Tolstoy. Arthur Miller wasn't driven to be better than Tennessee Williams. That was the wrong reason to tell a story, especially when there were so many right ones.

She opened a Word document. The blank screen stared accusingly at her. Who was she kidding? What could she possibly write about? What did she know besides the story of a well-bred New York City girl from a well-bred New York City family who decides to go live with her father in Beverly Hills for the second semester of her senior year?

She typed. Tentatively, then with authority:

Untitled Screenplay about <u>SENIOR YEAR</u>.
by Anna Percy

The Tallest, Coldest Mojito in History

Once Eduardo had convinced Sam that Gisella was *not* in New York, had *not* been at the embassy party, and in fact had not been in contact with him since the charity fashion show a few weeks ago, she enjoyed a fantastic—if chaste—week of restaurants, shows, concerts, and shopping, all worked around his busy schedule at the consulate and Peruvian mission to the United Nations. At first she'd been suspicious when he hadn't invited her to move into his hotel room at the Peninsula. But he'd explained that he didn't want to announce to his colleagues that he was engaged before they told their parents. Anna was right after all. As his "girlfriend," it would be inappropriate for her to be sharing a hotel room with him when he was here on business. Peruvians were much more formal about these things; they needed to plan a trip to Lima to tell his parents and his other relatives as soon as possible after their return to Los Angeles. Would the end of August be okay with her? Eduardo had even talked about having Jackson fly to Peru so that both families could share in the joy at the same time.

Sam had seen people do all kinds of things in hotel rooms and be perfectly up front about it since she'd been old enough to spell *room service*. But then, she was a child of Hollywood. And Eduardo was . . . not.

She decided that she liked his sense of propriety, even if it meant that they would not get up close and personal while she was in New York. But the fact that they were forced to be creative—and limited—about their passion turned into an erotic game. They'd had a great make-out session in the back of the Lincoln Square cinema on the Upper West Side two nights earlier, and another in the rear of a taxicab coming home from a club on Rivington Street last night.

Today, they had plans to meet for lunch near the Museum of Television and Radio, the New York branch of a museum that Sam adored because of its extensive collection of classic television episodes and films. When she read in *Time Out* that the museum was doing a retrospective on the work of Rod Serling, the creator of the classic 1950s sci-fi show *Twilight Zone*, Sam cabbed from Anna's to the museum on West Fifty-second Street so she could take in the whole thing, including the screening of two newly discovered episodes that had never been aired, and an interview that Serling did in the weeks before he died.

She was supposed to meet Eduardo at one thirty. At twelve forty-five she left the world of *The Twilight Zone* and headed into the humid New York summer heat. Sam had decided to wear another of the new outfits she'd acquired—an Ann French Emonts vintage-inspired white blouse, skirt, and jacket combination she'd purchased on a whim at Darling—but she hadn't walked more than a hundred feet before it was sopping with perspiration, and she felt her hair, which had been newly blown out at the John Frieda salon, start to superglue itself to the nape of her neck. Ugh. Horrible. Though she could almost hear Eduardo's protests that she looked just fine the way she was—he always said that, as if she were the most beautiful creature on the planet—a quick glance in the plate glass of a locksmith shop she was passing gave a truer picture of how she looked. Her makeup had oozed into her oversize pores. Describing her as looking like melting dog shit, Sam thought, would have been on the kind side.

Just as she was wallowing in self-criticism, she heard the shrill bell tones of her Razr V3. She plucked it from her Kate Spade bleached straw bag without bothering to check caller ID. "Hello?"

"Sam, it's Dee!" Dee's breathy little voice sounded full of excitement.

Sam dodged a couple holding hands on in-line skates. "Dee! Where are you?"

"Hawaii, remember?" she chirped in her sweet voice. "Jack and I are on the beach and the sun is just coming up. And I thought to myself: I have to call Sam and tell her how happy I am."

Sam couldn't help but think that if she were on a beach in Maui with Eduardo at sunrise, calling Dee to tell her about it *during* the experience would have been really far down on her list of priorities. But then again, Dee always did things the Dee way. "So, you're having fun?"

"The best time of my life," she replied enthusiastically. "We never even went to sleep last night! We danced and then we went for a nude swim—our suite has this private pool—talk about romantic."

"Sounds fantastic." Sam used her forearm to swipe the sweaty hair from her face. Hundreds of New Yorkers out on their lunch hours in equally sweaty condition swarmed around her. As fabulous as New York was, at this particular moment she'd kill to be taking nude swims in a private pool and watching the sun rise on a deserted private beach.

"So, anyway, how are you?" Dee asked eagerly.

"Good." Sam wasn't about to go into her engagement, or why she'd come to New York in the first place, or her suspicions about Eduardo when Dee was blissing out with Jack. That was a long discussion, and if Sam opened the topic she knew that Dee's next call would be to Cammie. After that, it might as well be on the front page of *Daily Variety*.

Sam ended the call quickly so Dee could get back to her parallel universe, which did not reek of dog shit steaming under a tiny tree planted in a tiny square of grass surrounded by asphalt, as her own world did at this moment.

She passed two slender, perfect girls—the East Coast version of, say, Cammie—who managed to look cool, fabulous, and completely pulled together despite the crushing heat. How did they *do* it? Sam wondered. She wanted to be one of those girls. But whatever their magic formula was, she didn't have it. And it certainly couldn't be bought, or else she'd already have purchased it.

She lifted the hair from the back of her neck and fanned herself. At least the restaurant they'd picked—a

French-American place called Mauvais Accent that had opened recently—wasn't far. It had a small sidewalk area that was largely deserted because of the heat. Sam decided she'd go inside and order the tallest, coldest mojito in the history of tall, cold mojitos, then go into the ladies' room and do her best to repair the dog-shit damage before she saw Eduardo.

When she pushed through the front door she was hit with a welcome blast of icy air, and headed straight back for the smaller bar. There were only six stools, done in industrial gunmetal.

"What can I get you, mademoiselle, on this very hot day?" The bartender had a cute—not *mauvais* at all—French accent and an even cuter thin dark moustache. He put a glass of ice water down in front of her without her even asking. Sam liked this place already.

"I'd like a moji—"

She froze. Behind the bartender was a classic bar mirror; she could see the entire restaurant without turning around. The place was incredibly busy, with practically every table filled. There was an empty seat at one two-seater table close to the window facing the street. Fine. No problem. But the person sitting in the other seat was a big problem.

Sam stared into the mirror to be sure, blood pounding in her ears like a 767 barreling down the runway at LAX. She considered all the rational explanations. She was here in New York by coincidence. She'd just arrived and hadn't been at the embassy party at all. Eduardo hadn't planned for her to be at this particular restaurant at this particular time. That was a coincidence too.

"Your mojito, mademoiselle." The bartender slid the tall, frosted white glass across the bar to her.

"Know what?" Before the two words were out of her mouth, Sam dismissed all the cockamamie, rationalizing theories and landed on the most rational of all. Gisella was here now for a reason: because Sam was here now. "Send it over to the chick with the dark hair by the window. In five minutes."

"*Très bien.*" The bartender nodded, after Sam tossed some bills on the bar. Then she stormed across the restaurant, heading straight for Gisella, who wore a fitted black-and-red sundress with spaghetti straps—one of her own designs, no doubt. She looked perfect. And thin. Not a hair was out of place; not a bead of perspiration from the day lingered on her shoulders. That. Bitch.

"*Hola Gisella, que hay chiquita?*"

Sam's slang was perfect. Gisella turned to see who was calling. Sam saw the look of shock when she realized who it was. "Samantha . . ."

"Samantha!"

Sam whirled. Eduardo was cutting across the restaurant toward her, apparently coming back from the men's room. He wore a dark beige, hand-tailored, summer-weight wool suit; his suit jacket was slung over his shoulder. "You're . . . early!"

"And you're a fucking asshole," Sam hissed.

Eduardo looked from Gisella to Sam. "I can explain!"

"You've been out in the heat," Gisella observed calmly, looking Sam over from head to toe and back again. "Why don't you cool down and then—?"

"Shut the hell up," Sam snapped, then turned back

to Eduardo. "And you? Go to hell. With her. You two deserve each other."

Eduardo shook his head. "You are too upset over something in your imagination!"

"Right, just like at the embassy party the other night. Do you think I'm an idiot?" Her hands shook from sadness and anger.

"Of course not," he replied. "And if only you will calm yourself and listen, I really can explain."

"I don't want to hear your explanation." Her sweaty hands were balled into fists. She *willed* herself not to cry in front of him. "In fact, I don't want to hear from you ever again."

Then she turned around, and walked back out into the afternoon. This time, she didn't even feel the oppressive sun as it beat down on her.

"You've got John Carlos signed to the agency yet, Dad?"

Clark Sheppard laughed his deep, booming laugh. "You think I'm a miracle worker?"

"I think you're utterly ruthless and if you go after something or someone you'll do pretty much anything to get it. Or him."

Cammie was talking with her dad via her hands-free headset, since the LAPD was cracking down on people driving while celling—which, in her opinion, was just plain idiotic. She had seen women driving while putting on false eyelashes, for God's sake. Why wasn't there a no-driving-while-eyelashing law? Or a no-driving-while-having-sex law? Really, it was just ridiculous.

Instead of getting angry, her father sounded proud. "You got that right. And no, I don't have him signed yet, but he's set for your club opening night, and the rest of the deal should move along quickly."

"That's great!" Cammie exclaimed, as she cut around a slow-moving teal Ford Taurus on Venice Boulevard with a maneuver worthy of a Formula One driver. Since she was behind the wheel of her current favorite of the vehicles in her father and stepmother's garage—a cherry red Lamborghini that retailed for something north of the salary of the president of the United States—such a maneuver was a piece of cake.

John Carlos had finally come into Apex to meet with Clark that same morning. Cammie had volunteered to be at the meeting, but Clark had thought he'd be more persuasive and less intimidating one-on-one.

"So, just out of curiosity, how'd you do it?" Cammie genuinely wanted to know.

"It wasn't hard. He's freelancing and he can still freelance. But he's also now an Apex employee. If he works at clubs that we approve, we'll guarantee his salary up to a certain number each week. He can choose artistically where he wants to be, and money won't be an issue."

Cammie stopped at a red light at the corner of Venice and McLaughlin. "And my club is on your approved list, I take it."

"The first and only one."

Cammie had to admit it—she was impressed. There was a reason her father was known for both his ruthless negotiations and his brilliance.

"What about his gig at Montmartre?"

"You let me worry about that. Just get that club in shape for your opening. How many days left?"

"A week."

"I'll be there," Clark promised. "Margaret, too. We're bringing our whole client list under penalty of death."

Cammie thanked him again and ended the call. Again, she couldn't quite fathom why her father was being so nice to her. Maybe it was everything she'd gone through in learning about her mom's past during the last few months, or maybe he was mellowing in his old age. Or maybe her original suspicion had been correct: he was responding to her because she was showing some initiative with her life. Cammie didn't know the precise reason, and Clark wasn't the kind of dad whom you'd ask about it directly, but she did know she liked it.

She was practically at the club, but since she knew the parking lot was still a mass of construction equipment, she pulled into a pay lot just a little up the street. They'd already contracted with this lot for their parking needs, and the owner had said he'd be all too happy to put on an evening shift of employees.

"How are you, Miss Cammie?" The owner was on duty today, and he virtually ran to the Lamborghini to take the keys.

"Very good, Artoosh."

"A week until opening! Break a leg! I'll be there at the opening!" Artoosh's bearded head bobbed so fast that Cammie feared it might fall off.

"Cool. We'll talk about it." She trotted off on foot toward the club. She was serious about maybe having Artoosh as one of the VIPs on opening night. She'd been to a lot of club opening nights, and couldn't recall one where the parking manager was a guest. It would be a hoot, especially because Bye, Bye Love was located in a former auto body shop. Maybe she could ask him to wear his parking attendant uniform. Her club opening would be—

No, wait. It wasn't her opening. It was Ben's. But the more she'd worked on it with him, the more excited she'd gotten about it. Making things happen, having that kind of power, was exhilarating. That her friends were just now gearing up to start college struck Cammie as borderline bizarre. Why go sit in dusty classrooms and listen to boring old farts lecture to you about things in which you had zero interest when you could start your real life instead?

She was still musing on this when she ran into Ben, surrounded by a half dozen workers just outside the door. That wasn't unusual. What was unusual was the torrent of water—a gusher, really—pouring out the front door, and at the same time leaking from the exterior walls of the building.

"What's going on?" Cammie had to negotiate the water as the workers parted like the Red Sea, and made her way to Ben.

"Some kinda leak. It just started." He looked harried and stressed.

"That's not a leak. That's a tidal wave!"

"Whatever. I'm going in."

Heedless of the water gushing out, Ben sloshed inside. Cammie thought for a moment about joining him, but realized that her white leather Stuart Weitzman sandals, dark brown Jil Sander silk skirt, and beige silk

Michael Kors top were not exactly work clothes. As the flood continued unabated, she couldn't help picturing what this water had to be doing to their hard-won and expensive renovations. The new floor would be ruined. The walls, too. Probably all the fixtures. What about the basement? The sub-basement? All the electrical equipment that was resting on the floor. Gravity was at work; the water would pool at the lowest possible point. *God.*

This was a disaster. No. This was worse than a disaster. This was catastrophic. To add insult to injury, she saw that many of the workers were packing up the tool bags and belongings that they'd managed to salvage.

"What are you doing?" Cammie demanded. "You're not done for the day!"

"Oh yeah, we are." An elderly painter with a scruffy white beard took off his apron. "You're not gonna be able to paint in there at least for two weeks. Probably more. Too much moisture."

And still the water continued to pour out. She heard Ben shouting instructions to the workers who were still inside, about main cutoff valves and piping. Finally, after what seemed like an eternity, the water was cut from a river to a stream, and then to a brook, and then, to an almost piteous trickle. By that time, all the workers were gone.

"Seems like you've got a problem."

Cammie turned. Standing about ten feet from her, arms folded over his chest, wearing baggy plaid pants, black Converse All-Star high-tops, and a black bowling shirt, was John Carlos. He looked as wary of the deluge as Cammie was.

"Just a little plumbing hassle," she fudged, flipping out inside. Did this guy have to show up now, of all times? But she knew she had to keep her cool. Panic tended to put people off, especially when it was over an obvious flood in their new place of business.

John Carlos surveyed Venice Boulevard in front of the club. It was covered in several inches of water; cars were poking through the man-made lake with great caution.

"More than a hassle. Looks like you decided to import the Marina del Rey."

Cammie waved a hand dismissively. "We'll be fine."

"I don't think so. I think you're fucked."

She put her hands on her hips. "We are not fucked."

"You're fucked," John Carlos repeated evenly. "I was at a club in New York when a water main broke a block away. They were out of business for two months. You've got seven days to get it together."

"Well, it shouldn't matter to you. Your salary is guaranteed."

Thank God her father had met with this guy earlier.

"That's one of the reasons I'm here."

"What do you mean?"

John Carlos shrugged. "It's like this. I know I saw your dad today, and I know we worked out an arrangement, but I got a call an hour ago from some dudes in Moscow. Like, fucking Russian mafia. They didn't say so, but they implied it. They're opening a new club on Tverskaya Prospekt and they want me to do the music. And for a whole lot more money than what you're gonna pay me. I'm flying to Russia tonight."

"But we've got a deal!" Cammie protested. The water

on Venice Boulevard was overflowing the curb now; she and John Carlos had to take a few steps to find dry ground. "You can't do that!"

"I just did. Like I said, my boys over there, they're in the Russian underworld. I suppose you could sue me, but that wouldn't make 'em happy. And you don't want these guys unhappy."

Cammie was incensed. "Maybe you don't realize who you're fucking with here. My father is—"

"I know who your father is. He's a fuzzy little kitten compared to these Russian cats."

"Then why the hell would you want to work for them?"

John Carlos swiveled his thumb against his middle finger. "It's all about the green, baby. Hey, good luck with whatever. You're gonna need it."

He turned back toward his shiny black Beemer, which he'd parked on dry asphalt.

"You have a contract!" Cammie screamed at his skinny back.

He turned again to her, bemused, hands shoved into the pockets of his plaid pants. "Yeah, well, we both know that don't mean shit. You said so yourself. See ya."

He turned again, whistling, and strode to his black car.

The nerve. The audacity. Cammie simply could not believe it. She knew every Hollywood trick in the book. But . . . she had just been out-Hollywooded. And she had no clue what to do about it.

An Ace Up the Sleeve of Her Chloé Baby Doll

"**M**aybe John Carlos was right." Ben shook his head slowly as he stirred a heaping spoonful of sugar into his Nate'n Al's coffee. "Maybe we *are* totally fucked."

Cammie smiled smugly. Yesterday she would have wondered if Ben was right. Today . . . well, today she was ba-ack. There was no way she was going to let a skinny, skeevy DJ in an ultra-bad-taste bowling shirt wreck their club.

It was the morning after the double disasters. After the flood had slowed to a trickle yesterday, Ben had picked up a couple of carloads of undocumented workers at the corner of Venice and National and offered them ten bucks an hour each, in cash, plus all the squeegees and work towels they could find at the Culver City OSH hardware store. The goal was to try and restore the interior of Bye, Bye Love to some semblance of dry. Cammie had even pitched in, meaning she had indulged in actual physical labor. Their efforts had proved only marginally successful, and Cammie had ruined her white leather sandals in the process. But there was something satisfying in trying

217

to put the club back in action. She felt like she'd at least done something, however paltry.

By the time midnight came around and the new workers were gone, there was a four-foot-high pile of sodden towels in the kitchen, and the club interior still looked like the aftermath of Katrina. Cammie and Ben had locked up—though who would want to break in now was anyone's guess—and agreed to meet for breakfast the next morning at Nate'n Al's in Beverly Hills.

And now . . . here they were. That was then, this was now, and Cammie had an ace up the sleeve of her bubble-gum pink Chloé baby-doll dress. Nate'n Al's was one of the most famous delis in the city. There was a baked-goods and takeout counter to the left, and a bustling and noisy wood-paneled dining room to the right. As usual, it was filled with Hollywood types drinking coffee, eating breakfast, and making deals.

"I wouldn't give up so quickly," she advised. She'd ordered a toasted English muffin and black coffee. She considered adding fresh strawberry jam to the muffin, and then decided she'd prefer the calories in some other way. All around her the young and beautiful women of Hollywood, for whom Nate'n Al's was the prework equivalent of the Warner Brothers canteen, were making the same decision.

Ben rubbed his forehead wearily. "At some point, you've got to face reality."

Cammie sipped her black coffee and gave him a cool look. "So you'd give up on your dream, just like that, because of some setbacks?"

"Maybe what you took to go to sleep last night isn't what I took."

"I didn't sleep much," she admitted. "I was working."

"On what? The club?" Ben had raised a bite of his turkey, avocado, and green apple omelet to his mouth, but mention of the club seemed to make him lose his appetite, and he steadily lowered the forkful down.

Cammie nodded. This was actually true. Her father had been awake when she'd come home. She'd found him on the couch in the living room, reading through a stack of spec scripts by writers he was considering bringing on to *Hermosa Beach,* the hit TV show he'd packaged, set in a beachfront hotel in the town of the same name. Packaging meant he was responsible for the writers, directors—the whole production team. It also meant that his agency, Apex, earned a larger-than-average commission on the deal. He'd seen her bedraggled state and had sat up in concern. After she showered and changed into jeans and a T-shirt, they'd talked long into the night about an action plan. At first, Cammie had been as depressed as Ben, though she wouldn't let it show. But the longer she talked to her father, the more she thought that there might be a smidgen of hope.

"My father gave me some good advice. He said he'd help us." She took another sip of coffee. "But if you're going to give up over some bad luck—"

"Cammie." Ben reached for her hand across the metal-top table. "It was my knee-jerk reaction. The little voice in my head that agrees with my father and says this whole notion was insane and I should be going back to Princeton. But now the little voice is going back in his little box." He gave her a winning smile.

And, she couldn't help noting, he was still holding her hand.

"Okay, so," Cammie began, "no venue and no DJ . . ."

"Thanks for that recap," he muttered grimly.

"Daddy dearest suggested we turn the negative into a positive."

"Like calling the bomb that fell on Hiroshima an instant urban renewal project," Ben scoffed.

"Not exactly." She laughed. "But he had some pretty cool ideas."

She had actually been stunned by how quickly her father had assessed the situation and made his pithy suggestions. He hadn't even been that shocked by how John Carlos had betrayed him and flown off to be a DJ for the Russian mob. Shit happens in the business, he'd said, with a shrug of his muscular shoulders. Entertainment wasn't like accounting or selling commercial real estate. It attracted personalities, and more than a few of them weren't very stable or loyal. It attracted unforeseen disasters. Sets on movies came crashing to the ground because local workers were incompetent. Hurricanes and thunderstorms interrupted shooting. Actors and actresses were caught driving the wrong way on the 405 and then promptly checked into rehab.

In the scheme of things, a burst pipe and a disappearing DJ were only middling problems, Clark maintained. The important thing was to keep them in perspective and deal with them one step at a time. In this case, he thought that the solution to both problems could come from the same place.

"Cammie, you're driving me insane," Ben interrupted, his coffee cup wrapped in both hands. "Enough recap."

"I'll let him tell you."

She took out her cell and, ignoring Ben's quizzical look, made a quick one-way phone call. "Dad? Yeah. We're in the back left corner. I'll pull up a chair for you. See ya."

"Your father is here?" Ben suddenly looked around.

"Clever deduction." Cammie waved to her father, who was working his way up the narrow aisle toward them. She always admired that quality that set him off from the people around him. Sure, he had the same robust, tanned, and relaxed stride of his regal Hollywood clientele, but something about him sharpened his features. Not just how he dressed, which today was in casually impeccable Ralph Lauren, but the way one hand held his shark-gray jacket over his shoulder while the other always had a surplus of hands to shake. Six feet tall, rangy build, slicked-back blond hair when he went to work, always in a suit when he was seen in public, Clark was the epitome of a hard-driving, respected Hollywood agent. He stopped to shake hands warmly with Jude Law, who was having breakfast with the director Stephen Frears, and then to exchange a hug with Gail Berman, with whom he'd done numerous deals when she was at Paramount. Cammie knew all these people. Most of them had been guests for dinner or drinks at the Sheppard house at one time or another. Her dad's philosophy was that unless you were in negotiations—where you could be as big a son of a bitch as you wanted—you should be nice to everyone. Today's gaffer was tomorrow's studio head. And vice versa.

"Hey, Dad!" She stood and embraced her father, though she'd seen him not long before for coffee at home. Still, she knew that many people would be watching to see what she did, and if her father was doing a favor for her, she wanted to do one right back.

"Hey, sweetie. Hey, Ben. Heard you got fucked yesterday."

"Heard you had some way for us to maybe enjoy it," Ben shot back.

Clark laughed and clapped a hand on Ben's shoulder. "Good to see you." He slung his steel gray double-breasted suit jacket over the back of his seat. Like most agents, he dressed far more formally than most male Hollywood creatives, who favored T-shirts, torn jeans, and baseball caps—as did a fair number of females as well. Female writers tended to dress as informally as the guys, but for some reason directors and producers took it a notch up, meaning their jeans were never torn.

"Okay, so here's the plan," Clark began as the waitress placed the steaming cup of black coffee he must have already ordered—or had his assistant call in—in front of him. "I talked to Margaret, my partner at Apex. We committed our client list to your opening night. We're prepared to revise that: commit them this afternoon—as many of them as are available, of course—to come down to the club and work on the renovation. Sound good?"

Ben drummed his fingers on the table impatiently. "They'll say no."

Clark's eyebrows furrowed. "Now you know my clients better than I do?" He leaned forward and dead-eyed him. "I've got one word for you, Ben: publicity."

"It makes the world go round," Cammie put in.

Ben shook his head. "Okay, I'm lost. Why would Hollywood's A-list dirty their hands getting our club ready to open, and why would they score publicity for doing it? It's not like they're doing it for—"

Cammie watched the light dawn on his face. It was a thing of beauty.

"Charity," he finished, looking at Clark expectantly. "That's it, isn't it?"

"We give the profits of Bye, Bye Love to charity!" Cammie sang out. "How brilliant is that? Every star in Hollywood will be begging to be involved because they want the good press."

"And the longer you run your club with all the profits going to charity, the more press you're going to get for your opening," Clark concluded. Ben scratched the day-old stubble on his chin. "Eventually we'd turn it back into a for-profit thing." He picked up the conversation where Clark left off. "But we could still do, like, the first Saturday of every month for charity—"

"I was thinking we could do the New Visions foundation," Cammie broke in.

"The one that sponsored the fashion show you and Anna were in a couple of weeks ago?" Ben raised an eyebrow.

She wasn't exactly turning cartwheels at hearing Anna's name on Ben's lips, but whatever. "Exactly."

"I'd recommend two weeks as the minimum time you dedicate to charity," Clark advised. "But—"

"But a month would be better," Ben finished his thought.

Clark smiled, tiny lines appearing around the corners of his mouth. "At least. I knew there was a reason my daughter likes you. Yes, a month would be better. Do we have a deal?" He held out his hand.

Ben shook it, his face breaking into a grin. "How can I ever thank you?"

"Be good to my daughter. And have your ass at your club by two o'clock. That's when my clients are going to show up. Also, TV vans from KCAL, KABC, and Channel 4 News. And possibly *Entertainment Tonight.* Now I need you guys to excuse me. I'm meeting Jackson in my office at ten." Clark stood and put his coffee cup down. "We're talking about *Ben-Hur.*"

"Sam's dad?" Cammie asked. "How come?"

"He's been at Endeavor since that agency was formed. And that's all I'm going to say."

"You're poaching him!"

"No one's poaching anyone. We're just going to have a discussion to explore common interests and directions. Good luck, you two. See you this afternoon."

Clark moved off. As he did, Ben leaned across the table, embraced Cammie, and planted a big fat kiss on her cheek. She was thrilled, though she would have been more thrilled if the kiss had been directed at some other part—or parts—of her anatomy. On the other hand, they were in a crowded deli—not that such a thing was likely to stop her, but she was somewhat more adventurous in that department than Ben.

"Your father just saved our asses." He reached across the table for her hand again. Cammie smiled.

She used the other hand to motion Tillie, a waitress in her eighties who had the body of an in-shape forty-year-old, thick gray hair in a bun, and an encyclopedic knowledge of Hollywood gossip. Rumor had it that she'd been one of Jack Warner's lovers late in his life, when Jack was getting on and Tillie was still searching for stardom. She'd waited on Cammie many times.

"Tillie! Can we order a real breakfast now?"

"You? Eating more than a plain English muffin?" Ben teased.

"Two things help me work up an appetite," Cammie answered coyly. "And a great save is the one we can do with our clothes on."

He shook his head and Tillie hustled over with a pink-lipsticked smile. "Your father restored your appetites?" She gave Ben an approving up-and-down. "A boy so handsome like this, he needs to eat." Then she winked at Cammie. "To have energy for a girl like you."

Cammie batted her eyelashes and puckered her lips. "Couldn't have said it better myself."

The Trout Pout

"It's funny that people don't walk in Los Angeles."
Anna's fingers were entwined with Logan's, and they were strolling down the stone steps to the Boat Basin Café, one of Anna's favorite hangouts in the entire city. Located at the Seventy-ninth Street Boat Basin on the Hudson River, the café overlooked dozens of moored sailboats and had an unobstructed view of the river and New Jersey beyond. On a hot summer night like this one, with the cool breeze coming off the water, it beat almost anyplace that she knew. A young woman in her twenties in lime green capris and a clashing sports bra ran by, pushing a hooded double baby jogger. A skinny boy without front teeth was throwing a battered pink Frisbee to his dog, a brown-and-white mutt of no discernible breed; a distinguished if diminuitive elderly man in a suit and his equally small octogenarian wife, in a formal dress and vintage hat, strolled slowly together, holding hands. Every so often, they'd stop and gaze into each other's eyes.

It struck Anna how un–West Coast the whole thing was, because none of the people had that rosy sheen of

Hollywood airbrushed perfection. They were just people, living their lives.

Anna was thrilled that Logan hadn't known about the boat basin; it was a chance to introduce him to something new. Plus, the Little Red Lighthouse was only a hundred blocks north. They could walk there along Riverside Park, if they chose. She was sure that with him, even five miles would go by in a heartbeat.

He grinned at her. "No, it isn't, it's that car culture. Here, a car is a terrible way to get around. Speaking of . . . how do you feel about going back to Los Angeles tomorrow?"

She shrugged as they reached the café and took one of the open white plastic tables and chairs. "I'll only be there a week, then back here for a few days, then up to New Haven." Anna heard the flatness in her own voice. "You won't need that," she advised as Logan reached for a menu. "Stick to the burgers. And watch out for the dogs. They allow them here."

"I'll keep certain parts well protected," he answered with a straight face, as a waitress appeared immediately to take their order—two cheeseburgers, two Absolut Citron martinis, and a side order of pickles. "Meanwhile, I can tell you're not filled with joy about going back to L.A."

Was that true? And if it was, which part of the scenario was it that she didn't like? The thing she felt most excited about was the screenplay she'd started. She finished twelve pages last night, and of course, had no freaking idea if it was any good. But at least she was *doing* something, instead of thinking everything to death.

They sat in silence for a while until an aging hippie

couple in tie-dye shirts and their Doberman sat down at the table next to them, and the dog—a friendly behemoth with a red bandanna tied around its neck—decided that he was in love with Anna. After several amorous advances, the hippie couple chatted them up. It turned out that they were visiting from an actual commune in Tennessee and were about to eat their first hamburgers in five years.

"I'll order one for the dog," Logan gestured humorously as the waitress brought them their drinks. They clinked glasses.

Anna studied his handsome face across from her. "When we're at school, we'll only be two hours apart," she started thinking aloud. "We can see each other on the weekends, and . . ." She let the rest of what she'd been about to say peter out, because of the shadow that crossed his face. "What?" she prompted.

"Nothing." He shook his head and instead took a sip of his drink.

Anna flushed. She sensed immediately that she'd gone too far, talking about getting together once school started. She'd only been in New York for a week and she was already making them into some kind of a couple? What was going on with her?

The waitress brought their food, and they ate practically in silence. Their table had just been cleared when they were interrupted by a voice behind them.

"Anna Percy? Is that you? It *is* you!"

A brunette with cut-glass cheekbones and the trout pout of overly enthusiastic lip enhancement—a woman of a certain age who'd had so much work done that her actual age was now entirely uncertain—approached their table. She wore vintage black-and-red Chanel. The toy poodle panting in her Hermès handbag was the same color as her suit.

"Marianna Saint Thomas. I was co-chair with your mother for the American Ballet Theater benefit for years."

"Right, nice to see you," Anna murmured. Evidently, folks from her side of Manhattan had found the boat basin restaurant, too.

"And you're Logan Cresswell," Marianna continued, pointing an elegant finger at him. "My niece owns the cottage next door to your parents on the Vineyard. Such lovely people. Well, isn't this a small world."

The toy poodle gave a toy bark, and Marianna stroked its twitchy head. "Hush, Precious," she chided. "She just loves attention," Marianna added for Logan and Anna's benefit, then lowered her voice. "I'd never be seen at this place, but my daughter Muffin graduated from Sarah Lawrence and we're having a little celebration before she leaves to study art in Venice. She's very bohemian. We have a table by the water. Would you care to join us?"

"We'd love to," Logan answered quickly, "but we have other plans."

"Some other time then. Kisses to your mother, darling Anna!" Marianna let her dove gray Prada pumps carry her away from the table. As she did, Logan tossed some money on said table and rose. "Let's get out of here."

His face was grim. "Are you mad about something?" Anna asked, stretching her long legs to keep up with his stride.

"Just . . . her. And the whole world of hers."

Anna arched a brow. "You mean, the world we grew up in?"

"Exactly. It's like she fits the mold exactly."

There was a time, Anna knew, when she fit that mold, too. But eight months in California had changed her. She hoped.

"I don't think where you're from makes you who you are. Not completely, anyway."

Logan shoved his hands deep into the pockets of his ancient khakis, and they started up the stairs to Riverside Drive. "I hope not. My father went to Harvard. His father went to Harvard. All I ever heard my whole life was, 'When you go to Harvard...'"

He captured her hand as they reached the sidewalk. "I've done what's expected of me my whole life."

Anna nodded silently, knowing exactly what he meant. They walked to Amsterdam, where there was a street scene to watch every night. Just as two elderly women in kerchiefs and support hose vacated a bench surrounded by pigeons, Logan slid onto it and patted the seat next to him. They observed the changing street scene of a hot New York night. People out walking their dogs, groups of teenagers from New Jersey looking for fun but not knowing where to look, Rollerbladers, night bikers, and an endless stream of honking cars and taxis.

"I thought we'd talk during dinner," Logan suddenly began in a low tone. "But we'd better do it now. I have something to tell you."

"Okay. Go ahead." She steeled herself. He was probably still freaked out by what she'd said at dinner, the plans for their relationship she'd blurted out without thinking. *I really like you,* he'd say. *But I'm just not ready for that kind of commitment.* How could she have thought differently after just a week?

"I'm not going to Harvard."

"You're *what?*"

"Not going," he repeated. "I've been thinking about it for weeks. And then when I went to the reception and couldn't find the enthusiasm I'd been hoping—"

"But . . . but it was just a cocktail party for incoming freshmen—it wasn't like actually being at Harvard!" Anna exclaimed.

"I just . . . I need some time to think. St. Paul's, then Harvard, then grad school. I feel like I'm in a car, driving ninety miles an hour to I don't know where."

Anna's throat tightened. She'd already pictured them together in New Haven or Cambridge. Even though she knew it was too soon to really talk about it, it felt all too natural that they'd continue to see each other once they were at school. It didn't have to mean they were a couple. It just made the thought of going off to Yale so much more bearable to know—

She stopped herself. *So much more bearable?*

That was what she thought about going to college, that she needed something—someone—to make it more *bearable?*

What if . . . what if he felt about Harvard the same way she felt about Yale? Yet she couldn't imagine simply blowing it off as he just had. Because without her plan of going to college, she had no clue what she wanted to do.

"I'm sorry if I didn't seem enthusiastic about what you said at dinner," he continued. "I would have been.

I just . . . it caught me off guard. I wasn't ready to tell you I wasn't going."

She turned to him again. "Maybe you should think about it some more."

Logan shook his head. "All I've been doing is thinking about it. And I know what I'm going to do instead."

"What?" She was unable to contain her curiosity. What did people like her and Logan *do* if they didn't go to college?

"Go to Bali. My dad just opened a new eco-resort there. A new hotel."

"And what exactly will you do at your father's new eco-resort in Bali?" Anna could hear the edge in her voice, which wasn't fair, but she couldn't help herself. It wasn't just that she suddenly felt abandoned. She cared about Logan. And maybe it could develop into something more. Evidently, he didn't feel the same way. They'd just been old neighbors hanging out for a few days.

"Think." He rubbed his temples. "Just be free and clear to . . . think. Figure out what I want."

"Okay," she replied softly. It wasn't like she could talk him out of it.

Logan put a hand to her cheek. "These past few days with you have been amazing, Anna. I want you to know that."

Her answer was very short and very honest. "For me, too."

When You Feel Your Worst, Always Look Your Best

Anna had been to the Academy Awards with Sam this past spring, when Sam's father had unfortunately lost—yet again—for best actor. But the scene on Venice Boulevard as she approached Bye, Bye Love rivaled it for celebrity and star-studded controlled chaos. The LAPD had actually blocked off the boulevard in either direction, snarling traffic in the somewhat scruffy Culver City neighborhood almost to the point of gridlock. Certainly, the neat frame houses, plumbing suppliers, temporary-labor storefront shops, and takeout Chinese joints had never seen anything like it.

"I'll say this for Ben and Cammie—they know how to do an opening," Sam commented as she and Anna crawled along in Sam's yellow Hummer. "Not that I care," she added, "about that or anything else."

That much Anna already knew. Sam had been in a deep depression ever since her breakup with Eduardo, and she couldn't seem to pull herself out of the funk. Anna had suggested many times that she pick up the phone when he called and hear what he had to say rather than just write him off. They had been engaged, for God's sake. But Sam refused. Clearly she'd been right in her suspicions about him and "that bitch" Gisella, Sam had decided. It wasn't like Eduardo was breaking down the gates of her house to get to her, trying to make things right. No, it was over, she insisted. She'd been a fool to believe that he loved her in the first place.

"Let's just try to have fun tonight," Anna suggested gently. She was as anxious as Sam was depressed, because she was about to see Ben again. She wasn't sure how she felt about it. She hadn't ever expected to meet someone new so quickly. Not that she was with Logan now, anyway. The night at the boat basin had been their last together. In the week since, he'd written her a few e-mails, saying that New York was boring without her—all he'd done for days was pack for Bali—and that he wished she were there. But all the wishing in the world couldn't change the fact that right now he was probably making his way across the world, and she was here, at the opening of her ex-boyfriend's club, once again alone.

"This could take forever," Sam groused as they slowed yet again for the intense traffic. Cammie and Ben had sent out official blue-and-white Bye, Bye Love opening night placards for attendees and/or their drivers to put on the dashboards below their windshields, in order to get past a first line of security, whose only job was to wave vehicles through with a grin or turn them around with a stern stare. Sam had decided to drive the Hummer rather than take a limo, for ease in departure at the end of the night. Sometimes at these affairs, the wait for your limo to arrive afterward was interminable.

Anna and Sam had been back in Los Angeles for a week, and in just one more week, Anna would go east again to start at Yale. Before she'd left Manhattan, she'd booked her flight home—a Delta flight late Saturday afternoon that would get her into LaGuardia at midnight. At least packing wouldn't be hard. She'd just take her Los Angeles suitcases and ship all her boxes to New Haven, to be waiting for her arrival. What she wouldn't put in her dorm room would go into storage.

God. What was wrong with her? Why was she still thinking *Yale* instead of *Yale!* At the present moment she had just about as much desire to begin freshman year at college as she had to see Ben at this opening. At least Ben wasn't a total obsession. She'd come home to articles in the *Los Angeles Times* and *L.A. Weekly* about the opening of the club, with photographs of Ben and the club under construction side by side with old pictures of the original business. Anna remembered what it had looked like on the night she'd discovered the place. The transformation, at least in the pictures, was amazing. That Cammie Sheppard was named in those articles as Ben's business partner was less than thrilling. That there was a small picture of Ben and Cammie in the *Times,* with their arms around each other, was actually daunting.

"We could make a U-turn," Anna blurted out before she could edit the thought. The Hummer inched along, wedged between two black stretch limousines and a white Jensen Interceptor. "I'm not sure either one of us is in a party mood."

Sam eyed her. "We look too fabulous to bail. Old

Hollywood saying: When you feel your worst, always look your best."

Anna couldn't argue with that. She wore a white eyelet lace Betsey Johnson baby-doll dress with white ballet slippers—it was simple and didn't look like she was trying too hard, which struck her as the right tone when seeing the boy who had so callously dumped her. Sam had on a fitted Blumarine shrunken silver silk jacket with new black cotton capris. The only sound in the car's well-insulated, black leather interior was Sam's Oscar de la Renta black alligator pumps tapping on the brake pedal.

Anna didn't respond, but just stared out the windshield of the Hummer at the chaotic scene beyond the police barricade in front of the club. Hundreds of rich and beautiful people in designer everything were milling around, with their publicists, personal assistants, and agents in tow. There was a bank of movie-opening-style spotlights cutting through the night sky, plus a lineup of television live-remote trucks with their on-air personalities waiting to go live on the ten o'clock news once the doors to the club were open. Off in the distance, Anna could see dozens of hangers-on with binoculars, hoping to do a little celebrity spotting. A return to such lavishly saturated L.A. culture after the concrete-jungle reality of New York felt almost surreal to her.

As Sam finally pulled the Hummer up to the first checkpoint, Anna saw Mrs. Virginia Vanderleer and her friend Victoria Chesterfield hurrying toward the front area of the club. They were two of the leaders of the New Visions foundation, and Anna knew them from the fashion show at the art museum, which they had organized. The profits of the first month of the club's operations would be entirely dedicated to New Visions. Anna knew this from the same article in the *Times* that featured Ben and Cammie. On an interior page, there'd been yet another photograph, of the two of them looking comfortable in workmen's clothes and tool belts standing in front of the combined casts of *Grey's Anatomy, Hermosa Beach,* and the new Vince Vaughn/Ben Stiller film, flanked by bevies of camera-toting teen fans. The actors and actresses were all in workmen's clothes too.

But it wasn't the A-list celebrities who caught Anna's eye—it was the image of Ben and Cammie that caused her gaze to linger. They looked almost perfect together, and so . . . happy. Anna could still recall the angry, stormy look on Ben's face when he'd dumped her, the nasty, mean tone in his voice. Having his apparent contentment confirmed in a photo didn't make it any easier to take—especially not when Cammie Sheppard was in that photo with him.

If Anna was going to be completely honest with herself, the thought of Ben even touching Cammie drove her insane. She knew it was silly. She knew he and Cammie had been a couple before she'd even known Ben. She knew there was no more Ben-and-Anna. No more. No more ever.

And it *still* drove her crazy.

The article had explained the inception of Bye, Bye in glowing and admiring detail: Cammie and Ben had set up a charitable organization called the Bye, Bye Love Foundation, to whom they were pledging a significant

long-term percentage of the overall profits of their club,
in addition to their first month's revenues. Celebrity
support had started with the Apex client base, but then
had spread through the Hollywood A-list. Donations
over and above the club profits had already been made
by most of the city's movie studios, record labels, and
television production companies. Without having sold a
single drink or taken a cover charge, Cammie and Ben's
foundation already had over two hundred thousand dollars
in pledged assets. Already, an aspiring impresario in Miami
Beach had approached them about franchising, with a percentage of his club's earnings also going to their charity.

"Credentials, please." The straight-out-of-central-casting,
shaved-head-and-goatee rent-a-cop approached Sam for
their invitation. Anna watched as he ran it under an ultra-
violet scanner to make sure that it wasn't counterfeited.
The security guy must have seen her questioning eyes.
"You can't imagine how many false ones of these I've
seen already tonight. You two are fine. Valet stand's just
ahead." He punched a few holes in the invite with a hole-
punch, then handed it back to Sam. "Have a blast. I heard
it's insane in there."

Sam pulled up to the crowded valet stand. The valet
who approached the Hummer wore a tuxedo and a black
cap emblazoned with the name of his parking facility,
instead of the usual baseball jacket and jeans. Sam handed
him the keys, and he gave her a receipt and reminded her
that parking would be free if she had the receipt validated
inside the club.

"Free parking." Sam nodded approvingly. "Or at least
the appearance of free parking, since they tack the price

onto the door charge. I'll say this for them: they're doing it right."

Anna took a step toward a line that was forming near the valet stand, and spotted the fashion designer Martin Rittenhouse and two other immaculately dressed men step out of a white limo. She knew Rittenhouse from the charity fashion show she'd been in where his designs had been shown—and from the dress scandal that had ensued afterward. Then she felt Sam clutch her arm.

"Do you have any idea who those two men are with Martin Rittenhouse?" she hissed.

"No clue," Anna admitted.

"Domenico Dolce," Sam said. "I've never seen him at an opening. And Stefano Gabbana. My ass would do cartwheels to fit into one of his dresses. Well, there's always the next life. Come on."

Anna inhaled deeply and blew the air out slowly. It wasn't the celebrity designer sighting that filled her with anxiety. *Okay,* she told herself. *You've got exactly one more week here in Los Angeles. Go in there, smile at everyone, and make some memories.*

Even if they won't be with Ben.

"Ladies and gentlemen!" Cammie shouted into her handheld microphone, the crowd below her pulsing with energy. "Welcome to the grand opening of Bye, Bye Love! It's a helluva night for a helluva club and a helluva crowd. Let's give it up for the star of tonight's show, the handsome, driven man who bucked his father, opened this club, and is gonna rock the hell out of Los Angeles . . . Mr. Benjamin Birnbaum!"

Sam stood on tiptoe so that she could attempt to see over the masses. They cheered as one of the old automotive lifts rose up from below the dance floor, hoisting Ben high over the heads of his opening-night throng. He wore a black Giorgio Valentini suit over a bloodred BYE, BYE LOVE T-shirt, which featured a razor slicing through the center of a heart. The place went wild as the lift hoisted Ben skyward, a sea of beautiful people applauding, whistling, and cheering.

Sam had to give Cammie credit: when she'd told Anna before that Cammie was doing it right, she had no idea it'd be as right as *this*. Just getting inside had reminded her of the security at her own father's wedding at the Griffith Observatory last fall, but with even more media. At Jackson and Poppy's wedding, *People* magazine had been the official news media outlet. Here, Cammie and Ben had welcomed the press; every major media outlet was represented. By barring the riffraff, putting down a red carpet walk as elaborate as that at any movie opening, and having the media cordoned off by a low silver barrier, Cammie and Ben had made it possible for their A-list opening night attendees to have the best of all possible worlds: live television, lots of interviewers and photographers, but no unofficial paparazzi. Though the doors were kept closed until 10 p.m., waiters and waitresses had circulated outside with trays of Flirtinis and the hors d'oeuvres specialties of Jason Travi of La Terza, including his famous glazed baby beets and roasted asparagus.

The doors had opened precisely at ten, and the crowd poured in. A discreet sign indicated that this week's interior was done by Professor Antonio de la Garza's design class at Cal State, Los Angeles. Sam had a feeling that the idea of rotating club designers would quickly be imitated by other clubs, because it was just so damn cool. You had both the comfort level of a club you knew, and the freshness of it always looking different.

The Cal State design students had taken the idea of an auto body repair shop and brought it to the next level. Signage and license plates from various states and countries dotted the walls and ceiling, and interior upholstering from cars through the years formed seating areas. Tables were hoods and steering wheels hung from the ceiling. The coolest touch of all was that the students had somehow run an enormous two-car slot-car racing track all along the interior walls and covered it in clear tubing so the cars couldn't be disturbed. Clubgoers could take their turns racing these cars, and people were lined up to do that almost from the moment the doors had opened. The students had even done work on the lights, which shifted colors and positions on overhead tracks.

The rest of the club was equally alluring. People were similarly lining up for a chance to be part of the fifteen-person audience for a series of five-minute monologues by Sarah Silverman, Keenen Ivory Wayans, Will Smith, and Chelsea Handler. Sam thought Chelsea's comedy show, *Girls Behaving Badly,* which had punked people way before Ashton Kutcher ever thought of it, was perhaps the funniest thing on TV. Leave it to Cammie to get the queen of mean comedy at a moment's notice. Maybe Chelsea had agreed to do it because she'd recognized a kindred spirit in Cammie.

Within five minutes of getting inside, the celebrity/
fashion designer/model/Beverly Hills A-list crush was so
great that Sam found herself immediately separated from
Anna. But it didn't matter, because she kept running into
people she knew, either through her father's showbiz
connections or from Beverly Hills High. Skye Morrison,
a gorgeous stoner who wore her hair in blond dreadlocks,
was wearing a dazzling mint green Vera Wang gown and
had taken out her multiple piercings. Skye reported that
she was going to Bennington. With her was their friend
Damian Williams, whose father owned a string of exotic
car dealerships stretching from Santa Barbara to San
Diego, and who was known for never driving the same
vehicle twice in the same month. Damian looked fantastic; he'd lost weight over the summer, and his olive skin
had tanned almost as dark as his curly black-brown hair.
They talked easily for a little while, getting caught up on
who was with whom, who'd broken up with whom—the
Anna/Ben bust-up was still big news. Yes, people had
heard that Anna and Ben had briefly gone through a "non-
exclusive" period. But no one had believed that would last.
It turned out they'd been right, but not in the way they
had imagined.

"How about Eduardo?" Skye asked, firing up a Marl-
boro Red. "Where is he?"

"Don't know, don't care," Sam answered coolly, lying
through her cherry red Stila lip gloss.

"Oh my gosh, what happened?" someone with a very
high-pitched voice cried.

Sam turned; there were Dee and Jack, back from
Hawaii. Dee threw herself into Sam's arms. "You broke

up with Eduardo? I'm so sorry! Why didn't you tell me when I called you?"

It was all Sam could do not to cry. When Dee and Jack had headed off to Hawaii, Sam hadn't been engaged. Then she had been. Then it had ended horribly. Dee's genuine heartfelt sorrow made her feel even worse.

She hadn't talked about her breakup with Eduardo with anyone but Anna since she'd come back to Los Angeles. It was as if speaking about it would make it more real than it already was. Once school started, she'd decided, and Eduardo was back in France, she would share the news. Now that she saw Dee, right there in her friend's thin and newly tanned arms, she decided she wasn't going to expand her circle of knowledge here and now either. What was the point? It would only make her feel worse. If there was one thing in life she didn't want, it was pity from Dee Young.

"Just one of those things," Sam replied breezily. She'd been around actors all her life; at this moment she was damn well going to act with the best of them. She stood taller and shook her silken almond hair—she'd had Raymond color it the day she'd come back from New York—off her face with a practiced gesture, keeping all angst out of her voice.

"Hey, it's great to see you. Did you have fun?" she asked Dee.

"It was fantastic," Jack responded eagerly, adding a hug of his own.

"I'll tell you all about it later," Dee promised, then grabbed Sam's hand. "But seriously, what happened with Eduardo?"

At that moment, the music cranked to another level. Sam put a hand by her ear and shrugged helplessly, as if to say she couldn't hear what Dee had asked, or that it would be too hard for her to answer. The last thing she wanted to do right now was let the floodgates open. Because she knew that once she did, she'd never get them closed again.

Sheer Showbiz Genius

"Well, that's it," Sam declared. "There's no club in L.A. but Bye, Bye Love. You pulled it off!" She hugged Cammie hard. "I am so proud of you!"

"Glad you like it." Cammie smiled. "'Cause you're on the permanent guest list."

"Me too?" Dee asked.

"Of course." Cammie turned to Anna. They were just a few feet away from the main bar, a semicircular affair made entirely from reclaimed automobile hoods, with their hood ornaments still adorning the metal. At the moment, the crowd at the bar was three deep. "And you would be too, if you were sticking around. But you're not. Too bad. You've made life more interesting. Really, you have."

Sam doubted that, because in her experience, wherever the party was, that's where you found Cammie. But Cammie could afford to be in a benevolent mood, since she was the center of attention tonight, and she looked even more amazing than usual in her lime green, Randolph Duke beaded mesh spaghetti-strap dress. She didn't disguise an iota of her body; the dress was practically painted on. Sam was happy for her and jealous as hell, both at the same time. It wasn't a new feeling—Cammie was forever showing off her perfect body.

The thought involuntarily came to Sam's mind: *I thought I'd be here with Eduardo, showing off my perfect engagement ring.*

"Hey, beautiful."

Sam turned, her heart beating faster. In that instant she knew she hadn't truly given up hope, and that she would take Eduardo back in a second if he'd only come for her. But her buoyed hopes sunk immediately when she realized it was Parker standing beside her. Still, she couldn't help but smile to see her good friend. He looked fantastic, with a new short, spiky haircut and the golden glow of a guy who had just spent two weeks on location shooting a Showtime original film down in Camp Pendleton. The gig—called *Boot*—was about a disparate collection of young men from around the country who come together for basic training as Marines. The director of *Boot* had been an assistant director on *Ben-Hur;* Parker had been hired immediately on the heels of wrapping his work on that film with Sam's father.

She was thrilled that her friend was finally getting some work on his own. No one deserved a break more than Parker. She threw her arms around him. "I'm so glad you're here!"

"I'll have to go away more often, if you're going to greet me like that," Parker said with a pearly white grin. "Hey, I want you to meet someone." He slipped an arm around the shapely waist of a girl who looked familiar to Sam. She had long, wavy chestnut hair, held back by a slender black ribbon, and impressive curves encased in a citrus-print baby doll—

"Citron. You're the waitress from the Polo Lounge," Sam filled in. She and Parker had met Citron there when she'd waited on them. Parker had been into the girl from the first moment he'd seen her; that had been clear to Sam. At the time, his preoccupation with her had been more than a little annoying, but now, seeing the grin on her friend's face, Sam couldn't help but be pleased.

"Citron Simms," the girl replied, laughing. "Lord, I can't ever remember people's names!"

She had that sweet, Southern accent that Sam remembered. Evidently Parker had moved in on her after all.

"She's Django's sister," Parker added.

Sam vaguely remembered that, too—that Citron was the younger sister of Anna's father's chauffeur. "So how long have you two been hanging out?" Why not rub salt in her own wounds and find out that everyone was blissfully happy and in love but her?

"Just since I got back from the shoot." Parker gave Citron that special look that Sam had seen him give to so many girls, and it always had the same effect—they melted. Citron, however, didn't seem to melt, but returned a similarly special look instead. Which was interesting.

Parker looked past Sam. "Where's Eduardo?"

"I don't want to talk about it." She stopped him quickly. "How was your film?"

"I don't want to talk about that, either," he replied ruefully. "I'm sunburned in places I didn't know you could sunburn. And no, it wasn't a porno—it was rated R. But all the R seemed to be me." Parker looked around. "It's nuts in here, huh?"

That was an understatement. It was an hour later, and the club's energy and excitement hadn't diminished at all. In fact, it was right at the maximum of its capacity, and the door crew was keeping a careful count on who was coming in and out. Sam knew that the worst thing that could happen would be a visit from the fire marshals and an order to empty the place out. She'd been in situations like that before, and they were never fun. Crowds tended to get ugly when their Dionysian reveling was interrupted and they were told to disband.

She surveyed the premises. The dance floor was a paparazzi's dream. In one corner alone, she spotted Jake Gyllenhaal, Natalie Portman, Mena Suvari, and Pink. One of Cammie and Ben's really smart touches had been a so-called Cone of Silence that lowered from the ceiling to the floor. VIPs could go inside the clear Plexiglas cone to talk without being bothered, while at the same time being admired by all the people outside the cone. Of course, there was also a more private VIP section for those moments when celebs really did not want to be gawked at. But Sam guessed that it would always be empty. Celebrities came to clubs to be seen. If they weren't seen, they felt as if they didn't exist. The cone was sheer showbiz genius.

They were inside the cone—it held a dozen people comfortably, as well as a stocked refrigerator and minibar—at that very moment. It was so soundproof that they could barely hear the beat of Kanye West that was driving the dancers. So soundproof, in fact, that Sam heard the beeper go off inside Cammie's Zac Posen citrus yellow beaded clutch handbag.

Cammie opened the bag, shut off her beeper, and found the small walkie-talkie communicator that linked her to Ben.

"Are you there?"

"Copy that." Ben's deep, familiar voice came through loud and clear.

"You handling the music change?"

"Already on it."

"Who's up next?"

"Wait and see. And fuck John Carlos!" his voice chortled. Sam saw him climb down a short ladder from the overhead catwalk to the DJ area.

She noticed that Anna was watching him. For the briefest moment, Ben's eyes met Anna's through the Plexiglas, and then she quickly looked away. So did Ben. It was strange. Sam felt for her friend, yes. But she thought it might be a good thing that Anna and Ben were history. When they'd first met, she'd been terribly jealous—especially because she'd had a crush on Ben since middle school. But the better she got to know Anna, the more she realized that the tumult of Ben-and-Anna wasn't good for Anna. And Anna was the person she cared about now. Especially with her going off to college, it was better that there'd been a clean break, no matter how ugly it was. At least Anna wouldn't be blaming herself for his assholian behavior.

"Let's listen." Cammie flicked a switch to an internal speaker, which allowed the sounds outside to be heard inside the cone.

Ben took hold of a handheld mike. "You welcomed her, now let's give her a big goodbye. Give it up for the last hour's DJ, Miss Beyoncé Knowles!"

The crowd cheered and whooped, as Beyoncé—dressed in a self-designed House of Deréon off-the-shoulder black satin crepe dress—took a happy bow.

"Bye, Bye Love will have a different guest DJ spinning every hour on the hour," Ben crowed into the microphone. "So let's welcome to the turntables for the next hour the star of the hit TV show *Hermosa Beach*, Miss Pegasus Patton!"

The crowd whooped as Pegasus, twirling her *über*-long, *über*-blond hair, in a strapless black toile gown designed by Gisella Santa Maria, blew kisses to the audience. After sizing up the daunting array of pots, switches, knobs, and sliders in the DJ booth, pausing twice to clear her stray flaxen locks from the console, she started her first song, Gnarls Barkley's "Crazy," and then leaned over the railing of the booth to pump her first at the crowd below.

"That's my cue to dance with Ben," Cammie exulted, then shot Anna an oh-so-innocent look—Sam could only imagine how much Cammie was enjoying Ben and Anna's breakup.

Cammie flicked the speaker off. "You guys want to come with?"

"I'll pass," Anna managed. She kept her countenance even.

Dee blew her shaggy platinum bangs out of her eyes. "I'm in. I need to find Jack,"

"Dance one with me first," Parker suggested. "Unless...?" He looked over his shoulder at Sam.

"I'll hang with Anna," Sam replied, and Anna gave her a grateful smile. What the hell difference did it make? The guy she really wanted to dance with was far, far away, probably in the arms of TBG, the same bitch who had designed the gown the skanky Pegasus was wearing that very moment. She couldn't even bring herself to think Gisella's full name.

On the other side of the cone, a skinny guy in a silk-screened Joan Jett T-shirt mashed his face against the Plexiglas and began to lick it.

"Wasted cone alert," Sam announced.

Anna made a face. "Let's get out of here."

"You're okay? With Ben, I mean?"

"Depends on which moment you ask me," Anna admitted. "I don't know what I feel anymore. He dumped me. Logan went to Bali. I'm leaving L.A. I hated the Yale thing."

"Pity party on aisle one," Sam droned like a voice over a supermarket's PA system. She'd heard Anna's litany of woes in New York, and again on the plane back to Los Angeles. It wasn't like her to bitch and moan. On the other hand, even she should have the right to whine now and then. But before Sam could temper her nasty joke, Anna spoke up.

"You're absolutely right. God. I'm becoming as self-involved as the people I loathe."

"Unlike me," Sam quipped, "who only thinks about the various ways I could kill Eduardo and TBG—I refuse to say her name out loud—without getting caught. We're out of here."

It took a minute or two to edge their way through

the dense crowd, but finally they were out the door and into the night. Even though the air conditioners inside had been working overtime, the cool air felt wonderful. There was a slight breeze blowing from the west, and Sam could smell the salt of the Pacific just a few miles away. The rotating spotlights still pierced the heavens overhead, and down the street she could see that a considerable crowd had gathered to stare at the celebrities and the riotous club.

"I'll miss this," Anna said simply. "Funny, isn't it. I was so skeptical when I got here in January. And now—"

Sam laughed. "Now you've been Californicated. You thought it wouldn't happen, and it happened. Watch out. Next thing, you'll be buying a Beemer."

"Doubtful. A Prius, maybe, if I were to—"

"I'm looking for Samantha Sharpe." Anna was interrupted by a loud voice somewhere behind them. "Can you tell me where I can find Samantha Sharpe?"

Sam whirled when she heard her name. There was a Latino gentleman in a black pin-striped business suit talking with the security detail at the entrance to the club. He was carrying a black-and-white-striped artist's portfolio in his right hand.

"We can't help you, sir," the biggest of the security guys said gruffly. "You'll need to leave if you don't have an invitation."

"But I need to find Miss Sharpe," the gentleman repeated. Tall, almost gaunt, and in his forties, he was definitely not Eduardo. Yet he didn't look dangerous.

"Hey!" she shouted. "I'm Sam Sharpe!"

The gentleman's face lit up as he ran over to her. "How

lucky, how lucky. I have a delivery for you. Some identification, please? I have a delivery for you."

"Careful, Sam," Anna cautioned.

"Are you kidding? There's an army of security here," Sam pointed out. She opened her silver bugle-beaded Hermès bag and took out her driver's license. "See? Samantha Sharpe."

"Ah, very good." He handed her the portfolio. It was elegant and leather-bound, easily four feet by three feet with a thick leather handle. It was zipped shut. As Sam took it from him, she was surprised at its heft.

"What is this?" she asked quizzically.

He smiled again. "It is self-explanatory. I bid you a good night."

With that, he turned into the crowd and was gone.

Sam shook her head wryly. "That was strange."

"Open it," Anna urged. Spotting a round stone table with matching granite benches that were in a lighted area to one side of the club, Sam headed for it, with Anna right behind her. She laid the portfolio on the cold stone, and unzipped it as Anna moved closer.

All the girls could do was look at each other. Finally, Anna motioned for her to turn the pages—there were eight or ten of them inside the portfolio. Sam did, lingering on each page for thirty seconds or more. When she was done, she went back to the beginning and started again.

Each one of the leaves of the portfolio contained a beautifully rendered two-by-three-foot sketch on creamy artist's paper, with the paper protected by a thin, clear plastic sleeve.

Each sketch was of a custom-designed wedding gown.

And the girl in each drawing wearing these amazing weddings gowns was Sam. Or, she thought, some romantic, idealized, much more gorgeous version of herself. In some her hair was in waves around her face; in others it was blown straight, or up in a French twist with romantic tendrils around her face. In each drawing, she had a mysterious Mona Lisa smile on her face.

The gowns, too, took her breath away. Her favorite was strapless, the bodice encrusted with pearls and diamonds and an Empire waistline.

Sam kept turning the pages until she came to the very last one. There, inside the plastic sleeve, was an envelope instead of a sketch.

"Open it," Anna urged.

Sam tore the envelope open and read feverishly.

Dearest Samantha,
You are a difficult girl to surprise. But when work took me to New York, I saw my opportunity. It was the hardest thing in the world to take my leave from you, to not invite you to come with me. Yet I knew in New York I would be able to accomplish my mission.

And then, there you were! Part of me was cheering, part of me was cursing. Because I knew Gisella would be in New York for a workshop at the Fashion Institute of Technology, and my plan was to enlist her help for your surprise. But once you showed up, it made my plan so much harder to pull off. Unfortunately, you saw her, and jumped to an obvious, but very wrong conclusion.

Somewhere in your family tree, there is hot Latin blood—of this I am certain.

I was with Gisella for only one reason: to consult on ideas for the design of your wedding gown. Her work is in front of you now, if you are reading this letter. It is not that you must wear one of these gowns, because a bride should always choose her own wedding dress, and you are not a girl to be dictated to! But in my mind's eye, I saw your beauty in these gowns, and described my ideas to Gisella. What you see before you is the beauty I see every time I look at you.

I've been trying for a week to get this explanation to you, but sadly you would not take my calls, and when I came to your house, your father's guards told me I would not be permitted near you. I am hoping very much that this will reach you tonight at your friend's party, and that you will find it a reasonable explanation for my behavior. If only I could explain away all the pain I must have caused you.

I'm at my condo now. Come to me if you can.

—Your Eduardo

"Oh my God." Sam could hardly breathe. "Check this out."

She pressed the note into Anna's hands and then read it again over her friend's shoulder. Images from New York flashed through her mind. Seeing Gisella at the embassy party. The ugly confrontation at the restaurant. All that time, she realized, Eduardo had been trying to arrange this for her. She'd been wrong to be suspicious.

Very wrong. Why was it that doubts were always stronger than trust?

"All I have to say is, that's about the most romantic thing I've ever seen in my life. Go," Anna urged gently, when she was done.

Sam hugged her tightly. "Why the fuck did Eduardo do that to me?" But even as she asked the question, she knew she couldn't possibly hold on to her anger. Her eyes filled with tears. She hadn't known it was possible to feel as happy as she felt at that moment. Her Eduardo.

Away from the Madding Crowd

Anna stood outside Bye, Bye Love. Life with a capital *L* swirled around her; the clothes, the celebrities, the gawkers; the deafening music spilling from the club, the searchlights illuminating the night sky. She didn't really feel she was a part of it. She didn't know where she belonged anymore.

"Anna?"

The familiar voice had come from behind her. The hairs stood up on the back of her neck as she turned toward the voice.

"But, but, but . . . what are you *doing* here?"

All of her usual poise fell away. And there wasn't a damn thing she could do about it.

"For the moment, all you need to know is that I'm here." A familiar smile curled Logan's lips.

It was him. Really him. The flesh-and-blood handsome pseudo-son of Daniel Craig. He was casually dressed, in faded jeans and a plain black T-shirt, smiling that fabulous little-boy smile. Logan. Here in Los Angeles. Here at Bye, Bye Love. Not in Indonesia.

She blinked, but he didn't go away. Logan was here.

Ben was inside, only about twenty yards away. Did life get any weirder than this?

"Why? How?" she stammered.

"In reverse order, the 'how' is I looked for you inside the club and your friend—I think she said her name was Dee?—said she'd seen you come outside. And the why . . . How about if we take a walk?"

He reached out a hand. A moment later, they'd negotiated their way past the security guards and away from the crowd. She kept sliding her eyes to Logan, as if to assure herself that this was really happening. As they stood together by one of the three spotlight machines in front of the club that were painting bright circles across the night sky, she couldn't avoid the obvious conclusion that he'd come to see her.

But how could that be? If he'd flown to Bali already?

The pounding noise of the club turned to distant thunder and then to a gentle wash, and they could hear night birds chirping in the eucalyptus trees of the modest residential streets on which they found themselves. This corner of Culver City was a universe away from either the mansions of Beverly Hills or the brownstones of the Upper East Side of Manhattan. Small frame houses and six-unit apartment buildings abutted one another. There were Chevys and Toyotas in the driveways instead of Beemers and Maseratis. It was a world—no, a *galaxy*—away from the Los Angeles she had come to know.

"No one I've met in L.A. has probably even been to this neighborhood before," she realized.

"I've only been in L.A. once before." Logan looked

around. "When my dad was scouting the hotel location in Bali. Back in January."

"That was right after I came here!"

"I knew you were here." He smiled. "I heard it through the Trinity grapevine."

"You should have looked me up."

"No, I shouldn't have." Logan shook his head. "That was the wrong time."

Anna pondered his comment. "I've never been much of a fatalist."

He stopped and looked closely at her. "If this sounds crazy, then I'm crazy. I've had a thing for you since the day at Trinity when Jillian Dubois peed her pants and you found an extra pair in the lost-and-found box for her to put on, so that no one would know."

Anna's mind raced back through the years. She remembered that day. Jillian had been the smallest girl in their class, and very shy. As successful as her ambassador parents were, they didn't seem to know how to dress Jillian so that she fit in with all the other little girls. By age six, Cassie Lancaster and Margaret Thornhill had already marked her as a geek. So Anna had taken Jillian under her wing. The fact that Logan remembered that was amazing.

"When I was in Bali—"

Anna held up a palm to stop him. "You were in Bali?"

"I was. Until about twenty-four hours ago. Then I turned around and flew back."

They were standing under a streetlight. He reached into his back pocket for a large manila envelope. "There's a flight back to Bali that leaves LAX at three this morning.

That's three hours from now. I've got to check in there in an hour."

Anna's head was pounding. None of this made any sense. "You're . . . going back?"

"Absolutely. The place—my father's new hotel—is paradise. There's no real town for five miles in every direction, there are only thirty-five thatched bunga-lows, and each of them is unique. Poster beds, and every bungalow has a little library. My dad put me in charge of acquiring the books. The resort's right on the beach. The catamarans and windsurfing are unbe-lievable. And the fishing. And the palm trees and the mountains. Everyone eats in this open-air dining room. There are three meals a day, and a seafood snack at midnight. They brew their own beer, and recycle everything." His eyes were shining. "For the very first time in a very long time, I felt like I could breathe. And think. About Harvard. About the future. About you. Come with me."

He put the envelope in her hand. "It's a ticket to Bali. Yours."

They were in front of a small brick house with a tidy yard, and a light went on in the living room. A shad-owy figure peered at the bay window. Then—apparently deciding that Anna and Logan were merely a couple out for a stroll—the light went off again and the figure dis-appeared. In the distance, a dog started barking. It was joined in a matter of moments by seemingly every other dog within earshot.

"I have a cheering section," Logan observed wryly. "So listen to the fans. Say yes, Anna. Come with me."

He'd just painted a beautiful portrait of how life should be. She had a plane ticket in her hand. And yet—

"I-I…I can't!" she blurted out. Because…well, because she wasn't a spontaneous, throw-away-the-future-you've-planned-since-forever kind of girl. "There's Yale."

"Of course you can," he insisted. "You can come back if you want, and still go to Yale. But I know I'm not crazy. You're just as confused about your future as I am about mine. You can *think* in Bali, Anna. Away from the madding crowd. I've known you since forever. You're all about thinking."

She thought for that blurring moment about what her expectations had been for her life and her expectations for her time in Los Angeles. She thought about starting Yale—it wasn't perfect by a long shot, but it was still Yale. And she thought about what might happen in Bali, where she would have a chance to think without the relentless clutter of New York, the incessant noise of Los Angeles, the chronic drama of the people she'd come to know and who'd become her friends.

But how could she go to Bali? "I wish I was the kind of girl who could just say yes," Anna began with hesitation. "In the movie version of my life, I'd get on the plane with you. But in real life—"

"Whose real life is it?" Logan pressed. "You can do anything, if you want to badly enough."

Could she? It made perfect sense—in theory. But in the real world . . .

"I'm so sorry," she whispered. "But I . . . I just can't."

There was so much more she wanted to say, about what she felt for him. How could she, though, when he'd come all this way just for her and she was turning him down?

"I'm not surprised." He finally replied. "Come on. Let's go back. I've got a limo meeting us—me—in twenty minutes."

They walked back to the club in silence, though a loud internal debate raged in Anna's head. As they neared Bye, Bye Love and the black limo that was waiting for Logan, her mind still hadn't changed.

He took her hands again. "One last chance?"

Anna observed their distorted reflection in the limo's tinted window. She shook her head sadly. At another time, in a parallel universe, he'd open the door for her and she'd get in. She didn't have clothes, she didn't even have a toothbrush, but it wouldn't have made a difference. It made her disappointed and sad to know she couldn't take such a leap. Cyn would have done it in a heartbeat. Sam, too, probably. But she was Jane Percy's daughter, and she seemed to have inherited the "proper" gene, much as she wanted to deny it.

"I can't." She shook her head again.

"You *won't*. There's a difference. A big difference."

"I want you to know, Logan, that coming back here like this . . . it's one of the nicest things anyone has ever done for me. We're going to stay in touch, right?"

His response was to give her one gentle kiss. Then her beautiful stranger—who wasn't really a stranger at all—got in the black limousine and Anna swallowed hard as she watched it pull away. She felt a tear roll down her cheek and quickly wiped it away.

She took a deep, fortifying breath. What would Jane

Percy do? Her mother would go back into the club, find
Ben and Cammie, and offer them the most hearty congratulations on the enormous success of Bye, Bye Love,
before going home for a quiet nightcap in the privacy of
her own home.

So that's what she decided on, followed by what Anna
herself would do—go home and commence working on her
screenplay. Even if her writing wasn't any good—and she
strongly suspected it wasn't—at least it belonged to *her*.

The club was still rocking when she went back inside.
Still wall-to-wall people, but P. Diddy had now taken
over for Pegasus Patton in the DJ space. Anna spotted
Champagne, dressed in white chiffon, holding hands
with a cute guy who looked like a younger Martin Rittenhouse. She waved and Anna waved back, but she kept
snaking through the crowd. Then Parker crossed in front
of her with a willowy model type on his arm, and Anna
touched his shoulder. As she looked closer, she realized
it was Django's sister, Citron. How they'd come to know
each other was beyond her, but it made Anna smile. "Hey,
have you seen Ben?" she asked.

Parker motioned toward the performing space. "Back
there. I think Gwyneth is about to do a set. How hot is
this place?"

"It's great. Have fun!" Anna gave the two of them a
little wave that she hoped wasn't too rude, then edged
through the dancing crowd—at this point, people were
getting down not just on the dance floor, but anyplace
they could find a little space. It took five full minutes to
go fifty feet, but finally she was at the end of the short
corridor that led to the little theater.

There she stopped dead in her tracks. She'd found Ben and she'd found Cammie. They were straight ahead. In a lip-lock to end all lip-locks. There were friendly kisses, there were romantic kisses, and then there were kisses that were just raw sex.

This would be the raw-sex variation. Times infinity.

Just Her Luck

Ben. And Cammie. Together. *Very* together.

Anna felt like retching. She knew those lips of his. What they looked like, how they felt against her own. To imagine them against Cammie's . . . well, it was unimaginable and horrifying all at the same time. She tried to make herself look away, but there was some dastardly rule of attraction happening between their lips and her eyes.

She was trying to discreetly slide backward into the crowd when she saw Cammie open her eyes. That was it. She was locked on, like a deer in headlights. She tried to move her feet, or even her arms. Movement was impossible.

Cammie grinned wildly at her. "Hey. Look who's here."

Ben turned around; his eyes registering only mild surprise when he realized it was Anna. "Hi." His eyes were dark and hard. "Having fun?"

"I can see I don't need to ask you the same question," Anna replied smoothly. She wasn't going to give either of them the satisfaction of seeing how much their kiss had shaken her. She felt like she'd just been punched in the stomach.

Be your mother. Do not let them see you sweat.

She put on her best, most controlled Jane Percy smile.

"I just wanted to say good night, and to thank you for inviting me. Best of luck with your club. I'm sure it will be a huge success. It already is."

"Why, thank you, Anna!" Cammie sang with exaggerated politeness. Her arms were draped over Ben's shoulders, and his hands were carefully placed around her slender waist. They were still practically wedged against the wall. It was clear just how very much Cammie was enjoying this moment, this victory. "That's just so thoughtful. You know, I might not get to see you often—you're going back east to college, right? Was that what I heard? And Ben and I, we're going to be incredibly busy over the next year. So let me tell you now how *fun* it's been getting to know you. I want to wish you all the luck in the world!"

What could she say to that? Especially because their pose told Anna she was only a brief interruption in their cataclysmic embrace.

"Okay," Anna replied. She was careful to avoid Ben's eyes. "So . . . goodbye." She pivoted away, concentrating on her footsteps in the hallway still crowded with partying clubgoers.

So this is what it feels like to lose your first love. Bye, bye, love. Bye, bye, happiness.

Oh, she'd already known it was over, that Ben didn't want her. But that he still had the power to hurt her, after the hurtful things he'd said when he'd dumped her, only made it that much worse.

"Anna!" Ben called.

She heard him but kept walking, wanting to get away as quickly as possible. She stumbled forward, only to find her way blocked by a commotion in the concrete corridor in front of her. Someone was pushing through in their direction, and people were shouting at whomever it was to slow down. "Take it easy, dude!" a male voice shouted.

"Fuck you!" another male voice shouted back. And then the person causing the commotion broke through the crowd.

His hair was short now, so that the blue star tattoo just below his right ear seemed to pulsate in the strobing lights. He was dressed simply in jeans, a yellow polo shirt, and his usual basketball shoes. There was a snarl of anger in his eyes; his jaw was clenched. He moved past Anna, not even seeing her, and headed straight for Cammie. Before he reached her, Ben stepped in front.

"Welcome to the party, Ad—"

Without a word, Adam Flood uncoiled a vicious right cross that caught Ben squarely on the jaw. Ben, who hadn't even moved to defend himself, crumpled to the linoleum floor as Cammie started screaming and three or four people launched themselves at Adam, tackling him to the ground.

"There's more where that came from, asshole!" he bellowed. "Lots more!"

Anna rushed to him while he struggled in the grasp of the bulky guys who held him fast. "Adam, what—?"

"Stay out of this," he yelled, not even making eye contact. "Get the hell away from here!"

Suddenly she couldn't take one more moment of the drama, the angst, the over-the-top cult of the superficial. She decided to take his advice.

"Ladies and gentlemen, this is the final boarding call for Delta Airlines flight 4949, to Jakarta, Indonesia, departing from Gate 87 at 3:02 p.m. Final boarding, flight 4949. If you're holding a ticket for Delta 4949, please board at this time. Thank you."

Anna tore breathlessly through the seemingly endless terminal of LAX, running as fast as she could. When she realized that her three-inch white Chanel pumps were holding her back, she pulled them off and ran with them dangling dangerously loose from her fingers. When she dropped one, she didn't stop to pick it up and just heaved its mate toward the nearest trash barrel.

At this hour—two-forty in the morning, to be precise—the international departure area at LAX was nearly deserted, save for the graveyard shift of floor-polishers, trash picker-uppers, bathroom-scrubbers, and window-washers, who looked after this strange sight sprinting toward the gate. Just her luck—Gate 87 was at the far end of the concourse. She couldn't even jump on the people-mover or grab a ride on one of the golf carts normally used by infirm passengers.

The PA announcement for Logan's flight was repeated again. She was never going to make it.

The irony. Just when she was finally doing something spontaneous, she was going to screw it up. The taxi she'd found near the club had gotten stuck on the 405 due to an accident. Two of the entrances to LAX were closed. At least she had her passport with her. It was her backup ID, so she'd stuck it in her purse before leaving for the club opening. But she was never going to make it to the gate in time so it hardly mattered.

Breathing hard, she spotted the gate up ahead. Finally! There were just a few stragglers waiting in line to check in. By the time Anna reached the flight attendant to hand over her boarding pass, she was the only one left.

"Can you tell me if there's a passenger named Logan Cresswell on this flight?" she asked, still panting, strands of blond hair stuck to her sweaty forehead.

The flight attendant—a beautiful Indonesian girl with raven hair down to her back, shook her head slowly.

"He isn't?" *What?* So where was he?

"I mean that I cannot tell you. Regulations prohibit our giving out this information," she explained in her lilting accent. "Are you ready to board, miss?"

Maybe he wasn't on the plane. Maybe she was crazy. For a moment the old Anna took over. She should turn around, get in a cab and go back to her dad's. Follow the plan. Don't rock the boat. Do what you know.

She handed her ticket to the flight attendant.

"First class, very comfortable." The Indonesian girl tore the pass in two and returned part of it to Anna. "Have a good flight."

"Thank you."

She stepped into the jetway, the last passenger to board the enormous, roaring plane, and heard the heavy security door shut and lock behind her. She wasn't even sure Logan was on this flight. But there was no turning back. The only way was forward, into the unknown. . . .

Q&A with Zoey Dean

Name: Zoey Dean

Nickname: No nicknames, thank you very much. Sometimes my closest friends call me Z.

First job: My first job out of college was as an A-List celeb's personal assistant—if you call scheduling mani-pedis and blow-outs a real job.

Worst job: See above.

Perfect date: One that starts with dinner in New York and ends with lunch in Paris.

Favorite place: The private stretch of beach outside my Caribbean hideaway. And no, I'm not saying where that is!

Guilty pleasure: *The Young and the Restless.* Oh, Cane...

Best friend's first name: Katya

Good luck charm: My smile.

Tuesday night activity: See favorite TV show, add best friend or boyfriend of the moment, and voila!

Last thing I bought at the mall: Zoey does not do malls. But the last thing I bought at Kitson was a pair of white Missoni slingbacks.

Favorite movie: *Casablanca* and *Clueless.* Both classics.

Biggest fashion blunder: I've worn some adventurous fashions over the years, but if I'm wearing it, it's instantly stylish.

Item atop your grocery list: Mangos, at the moment. I'm on a mango salsa kick. And so is everyone I make it for.

French fry dip: My secret sauce is quite simple: ketchup and honey mustard. Best if eaten while actually in France.

Astrological sign: Oh, please.

Favorite TV show: *American Idol.* I refuse to be snarky about this.

Lucky color: Blush pink. Try wearing a pink sundress for a day and you'll see why.

Midnight snack: Dinner. When you wake up at noon and go out every night, meals don't always happen at normal hours.

Celebrity crush: His initials are J. G. And that would be his crush on me.

Favorite book: *The Great Gatsby.* I would have made an excellent 1920s socialite.

Favorite Hollywood Hangout: Why in the world would I ruin LA's best-kept secret by revealing it here? My second favorite, however, is Park City, Utah, during Sundance.

Best California Beach: You'd expect me to say celeb-studded Malibu, right? But I honestly prefer Huntington Beach—cute surfers everywhere!

Life Motto: Fashion passes. Style remains. (Thank you, Coco Chanel.)

*Once upon a time on the Upper East Side of New York City,
two beautiful girls fell in love with one perfect boy. . . .*

Turn the page for a sneak peek of

it had to be you
the gossip girl prequel

and find out how it all began.

by the #1 *New York Times* bestselling author
Cecily von Ziegesar

gossipgirl.net

topics ◀ **previous** **next** ▶ **post a question** **reply**

Disclaimer: All the real names of places, people, and events have been altered or abbre-viated to protect the innocent. Namely, me.

hey people!

Ever have that totally freakish feeling that someone is listening in on your conversations, spying on you and your friends, following you to parties, and generally stalking you? Well, they are. Or actually, *I* am. The truth is, I've been here all along, because I'm one of you.

Feeling totally lost? Don't get out much? Don't know who "we" are? Allow me to explain. We're an exclusive group of indescribably beauti-ful people who happen to live in those majestic, green-awninged, white-glove-doorman buildings near Central Park. We attend Manhattan's most elite single-sex private schools. Our families own yachts and estates in various exotic locations throughout the world. We frequent all the best beaches and the most exclusive ski resorts. We're seated immediately at the nicest restaurants in the chicest neighborhoods with-out a reservation. We turn heads. But don't confuse us with Hollywood actors or models or rock stars—those people you feel like you know because you hear so much about them, but who are actually completely boring compared to the parts they play or the songs they sing. There's nothing boring about me or my friends, and the more I tell you about us, the more you're going to want to know. I've kept quiet until now, but something has happened and I just can't stay quiet about it. . . .

the greatest story ever told

We learned in our first eleventh-grade creative writing class this week that most great stories begin in one of the following fashions: someone mysteriously disappears or a stranger comes to town. The story I'm about to tell is of the "someone mysteriously disappears" variety.

To be specific, **S** is *gone.*

In order to unravel the mystery of why she's left and where she's gone, I'm going to have to backtrack to last winter—the winter of our sophomore year—when the La Mer skin cream hit the fan and our pretty pink rose-scented bubble burst. It all started with three inseparable, perfectly innocent, über-gorgeous fifteen-year-olds. Well, they're sixteen now, and let's just say that two of them are *not* that innocent.

If anyone is going to tell this tale it has to be me, because I was at the scene of every crime. So sit back while I unravel the past and reveal everyone's secrets, because I know everything, and what I don't know I'll invent, elaborately.

Admit it: you're already falling for me.

Love you too . . .

gossip girl

the best stories begin with one boy and two girls

"Truce!" Serena van der Woodsen screamed as Nate Archibald body-checked her into a three-foot-high drift of powdery white snow. Cold and wet, it tunneled into her ears and down her pants. Nate dove on top of her, all five-foot eleven inches of his perfect, golden-brown-haired, glittering-green-eyed, fifteen-year-old boyness. Nate smelled like Downy and the Kiehl's sandalwood soap the maid stocked his bathroom with. Serena just lay there, trying to breathe with him on top of her. "My scalp is cold," she pleaded, getting a mouthful of Nate's snow-dampened, godlike curls as she spoke.

Nate sighed reluctantly, as if he could have spent all day outside in the frigid February meat locker that was the back garden of his family's Eighty-second-Street-just-off-Park-Avenue Manhattan town house. He rolled onto his back and wriggled like Serena's long-dead golden retriever, Guppy, when she used to let him loose on the green grass of the Great Lawn in Central Park. Then he stood up, awkwardly dusting off the seat of his neatly pressed Brooks Brothers khakis. It was Saturday, but he still wore the same clothes he wore every weekday as a sophomore at the St. Jude's School for Boys over on East End Avenue. It was the unofficial Prince of the Upper East Side uniform, the same uniform he and his classmates had been wearing since they'd started nursery school together at Park Avenue Presbyterian.

Nate held out his hand to help Serena to her feet. She frowned cautiously up at him, worried that he was only faking her out and was about to tackle her again. "I really am cold."

He flapped his hand at her impatiently. "I know. Come on."

She snorted, pretended to pick her nose and wipe it on the seat of her snow-soaked dark denim Earl jeans, then grabbed his hand with her faux-snotty one. "Thanks, pal." She staggered to her feet. "You're a real chum."

Nate led the way inside. The backs of his pant legs were damp and she could see the outline of his tighty-whiteys. Really, how gay of him! He held the glass-paned French doors open and stood aside to let her pass. Serena kicked off her baby blue Uggs and scuffed her bare, Urban Decay Piggy Bank-pink-toenailed feet down the long hall to the stately town house's enormous, barely used all-white Italian Modern kitchen. Nate's father was a former sea captain-turned-banker, and his mother was a French society hostess. They were basically never home, and when they *were* home, they were at the opera.

"Are you hungry?" Nate asked, following her. "I'm so sick of takeout. My parents have been in Venezuela or Santa Domingo or wherever they go in February for like two weeks, and I've been eating burritos, pizza, or sushi every freaking night. I asked Regina to buy ham, Swiss, Pepperidge Farm white bread, Grammy Smith apples, and peanut butter. All I want is the food I ate in kindergarten." He tugged anxiously on his wavy, golden brown hair. "Maybe I'm going through some sort of midlife crisis or something."

Like his life is so stressful?

"It's Gra*nny* Smith, silly," Serena informed him fondly. She opened a glossy white cupboard and found an unopened box of cinnamon-and-brown-sugar Pop-Tarts. Ripping open the box, she removed one of the packets from inside, tore it open with her neat, white teeth, and pulled out a thickly frosted pastry. She sucked on the Pop-Tart's sweet, crumbly corner and hopped up on the counter, kicking the cupboards below with her size-eight-and-a-half feet. Pop-Tarts at Nate's. She'd been having them there since she was five years old. And now . . . and now . . .

Serena sighed heavily. "Mom and Dad want me to go to boarding school next year," she announced, her enormous, almost navy blue eyes growing huge and glassy as they welled up with unexpected tears. Go away to boarding school and leave Nate? It hurt too much to even think about.

Nate flinched as if he'd been slapped in the face by an invisible hand. He grabbed the other Pop-Tart from out of the packet and hopped up on the counter next to Serena. "No way," he responded decisively. She couldn't leave. He wouldn't allow it.

"They want to travel more," Serena explained. The pink, perfect curve of her lower lip trembled dangerously. "If I'm home, they feel like they need to be home more. Like I want them around? Anyway, they've arranged for me to meet some of the deans of admissions and stuff. It's like I have no choice."

Nate scooted over a few inches and put his arm around her. "The city is going to suck if you're not here," he told her earnestly. "You can't go."

Serena took a deep shuddering breath and rested her pale blond head on his shoulder. "I love you," she murmured, closing her delicate eyelids. Their bodies were so close the entire Nate-side of her hummed. If she turned her head and tilted her chin just so, she could have easily kissed his warm, lovely neck. And she wanted to. She was actually dying to, because she really did love him, with all her heart.

She did? Hello? Since when?!

Maybe since ballroom-dancing school way back in fourth grade. She was tall for her age, and Nate was always such a gentleman about her lack of rhythm and the way she stepped on his insteps and jutted her bony elbows into his sides. He'd finesse it by grabbing her hand and spinning her around so that the skirt of her puffy, oyster-colored satin tea-length Bonpoint dress twirled out magnificently. Their teacher, Mrs. Jaffe, who had long blue hair that she kept in place with a pearl-adorned black hairnet, worshipped Nate. So did Serena's best friend, Blair Waldorf. And so did Serena—she just hadn't realized it until now. Serena shuddered and her perfect skin broke out in a rash of goose bumps. Her whole body seemed to be having an adverse reaction to the idea of revealing something she'd kept so well hidden for so long, even from herself.

Nate wrapped his lacrosse-toned arms around her long, narrow waist and pulled her close, tucking her pale gold head into the crook of his neck and massaging the ruts between the ribs on her back with his fingertips. The best thing about Serena was her total lack of embarrassing flab. Her entire body was as long and lean and taut as the strings on his Prince titanium tennis racket.

It was painful having such a ridiculously hot best friend. Why couldn't his best friend be some lard-assed dude with zits and dandruff? Instead he had Serena and Blair Waldorf, hands down the two hottest girls on the Upper East Side, and maybe all of Manhattan, or even the whole world.

Serena was an absolute goddess—every guy Nate knew talked about her—but she was mysterious. She'd laugh for hours if she spotted a cloud shaped like a toilet seat or something equally ridiculous, and the next moment she'd be wistful and sad. It was impossible to tell what she was thinking most of the time. Sometimes Nate wondered if she would've been more comfortable in a body that was slightly less perfect, because it would've given her more *incentive*, to use an SAT vocabulary word. Like she wasn't sure what she had to aspire to, since she basically had everything a girl could possibly want.

Blair was petite, with a pretty, foxlike face, blue eyes, and wavy chestnut-colored hair. She let everyone know what she was thinking, and she was fiercely competitive. For instance, she always found opportunities to point out that her chest was almost a whole cup size larger than Serena's and that she'd scored almost 100 points higher than Serena on the practice SAT.

Way back in fifth grade, Serena had told Nate she was pretty sure Blair had a crush on him. He started to notice that Blair did stick her chest out when he was looking, and she was always either bossing him around or fixing his hair. Of course Blair never admitted that she liked him, which made him like her even more.

Nate sighed deeply. No one understood how difficult it was being best friends with two such beautiful, impossible girls.

Like he would have been friends with them if they were awkward and butt-ugly?

He closed his eyes and breathed in the sweet scent of Serena's Frédéric Fekkai Apple Cider clarifying shampoo. He'd kissed lots of girls and had even gone to third base last June with L'Wren Knowes, a very experienced older Seaton Arms School senior who really did seem to know everything. But kissing Serena would be . . . different. He loved her. It was as simple as that. She was his best friend, and he loved her.

And if you can't kiss your best friend, who *can* you kiss?

upper east side schoolgirl uncovers shocking sex scandal!

"Ew," Blair Waldorf muttered at her reflection in the full-length mirror on the back of her closet door. She liked to keep her closet organized, but not too organized. Whites with whites, off-whites with off-whites, navy with navy, black with black. But that was it. Jeans were tossed in a heap on the closet floor. And there were dozens of them. It was almost a game to close her eyes and feel around and come up with a pair that used to be too tight in the ass but fit a little loosely now that she'd cut out her daily after-dinner milk-and-Chips-Ahoy routine.

Blair looked at the mirror, assessing her outfit. Her Marc by Marc Jacobs shell pink sheer cotton blouse was fine. It was the fuchsia La Perla bra that was the problem. It showed right through the blouse so that she looked like a stripper. But she was only going to Nate's house to hang out with him and Serena. And Nate liked to talk about bras. He was genuinely curious about, for instance, what the purpose of an underwire was, or why some bras fastened in front and some fastened in back. It was a big turn-on for him, obviously, but it was also sort of sweet. He was a lonely only child, craving sisterhood.

Right.

She decided to leave the bra on for Nate's sake, hiding the whole ensemble under her favorite belted black cashmere Lora Piano cardigan, which would come off the minute she stepped into his well-heated town house. Maybe, just maybe, the sight of her hot pink bra would be the thing to make Nate realize that he'd been in love with her just as long as she'd been in love with him.

Maybe.

She opened her bedroom door and yelled down the long hall and across the East Seventy-second Street penthouse's vast expanse of period furniture, parquet floors, crown moldings, and French Impressionist paintings. "Mom! Dad? I'm going over to Nate's house! Serena and I are spending the night!"

When there was no reply, she clomped her way to her parents' huge master suite in her noisy Kors wooden-heeled sheepskin clogs, opened their bedroom door, and made a beeline for her mom's dressing room. Eleanor Waldorf kept a tall stack of crisp emergency twenties in her lingerie drawer for Blair and her ten-year-old brother, Tyler, to parse from— for taxis, cappuccinos, and, in Blair's case, the occasional much-needed pair of Manolo Blahnik heels. Twenty, forty, sixty, eighty, one hundred. Twenty, forty, sixty, eighty, two hundred. Blair counted out the bills, folding them neatly before stuffing them into the back pocket of her peg-legged Seven jeans.

"If I were a cabernet," Blair's father's dramatically playful lawyer's voice echoed out of the adjoining dressing room, "how would you describe my bouquet?"

Excusez-moi?

Blair clomped out of her mom's dressing room and reached for the chocolate brown velvet curtain hanging in the doorway of her dad's. "If you guys are in there together, like, doing it while I'm home, then that's really gross," she declared flatly. "Anyway, I'm going over to Nate's, so—"

Her father, Harold J. Waldorf, Esquire, pulled aside the velvet curtain, dressed in his cashmere tweed Paul Smith bathrobe and nothing else, his nicely tanned, handsome face looking slightly flushed. "Mom's out looking at dishes for the Guggenheim benefit. I thought you were out. Where are you going exactly?"

Blair stared at him. He wasn't holding a phone, and if her mom was out, then who the fuck had he just been talking to? She stood blinking at him with her hands on her hips, tempted to peek inside his dressing room to see who he was hiding in there.

Does she really want to know?

Instead, she stumbled out of the master suite, clomped her way across the penthouse, grabbed her blood orange–colored Jimmy Choo treasure chest hobo, and ran for the elevator.

Outside it was breathtakingly cold, and fat flakes fell at random. Usually she walked the twelve blocks to Nate's house, but today Blair had no patience for walking—she had just discovered that her father was a lying, cheating scumbag, after all, and a cab was waiting for her downstairs. Or rather, a cab was waiting for Mrs. Solomon in 4A, but when the hunter green uniform–clad doorman saw the terrifying look on Blair's normally pretty face, he let her take it.

Besides, hailing cabs in the snow was probably the highlight of his day.

The stone walls bordering Central Park were blanketed in snow. A tall, elderly woman and her Yorkshire terrier, dressed in matching red Chanel quilted coats with matching black velvet bows in their white hair, crossed Seventy-second Street and entered the Ralph Lauren flagship store. Blair's cab hurtled recklessly up Madison Avenue, past Agnès B. and Williams-Sonoma and the Three Guys coffee shop where all the Constance Billard girls gathered after school, and finally pulled up to Nate's town house.

"Let me in!" she yelled into the intercom outside the Archibalds' elegant wrought-iron-and-glass front door as she swatted the buzzer over and over with her hand.

Inside, Nate and Serena were still cuddling in the kitchen. Serena raised her head from his shoulder and opened her eyes, as if from a dream. The kiss they'd both been fantasizing about had never actually happened, which was probably for the best.

"I think I'm warm now," she announced and hopped off the counter, composing her face so that she looked totally calm and cool, like they hadn't just had a moment. And maybe they hadn't—she couldn't be sure. She grinned at the monitor's distorted image of Blair giving her the finger. "Come on in, sweetness!" she shouted back, buzzing her friend in.

Nate tried to erase the disturbing thought that Blair had

caught him and Serena together. They weren't together. They were just friends, hanging out, which is what friends do when they're together. There was nothing to catch. It was all in his mind.

Or was it?

"Hey, hornyheads." Blair greeted them with snow in her shoulder-length chestnut brown hair. Her cheeks were pink with cold, her blue eyes were slightly bloodshot, and her carefully plucked dark brown eyebrows were askew, as if she'd been crying or rubbing her eyes like crazy. "I have a fucked-up story to tell you guys." She flung her orange bag down on the floor and took a deep breath, her eyes rolling around dramatically, milking the moment for all it was worth. "As it turns out, my totally boring, Mr. Lawyer father, Harold Waldorf, Esquire, is like totally having an affair. Only moments ago, I caught him asking some random babe, 'If I was a wine, how would you describe my bouquet?' and they were, like, totally hiding in his closet." She clapped her hand over her mouth, as if to keep the words in.

Or her breakfast.

"Whoa," Serena and Nate responded in unison.

"He just sounded so . . . slimy," Blair wailed through her fingers.

Serena knew this might be even grosser, but she just had to get it out there. "Well, maybe he was just having phone sex with your mom."

"Sure," Nate agreed. "My parents do that all the time," he added, feeling a little sick as he said it. His navy admiral dad was so uptight he probably wouldn't have phone sex for fear of being court-marshaled.

Blair grimaced. The idea of her tennis-toned-but-still-plump, St. Barts–tanned, gold-jewelry-loving mom having any kind of sex, let alone cabernet phone sex, with her skinny, preppy, argyle-socks-wearing dad, was so unlikely and so completely icky she refused to even think about it.

"No," she insisted, wolfing down the uneaten half of Serena's Pop-Tart. "It was definitely another woman. I mean, face it," she said, still chewing, "Dad is totally hot and dresses really well, and he's an important lawyer and everything. And my mom is totally insane and doesn't really do anything and she has varicose veins and a flabby ass. Of course he's having an affair."

Serena and Nate nodded their glossy golden heads like that made complete sense. Then Serena grabbed Blair and hugged her hard. Blair was the sister she'd never had. In fourth grade they'd pretended they were fraternal twins for an entire month. Their Constance Billard gym teacher, Ms. Etro, who'd gotten fired midyear for inappropriate touching—which she called "spotting"—during tumbling classes, had even believed them. They'd worn matching pink Izod shirts and cut their hair exactly the same length. They even wore matching gold Cartier hoop earrings, until they decided they were tacky and switched to Tiffany diamond studs.

Blair pressed her face into Serena's perfectly defined collarbone and heaved an exhausted, trembling sigh. "It's just so fucked up it makes me feel sick."

Serena patted Blair's back and met Nate's gaze over Blair's Elizabeth Arden Red Door Salon–glossed brown head. No way was she going to bring up the whole being-sent-away-to-boarding-school problem—not when her best friend was so upset. And she didn't want Nate to mention it either. "Come on, let's go mix martinis and watch a stupid movie or something."

Nate jumped off the counter, feeling completely confused. Suddenly all he really wanted to do was hug Blair and kiss away her tears. Was he hot for her now, too?

It's hard to keep a clear head when you're surrounded by beautiful girls who are in love with you.

"All we have is vodka and champagne. My parents keep all the good wine and whiskey locked up in the cabinet for when they have company," he apologized.

Serena slid open the bread pantry, where most families would actually keep bread, but where Nate's mom stored the cartons of Gitanes cigarettes her sister sent from France via FedEx twice a month because the ones sold in the States simply did not taste fresh.

"I'm sure we can make do," she said, ripping open a carton with her thumbnail. "Come." She stuck two cigarettes in her mouth like tusks and beckoned Nate and Blair to follow her out of the kitchen and upstairs to the master suite. If anyone was an expert at changing the mood, it was Serena. That was one of the things they loved about her. "I'll show you a good time," she added goofily.

She always did.

The Archibalds' vast bedroom had been decorated by Nate's mother in the style of Louis XVI, with a giant gilt mirror over the head of the enormous red-and-gold toile canopy bed, and heavy gold curtains in the windows. The walls were adorned with red-and-gold fleur-de-lis wallpaper and renderings of Mrs. Archibald's family's summer château near Nice. On the floor was a red, blue, and gold Persian rug rescued from the *Titanic* and bought at auction by Mrs. Archibald for her husband at Sotheby's.

"*Bus Stop? Some Like It Hot?* Or the digitally remastered version of *Some Like It Hot?*" Serena asked, flipping through Nate's parents' limited DVD collection. Obviously Captain Archibald liked Marilyn Monroe movies—*a lot*. Of course, Nate had his own collection of DVDs in his room, including a play-by-play of the last twenty years of America's Cup sailing races. Thanks, but no thanks. His parents' taste was far more girl-friendly. "Or we could just watch Nate play Nintendo, which is always hot," she joked, although she kind of meant it.

"Only if he does it naked," Blair quipped hopefully. She sat down and bounced up and down on the end of the huge bed.

Nate blushed. Blair loved to make him blush and he knew it. "Okay," he responded boldly, sitting down next to her on the bed.

Blair snatched a Kleenex out of the silver tissue box on Nate's mom's bedside table and blew her nose noisily. Not that she really needed to blow her nose. She just needed a distraction from the overwhelming urge to throw Nate down on his parents' bed and tackle him. He was so goddamned adorable it made her feel like she was going to explode. God, she loved him.

There had never been a time when she didn't love him. She'd loved the stupid lobster shorts he wore to the club in Newport when their dads played tennis together in the summer, back when they were, what—five? She'd loved the way he always had a Spider-Man Band-Aid on some part of his body until he was at least twelve, not because he'd hurt himself but because he thought it looked cool. She loved the way his whole head reflected the sunlight, glowing gold. She loved his glittering green eyes—eyes that were almost too pretty for a boy. She loved the way he so obviously knew he was hot but didn't quite know what to do about it. She loved him. Oh, how she loved him.

Oh, oh, *oh*!

She blew her nose with one last trumpeting snort and then grabbed a pink, tacky-looking DVD case from off the floor. She turned the case over, studying it. *"Breakfast at Tiffany's.* I've never seen it, but she's so beautiful." She held the DVD up so Serena could see Audrey Hepburn in her long black dress and pearl choker. "Isn't she?"

"She is pretty," Serena agreed, still sorting through the movies.

"She looks like you," Nate observed, cocking his head in such an adorable way that Blair had to close her eyes to keep from falling off the bed.

"You think?" Blair tossed her dirty tissue in the general direction of the Archibalds' dainty white porcelain waste paper basket and studied the picture on the DVD case again. In the movie that began to play in her head, she *was* Audrey Hepburn—a fabulously dressed, thin, perfectly coiffed, beautiful, mysterious megastar. "Maybe a little," she agreed, removing her black cashmere cardigan so that her hot pink bra was clearly visible beneath her blouse.

Blair picked up the DVD case again. Audrey Hepburn

looked so fabulous in the pictures on the back, but also sort of prim and proper, like she wore sexy underwear but wouldn't let a guy see it unless he was going to marry her. Blair pulled her cardigan back on and buttoned the top button. From now on, her life's work would be to emulate Audrey Hepburn in every possible way. Nate could see her underwear, but only once she was sure that one day they'd be married.

That makes sense—to her.

"I watched that movie with my mom," Nate confessed, causing both girls' hearts to drip into sticky puddles on the floor. "It's kind of bizarre, actually. I think it's supposed to be romantic, but I'm not sure I even understood it."

That was all the girls needed. Blair stuck the DVD into the player while Serena mixed martinis at the wet bar in the adjoining library. This involved pouring Bombay Sapphire into chilled martini glasses and stirring it with a silver letter opener. It was only 11 A.M.—not exactly cocktail hour—but Blair was in crisis, and Nate tended to take off his shirt when he got drunk. Besides, it was Saturday.

"There," Serena announced, as if she'd just put the finishing touches on a very complicated recipe. She handed out the glasses. "To us. Because we're worth it."

"To us," Blair and Nate chorused, glasses raised.

Bottoms up!

Before **Vanessa** filmed her first movie,
Dan wrote his first poem,
and **Jenny** bought her first bra.

Before **Blair** watched her first Audrey Hepburn movie,
Serena left for boarding school,
and before **Nate** came between them. . .

it had to be you
the gossip girl prequel

Coming October 2007

Blair Waldorf and Serena van der Woodsen were the reigning princesses of the Upper East Side.

Until now.

Something wild and wicked is in the air.
The Carlyle triplets are about to
take Manhattan by storm.

Lucky for you, Gossip Girl will be there
to whisper all their juicy secrets....

gossip girl

A New Era Begins May 2008

THE FIRST ADULT NOVEL BY ZOEY DEAN,
AUTHOR OF THE BESTSELLING **A-LIST** SERIES

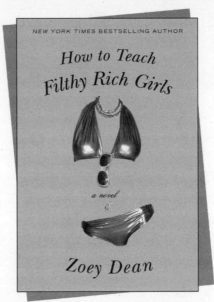

When recent Yale grad Megan Smith is fired from her assistant job at the trashy tabloid *Scoop*, she takes a position that's a little more suited to her skill-set: tutoring seventeen-year-old identical twins Rose and Sage Baker of Palm Beach, Florida—yes *the* infamous Baker heiresses. Unfortunately for Megan, the Baker twins aren't about to bend their social schedules to learn basic algebra. And they certainly aren't going to sit down for a study session with Megan, who associates the words "Seven" with *math* and "Diesel" with *fuel*. Megan quickly discovers that if she's going to get the $75,000 bonus she's been promised if—and *only* if—the girls are admitted to Duke University, she'll have to know her Pucci from her Prada to get in good with her very special students. And if she can look the part, maybe—just maybe—she can teach them something along the way.

How to Teach Filthy Rich Girls
Available now!
www.howtoteachfilthyrichgirls.com